Dreaming of Grace

Dreaming

of

Grace

Karen Nettles

Total Fusion Press
Strasburg, Ohio

Karen Nettles recently moved from Florida to her own "Cabin in the Woods" in North Carolina. She resides there with her husband, two Shelties, and four cats. *Dreaming of Grace* is Karen's debut novel that was inspired by her dream of sharing her love of the mountains and the awe-inspiring magic they hold. In addition to living her dream and working on her next novel, Karen and her husband are in the process of creating a smaller version of the McCullough Ranch and Youth Camp that includes experiences in camping, organic farming, and outdoor survival skills. A lot of healing and clarity can happen among the quiet of the trees or on the mossy banks of a sparkling waterfall, and then there's that peaceful stillness of a pine-thatched trail beckoning you to come and just wander for a while…

Copyright 2015 by Karen Nettles

ISBN-10: 1943496099
ISBN-13: 978-1-943496-09-9
Library of Congress Control Number: 2015952823

Published by Total Fusion Press
6475 Cherry Run Rd., Strasburg, OH 44680
www.totalfusionpress.com

Dreaming of Grace is a work of fiction. Names, characters, businesses, places, events and incidents are either the products of the author's imagination or used in a fictitious manner. Any resemblance to actual persons, living or dead, or actual events is purely coincidental.

Edited by Andrea Long
Cover design by Kara Starcher

Published in Association with Total Fusion Ministries, Strasburg, OH.
www.totalfusionministries.org

Printed in the United States of America
24 23 22 21 20 19 18 17 16 15   1 2 3 4 5

Dedication

This book is dedicated to my wonderful and patient husband. He keeps me laughing and always has a lovingly strong grip on my hand when I tend to stray off the path and need reeling back in. And a big hug goes to my sister, Ginny Juhl, for being my best friend and also my technical support when I'm having a sanity meltdown over computer issues.

Tremendous appreciation also goes to my mom, family, and friends for their love, forgiveness, patience, and continued support in all my crazy endeavors.

A special thanks also goes to my three earthly angels. The first being Susan Griffin for her undying support and spiritual mentoring. She never gave up on me, and that was no easy task. Susan is my real life Glory! My second earthly angel is Miriam Hill for all her love, literary support and mentoring. She is also my biggest fan and cheerleader. My third earthly angel is Tina Levene for her huge heart and many outreach ministries that she tirelessly leads and supports to bring the children and lost souls unto the Lord. The spiritual light inside her is so bright it gives me a sunburn. Without her help, this book may have never been published.

But, most importantly, I dedicate this book to my Father in Heaven. I am eternally grateful for His support, love, guidance, encouragement, and especially forgiveness despite the years it took me to finally trust in Him above all. Nothing in my life would be possible without His grace and love.

Thank you, Father, for the people and blessings You continue to bestow upon me every day and for the great honor of being Your beloved daughter.

Table of Contents

Preface

I have always loved writing, and I have written many stories over the years just for the enjoyment of it. I started this book probably about seven or eight years ago with the intention of possibly getting something published. This story started out as a very steamy romance novel full of...um, let's just say stuff I wouldn't want my mother to read! If you knew me then, you would know that I fully intended to be the next Jackie Collins!

Excuse me for a second while I stop laughing at myself. When you read the story now, you should get a chuckle over that as well. Obviously, the book is a bit different from when I started, and I don't care how many times I share that with someone these days, I still laugh my head off at the irony. I adore God's sense of humor especially when the joke's on me! Maybe I should have called it *Fifty Shades of Grace* to really drive the point home! I'll just throw that out there for a mental bookmark.

This story is NOT about religion, and I address that point many times herein. Religion has all manner of man-made rules and oppression, and it's something I grossly despise as a tool of deceit. Due to past experiences, I was constantly put off with the hypocrisy, false piety, "church lady" syndrome, the whole hellfire and damnation judgment nonsense, and the negative stigma that accompanies the whole religious facade. I like baloney on my sandwiches, not in my life.

I also used to be burdened with "what the purpose or point of my life" was. The older I got, the more that query chafed at me. I was in my late-forties, and I still didn't know what I wanted to be when I grew up. Although I was good at lots of miscellaneous things, not one particular achievement really stood out that was truly satisfying, fulfilling, or invaluable. What had I really accomplished that mattered or made a difference? I was surrounded by all the material things society deems as successful, but that wasn't enough. I still felt anxious and empty like I had absent-mindedly missed something bigger and better, or that maybe I would never achieve anything bigger and better. And, by the way, why do we feel the need for that "bigger and better" thing anyway? Would I ever figure that out? Then I would surmise that I was probably just overthinking things and getting all whipped up about nothing. Then the hormones would kick in and these questions would once again rub me back into this angry and unsettled half-life of longing and confusion. Side note: Hormones are definitely the devil's clownishly, unnerving Jack-in-the-Boxes, popping up with all kinds of crazy and emotional warfare when you least expect it!

Lucky for me, in the middle of all this emotional ping pong, I was blessed with some grace-filled women that showed me a genuine example of what true fulfillment looks like. I wanted that calm serenity that seemed to emanate from their pores like perfume. So, despite my doubt, arrogance and ignorance, I jumped in. To my complete bafflement and wonder, I discovered not only the answers, but also something so beautifully unexpected that it became something else entirely. The resulting changes in my character and heart were not only surprising, but also a bit overwhelming. I was inspired, excited, fulfilled and humbled all at the same time. These were the types of emotions that I could embrace and work with!

I finally had a purpose and a well-defined point to move forward and evolve from. This purpose proved to be infinitely boundless in the flawless beauty of its endless possibilities. I was so beside myself that I just had to get my elucidations on paper. This book is the result of my bigger, better thing I was looking for along with the chance to share it with you.

How cool is it that your past doesn't have to be a guilty or debilitating thorn that keeps impaling you with pain or definition? How empowering is it that your sorrows and regrets can be used as a formidable exhortation of strength and wisdom for others to identify with? How I love to wield my past regrets as a walking, talking, teaching, and writing testament that miracles really do happen every single day.

And what about your current life? It doesn't have to be a robotic loop of monotonous confusion or purposeless drift. It can have a well-defined understanding and valuable intention. You can find your bigger and better, too. I have received the grace and freedom to see that now. *And that...well, that changed everything!*

~ 1 ~

A Mossy Burden

Ginger's head slumped heavily into the darkly stained, concave oval that was worn into the back of the old leather chair. Her eyes were frozen in an unblinking stare, like two nickels in a fountain of forgotten wishes. Her mouth hung slightly ajar as small breaths wafted in and out in shallow puffs. Her body was flaccid with one hand tightly curled around the cool plastic of her computer mouse, and the other lying limply in her lap as she drifted off.

The loud rhythmic clicking of the wall clock's *tick tock, tick tock,* had lulled Ginger into a hypnotic haze of semi-consciousness. She was in that catatonic state of woozy daydreaming between reality and the vaporous pull of unhinged imagination. *Tick tock, tick tock.*

As she became increasingly bored with the monotony of her days, the daydreams were occurring more and more often. She had been gazing out her windows when she became fixated with the moss growing on the trees just outside. She loved the strangely beautiful composition of the mosses and always marveled at the way the intricate little forests of green laciness clung to the damp and shady places.

It wasn't long before her mind had wandered off and her office surroundings began to melt away. Her nostrils picked up the faint and pungent scent of a sweet and musty mixture of decomposing forest undergrowth that soon permeated her senses. The familiar and comforting smell channeled her memories of blue-green mountains, icy cold streams, and the softness of fern-filled hollows.

Her mind continued to travel farther and farther away from her office as the scents of the forest became sharper. A lushly wooded scene began to materialize before her as she felt her body floating leisurely into the picture. The smell of pine was intoxicating as the uneven terrain of small twigs, leafy brush, and spongy dampness slowly manifested itself beneath her body as she realized she was lying in the warm sun, surrounded by hemlocks and knotty pine trees. She languidly brushed her hand over the dark green softness of the moss surrounding her as the soft breeze danced and played over her skin. The peaceful joy of the moment felt wonderful as she reveled in the warmth of the sun mixed with the cool softness of the breeze.

Ginger released a deep sigh as she breathed in the fresh mountain air. There was nothing like the smell of the mountains; to her it was right up there with the kind of smells that made her knees a little wobbly, like freshly baked bread or Thanksgiving turkey just out of the oven.

She smiled to herself as the warmth of the sun began to slowly subside. Large clouds had begun to move in, covering her with ominous shadows that crept over her like feral ghosts rummaging around for someone to possess. The warm breeze suddenly turned chilly and slithered across her neck like a snake, sending a cold shiver down her spine. A disoriented panic started to rise within her as she realized that the sun was setting and the darkness of night would soon devour the last of the lingering light that surrounded her.

Her body began to shudder as the rays of the sun began fading more rapidly. Her mouth felt dry and her mind struggled to clear the hazy thickness that was now making it impossible to focus on anything clearly. The chill struck her again like an icy hand and her teeth began to chatter as the cold began to settle into her bones.

Ginger was longing for warmth when she noticed there was still a bit of sunshine stretching out like a golden carpet of refuge just beyond where she was lying. She desperately needed to get to the sunshine, but her body felt heavy, her mind was thick with confusion, and she became dizzy as sweat broke out on her brow and nausea rose violently in her gut…

RINGGGG! Ginger's body jerked forward with such a force it caused her heart to jam into her throat with a choking strength. The frantic motion also sent the computer mouse flying into the base of her water glass and she fumbled to grab the glass just before it toppled over. She was still choking when the phone rang again. The pounding of her heart created a thickness in her chest that made her gasp for air. She gulped down what little water remained in her glass. *RINGGGG!* She shook her head, took another deep breath, trying to readjust her focus. *RINGGGG!*

"Okay, okay!" she shouted as she quickly picked up the phone and tried to sound calm. She squeaked out, "Ginger Thomas, may I help you?" as her heartbeat still hammered in her ears.

When she finally finished the call with the overly chatty woman that insisted on sharing more of her private life than necessary, Ginger's heart rate had returned to normal and the nausea had subsided. She hung up the phone and gazed around the tiny insurance office, recoiling in distaste as she did every day. The faded décor and ancient furnishings made her feel just as dusty and worn out. She closed her eyes, laid her face in her hands, and let out a sigh that contained the weight of the world.

The application forms lying in front of her held as much interest as the fly strip hanging in the corner of her office. She empathized with the fly's dilemma of being lured in by a sweet promise only to be trapped—feet hobbled, wings flailing furiously, and buzzing in panicked madness while everyone else just went happily through their day.

She glanced at the calendar and realized it had been a whole year since she had moved from Florida to her little Georgia town. How had a whole year slipped by so quickly? She could see the minutes of her life ticking away on the big industrial clock as she stared at the ugly white face mocking her. It was almost five, which was the only time of day Ginger liked the clunky old relic. She robotically tidied up her desk, irritated that she still couldn't ignore the ear piercing shrillness of the old chair that creaked with her every movement. Despite the gallons of silicone she had applied to its hinges, it still screamed like an arthritic old cow.

Her speaker phone beeped, "Ginger, are you going with the girls tonight for drinks?"

"Oh, hey Heather, I think I'll take a rain check, I'm really tired and not feeling that well today."

Heather let out an exaggerated laugh. "Ha, ha, very funny," she drawled in her exaggerated Georgia accent, "is that just a pardon-the-pun excuse because it really is rainin', or are you really not feelin' well?"

Ginger heard drops against the window and gazed out to check the weather. She hadn't even noticed that it had started to rain and the big trees had begun to sway with the increasing winds of the oncoming storm. She stared at the gnarly old oaks as they shifted and groaned like tired old men in the wind. She loved those ancient trees and the beautiful way the emerald carpets of moss painted themselves along the hollows of the branches which suddenly reminded her of her earlier daydream.

She flinched at the way she had so easily faded into such a deeply realistic occurrence. Weird nightmares were one thing, but these daytime episodes were getting a little too tangible. Furthermore, up until today, her daydreams didn't include smells, weather changes, or nausea. Why would the moss trigger such foreboding musings in the middle of a workday? Her eyelids felt heavy and she fought back a yawn that was followed by several more.

"Hello…? Earth to Ginger. Are ya still there, honey?" Heather's voice on the speaker phone suddenly brought Ginger back to reality.

"Oh, I'm sorry, Heather. As you can hear by my repeated yawning, I'm actually really tired. I just need to make it an early night tonight, but I'm fine. Say hi to everyone for me and I'll catch up with them on Sunday."

"You have been a little less peppy than usual, now that I think about it. If you don't start to feel better tonight, give me a call and

I'll bring you some soup or somethin' before I go home. I have some awesome detox tea here at my desk. It will help clean out any bugs that may be stickin' to ya. I'll be down to your office in just a minute, so wait for me."

Ginger clicked the hands-free speaker off. She yawned again. Sleep deprivation might be a possibility for the realness of the dreams, but it couldn't be the only issue. Her thoughts were interrupted as her breath suddenly shortened and her office seemed to be shrinking. A stuffy, cloying feeling of closed-in-ness and restraint crept up her spine and constricted her lungs. She closed her eyes and took several deep breaths to calm herself. *What on earth was that, and when did I suddenly become claustrophobic?* Maybe the tuna sandwich she had for lunch was a little spoiled—could bad fish give you hallucinations? Or maybe she was coming down with some kind of feverish flu. She felt her head; it did feel a little clammy, but not hot. The detox tea was starting to sound better and better and hopefully it would help if she did have some sort of bug.

Heather came bustling through the door and stopped short, "Whoa, you are lookin' a little green. Are you sure you don't want me to call your doctor?"

"No, I think I may have a stomach bug or maybe coming down with the flu. I just need some rest, and the tea should help," Ginger insisted.

Heather looked doubtful. "Here, just keep the whole box. I have more at home. Drink a couple of cups tonight and several tomorrow. I brought you a couple of muffins, too. Are you sure you're gonna be okay?"

"Yes, *mother*, but thank you for worrying."

"Okay, I gotta run, the girls are waitin'. Call me in the morning if you don't feel well enough to go to the farmers' market tomorrow. I can pick up what you need and drop it by. We can always do lunch another time."

Ginger smiled at her friend. "I'm sure I'll be fine. Have fun tonight and I'll call you first thing tomorrow."

Heather paused at the door and turned back, "If you aren't any better by Sunday, you *are going* to the doc on Monday, okay?"

"Yes, yes. Okay," Ginger agreed, "I'll talk to you tomorrow."

Heather gave her a warning look to make sure she knew she was serious about the doctor and then headed out to meet the other women. Ginger actually loved Heather's bossy ways. Her southern demeanor made the "mother hen" type charming. She was the owner's daughter and official bookkeeper, but she was really more of a social director and a big round bundle of fun. She always had a smile on her face and some kind of homemade sugary and delicious thing that she seemed to bake each day. Ginger gained five pounds in her first month of employment thanks to Heather's heavenly muffins. She eventually stopped eating the muffins and instead gave them to her dry cleaner or left them for the mailman. They were very grateful men.

Ginger noticed the rain was getting much heavier and the drops were starting to run trails down the windows. She rose and still felt a little woozy. After she steadied herself and packed up her things, she headed out to get some fresh mountain air into her lungs. Once outside, she breathed in the smell of the fresh rain and remembered someone saying that the smell of rain was like the breath of God. She smiled and pulled more of it into her nostrils as she opened her umbrella. She rushed to her little SUV while sending a silent word of praise that she had the whole weekend to figure out what to do about this mossy, delusional bad-fishyitis, before she officially became the new Mayor of Crazy Town.

~ 2 ~

Soup for the Soul

Once home, Ginger maneuvered clumsily through the door, trying to get her wet shoes off before she entered, and piled her computer case and dry cleaning on the small dining table. Her Sheltie, Puck, was jumping frantically below her, barking joyous greetings in frenzied excitement. His tail was wagging anxiously until she knelt down to encase him in hugs.

"How's my good little boy? Mommy missed you, too. Are you ready for dinner? Did you have a good walk today with Mrs. Tobias?"

She moved to the kitchen and filled Puck's bowl with food and prepared some of the detox tea for herself. Ginger then collapsed on the couch to watch the rain while the tea steeped and cooled. The rain was light and steady and she loved the sound of it on the tin roof. She laid her head back against the pillows and closed her eyes to listen to the soft *tat tat tat* of the droplets when she caught a whiff of the mossy odor again. Her breath became shallow and her head swam with dizziness as a wave of nausea passed over her.

She put her hand over her eyes as a heavy, disoriented feeling of dread descended upon her. She started to itch when she felt feathery fingers of moss tickling her arms and legs. It was happening again. She began to struggle against the sensation when a sudden weight flattened her stomach. The smell of dog food infused her senses as Puck licked her cheek. She snapped out of the daze and pushed him away from her face.

"Oh, yuck! You have dog food breath, silly boy. I know you want to give me some lovin', but Mommy doesn't want those stinky kisses."

She hugged him close to her until the queasy feeling passed. She buried her cheek against his neck and stroked his soft fur as a tear rolled down her cheek. *What on earth is happening to me? That was not a daydream! Lord, I need your help, this is really scaring me, please help me understand this affliction and how to make it go away!*

Puck snorted and licked her cheek again. She could not resist his silly little smiling face and soft brown eyes when he wanted attention. He rolled over onto his back and she scratched his tummy until his head rolled sideways and his tongue lolled out of his mouth in contentment.

"You are such a good boy. I love you so much."

Ginger took several sips of the tea and then sat back and continued to stroke his soft belly. She was so glad she had Puck. He had been her sanity savior so many times when the emotionally-draining twins named *loneliness* and *depression* tried to creep into her psyche with all their gloomy baggage in tow. He cheered her up with his silly antics and shared his comforting nuzzles when she occasionally succumbed to watching romantic comedies and ended up crying like an idiot all the way through.

She never thought she would get a dog, as she'd worried about her long hours at work, but Glory Tobias, her widowed next door neighbor, said she would be glad to fill in whenever needed. Puck loved walking with Glory in the afternoons while he collected treats from the neighbors, who couldn't resist him, either. Puck also loved to play with Glory's grandson, Kyle, who came to stay with his grandma a couple of afternoons a week. Ginger and Glory had become very close friends the moment they met. It pained Ginger to witness how much Glory missed her late husband, Gus. They had been married for fifty-two years before he died. God had really shown her how rewarding a true love relationship could be.

Puck jumped up and ran toward the front of the house. They both heard a car door slam and then a knock at Ginger's door. She got off the couch and answered the door. It was Glory.

"Hi Honey, did you still need me to take Puck this evenin' so you can meet with your friends?" Glory greeted Ginger warmly.

Ginger smiled in return, "I was just thinking about you!"

Puck was circling Glory and waiting for some attention. The older woman knelt down and gave him some much-appreciated hugs and rubs. "Sorry I'm runnin' a little late."

"No, it's not that! I changed my mind and decided to stay home; I'm a little tired tonight. I'll see them later this weekend."

Glory nodded, "Are you feelin' all right, sweetie? You look a little pale."

"I'm fine. My stomach is feeling a little queasy, though. I think I just need to catch up on some sleep."

"Well, I've got some soup I could bring over, if you don't feel like cookin'," Glory offered generously.

Glory was a fantastic southern cook and all her soups were delicious. Ginger figured it may just cured what ailed her, so she responded, "That sounds good. Can I come over with you right now and get it? Are you sure there's enough?"

Glory giggled, "Honey, you know I always make too much for just myself."

Ginger and Puck followed Glory next door and helped her get some groceries out of the car. When they entered the house, Ginger was overcome with warmth and coziness, just like every time she entered Glory's welcoming home. She loved looking at the family pictures scattered all over the house in various stages of their wonderful life together.

Ginger treasured the times when Glory adoringly shared countless stories of her beloved husband's devotion and romantic gestures. When she spoke of him, her face glowed with a combination of wistful joy and bittersweet heartache. Even though he had been gone for four years, she still wore her beautiful memories of him like a gown of blush- colored roses in which each and every silken petal held a cherished moment in time. Glory was a woman that had been well-loved by her husband and by her Father in Heaven and it showed in everything she did.

Glory brushed past her and pointed to the buffet server. "Grab that container over there so I can ladle you some soup. It's probably still warm. I just turned it off before I went out to pick up a couple things before the kids come over tomorrow. And I bought Puck some of those organic cookies he likes so much. They are in my red shoppin' bag on the table."

"Thanks, Glory! You are so good to us, isn't she, Puck?"

Puck barked and yipped when he spotted the cookies, and she tossed him a piece while Glory ladled enough soup for three meals. Ginger's mother was a good cook also and loved to make big pots of soup like Glory. Before her parents had passed away, they enjoyed cooking together and had a good and loving relationship, but it wasn't quite as romantic or deep as Gus and Glory's had seemed to be.

Ginger sat down in the kitchen chair to wait while Puck waited longingly for another cookie. She tossed him another piece and gazed into Glory's small living room as her friend grabbed crackers and various other goodies to put in the bag with her soup. She was always struck by how the unseen reminders of Gus and Glory's marriage were still so palpable throughout their home. They emanated softly through the air like the smell of a freshly baked pie. Glory's love was interwoven into each delicate stitch in the gently worn pillows of her husband's favorite old chair, holding endless accounts of one enchanting story after another. The recollections of hopes, dreams, and celebrations echoed softly among the patterns of the faded wallpaper that caressed each framed photo of their treasured past. Their devotion to each other was so strong it became forever entwined with the dust bunnies under their bed as they weathered the joys and sorrows of life for over fifty years together. Ginger couldn't help but be overwhelmed with hope whenever she was in Glory's presence, which helped her overcome the loneliness. Glory and Gus also had kept God as the center of their relationship, which is what Glory claimed to be the secret of their successful marriage. Ginger admired that Glory continued to offer solemn and thankful praise for their long-lived happiness in faith. While it warmed her heart immensely, it also made Ginger really miss her parents.

Glory suddenly interrupted Ginger's line of thought, "You okay, honey? You look like you were a daydreamin' somethin' painful there."

Ginger smiled at her friend, "I'm okay, just thinking about how good that soup smells."

"Well, I'd have ya sit right here and gobble it up, but I have to get some things baked and prepared for tomorrow, so I wouldn't be very good company."

"No, no. I know you are busy tonight. I'm just grateful that I don't have to eat the measly leftovers I was planning on heating up."

"Why don't you join us tomorrow for dinner?" Glory asked warmly. "I know they would all love to see you!"

Ginger considered the invitation for only a moment. "I would love to see them, too, but I'm supposed to go to the farmers' market with Heather and I'm not sure when we'll get back. And if I do have the flu or something, I wouldn't want Kyle to catch it. I'll let you know tomorrow, but please give them my love anyway."

"Okay, sweetie, but if you change your mind, just head on over. Here's your soup and goodies. I know they'll make ya feel much better."

Ginger hugged Glory good-bye and went back to her own little house with Puck trailing along behind her. After dishing out some soup and crackers from Glory's care package, she settled back down on the couch. *Thank you, Father, for this wonderful meal and my loving friends for being there and caring for me tonight. Please don't let me have any more of those weird episodes again. In Jesus' name, Amen.*

After she had finished her soup and fed Puck most of her crackers, she washed up the dishes and went to put away her dry cleaning. She noticed Glory through the side window. The older woman was still bustling around in her little kitchen preparing for her family with such love and anticipation. Ginger's heart dripped another small drop of sadness. She longed for the luxurious feeling of her own blush-colored gown of roses just waiting for her to water them with her own loving memories. *Where is my Gus, Father? When will you send him?*

The memories of her past relationships raised their ugly heads and she winced at how sordid they had been. She shook them off and reminded herself that she had been forgiven by her heavenly Father for her past sins, which enabled her to leave the guilt behind like an old snakeskin hanging shamefully on the thorny branches of the past.

Her belly was full and the exhaustion of the day had finally caught up with her. Ginger's eyelids were heavy and her neck felt tight. She prepared for bed quickly, and she and Puck were soon fast asleep.

~ 3 ~

Rainy Day Reflections

Ginger's sleep was pretty uneventful and she was thankful for that. It was still a little rainy that morning and after showering and walking Puck, she called Heather and told her that she wasn't in the mood to deal with the rain. Heather agreed that the farmers' market was probably not going to have much activity and that maybe they would try again after church on Sunday.

Ginger definitely felt a little better today, but decided to take a do-nothing-in-particular day anyway. She heated up another bowl of Glory's soup for lunch and steeped some more of the tea that Heather had given her.

When she finished lunch, she lay on the couch and picked up a book on gardening and cooking. The book was her father's, and her mind soon wandered to bittersweet thoughts of him. The tragic loss of her father was so painful, but she was ever thankful for the path it led her to.

A single tear rolled down Ginger's cheek as the past leapt up before her. Losing her father so suddenly and without warning had knocked her totally off balance. Her life had spiraled way out of control and caused her to turn to all the wrong vices and bad relationships, looking for comfort and answers that would never come. She was like a three-legged table that could not support itself sufficiently when the weight of her despair came crashing down. Her last failed relationship ended over two years ago in all manners of deceit, infidelities, and insecurities.

After an embarrassing tantrum and hysteria-filled break up, she finally reached her lowest point and literally ran to the only place she could find comfort—her father's gravesite. She hadn't been able to go there since his funeral and hadn't realized until she collapsed on the grassy lawn in front of his headstone that she had been drowning in an ocean of guilt and despair. After hours of sobbing regrets and countless apologies for letting him down, she realized that it was time to dramatically change her life. She just didn't know how. She felt so helpless and exhausted after pushing all her emotions to their limits that she scooted up and laid her head against his headstone, wrapping her arms around it just like she had done against his chest so many times during her life. As her cheek rubbed against the cold surface of the stone, she suddenly noticed the engraved scripture. Her father must have said it to her over a thousand times. She had been so distraught at the funeral that she hadn't even noticed what had been etched into the shiny new granite. As she read it aloud, she remembered him saying this verse over and over again throughout her entire life: *Ginger, always remember to love the Lord with all your heart, all your soul, all your mind, and all your strength.*

Ginger's breath stopped short with the memory of his smile and the sincerity in his eyes when he spoke it to her as she struggled that day to recall the last part of what he always said. And then she heard the words as clear as a bell. It was as if her father was standing right there beside her that day: *If you always put God's love for you and your love for Him first, He will reward you with a life greater than you could ever imagine. Never forget that wherever you are and whatever you are doing, He will always be there to guide you and comfort you. If you keep your faith and trust in Him above all, you will never be alone. Always remember that He dwells within you right here. All you have to do is believe!* She remembered he would always point his finger at her heart when he said *right here.* She put her hand on her heart that day and for the first time she understood what those words meant—what her father had been trying to tell her since she was a child. She felt a flush of peace and warmth and radiance come over her like a blanket. She now realized why her father had been such a blessed and kind man. He had the light of the Lord within him. And that's when her whole life and her spiritual understanding had changed.

Ginger smiled again at the memory and ran her hand over the front of her father's book with fondness. The phone rang beside her and made both her and Puck, who had been slumbering beside her, jump. She picked the phone up quickly.

The voice on the other line spoke first, "Hi, sweetie, I noticed that you didn't go to the market today. How are you feelin'?"

"Oh, hi, Glory." Ginger shook off the memories as she considered Glory's question. "It was more about the rain than how I felt which is much better thanks to your magic soup."

"That's so good to hear. The kids will be here soon, and the invitation is still open to join us."

"You know how much I love your family and appreciate your invitation, but I'm just not feeling very social today," Ginger paused. "Do you know what I mean?"

"Of course I do!" Glory answered reassuringly. "You don't have to explain the melancholy days to me, sweetheart. Just have a good, long chat with the Father, and you'll feel much better. I'll drop some dessert to you later when the kids leave."

"Thanks, and be sure to give my love to everyone. Oh, and Glory..." Ginger's thought trailed off a moment.

"Yes, my dear?"

"Thanks for being such a good friend to me."

Glory responded, "Right back at 'cha, love."

As they hung up the phone, Ginger thought about how nice it was that Glory had faith like Ginger's father had. Before her mother died, Ginger had tried several times to explain her spiritual revelations about herself and her father to her mother, but she would just smile and say, *"That's nice dear..."* and *"Yes, your father was a saint..."* Ginger realized that her mother was a strong believer, but church on Sunday was as far as she was going to go with her faith. For her mother, it was something you were just expected to do.

Her father's faith was different—he was always reading the Bible and attending Bible studies with other members of the church. He faithfully attended church, even when he traveled, and was always looking for ways to serve others.

When Ginger decided she wanted the light that her father had, it was hard at first and she didn't know where to start. So she did what her father did and started reading her Bible every day and prayed for God to help her. She started going back to her father's church where each week it seemed like every sermon was written specifically for her, which she had never experienced in all the previous years she had attended.

After her father passed away, she had turned totally away from the church and what she thought was faith, and in those actions she had actually lost two fathers—one in the flesh and One in the Spirit. When she sincerely committed her heart to the Lord, the words He spoke to her through the Bible and her pastor gave her the peace to finally deal with her father's death. She also gained the wisdom to stop focusing on her needs and issues and be more concerned with the needs of others.

Her failed relationships were previously built out of desperation, low expectations, and loneliness. She had been looking to fill a void that would never get full with earthly pleasures, pursuits, or people. She had been reacting to her life instead of trusting the Lord's plan for her. She knew now that when the time was right, God would send true and lasting love to her. It was a matter of faith and patience, and the world continually tested her on that. But she kept her focus and trusted that God was building her strength and character for some larger purpose and the reward of someone very special. She finally adopted the state of mind that she would rather be alone and occasionally lonely than settle for less than what God thought she deserved.

When she did get lost in a pity party for herself, the rewards of helping others through the ministries of her church in Florida and now in Georgia were so humbling and fulfilling and that always put the fourth leg back under her table again. So many people were in real crisis, and seeing their struggles always helped to put her issues into perspective. It was also nice to know that her church body was full of compassionate believers that understood the ways of the Lord and would always be there for her if she was ever in real need. Occasionally she missed the loving people she had known from her father's church in Florida, but she loved Glory's little church and the people here even more. The mountain church was strictly Bible-based teaching, and the pastor was so humble and compassionate. The people seemed much more spiritually mature, and she continued to learn a lot from them. Ginger had also grown substantially in her faith, wisdom, and relationship with the Lord through Glory's guidance and counsel. Thinking of church reminded her of a sick child mentioned on Sunday, so she began a silent prayer of healing for the boy when Puck burped rather loudly. She burst out laughing.

"Well, excuse you!"

Puck sneezed and then flashed a big guilty smile. When she finally stopped laughing, she finished her prayer and heard the birds singing outside and noticed the rain had subsided again. The sun decided to make one more appearance before it started to travel west for the night. Puck bumped her hand with his nose and licked her palm. She smiled down at him, and he cocked his head. He knew she was feeling out of sorts, and she stroked his head and gazed into his big brown eyes.

"We have so much love to give, don't we, boy? I just pray we have a big family to share it with soon." Ginger finished scratching Puck's ears. "Want to go for a quick walk before it starts raining again?"

He jumped down from the couch and ran toward his leash by the door. After they had returned from their nightly walk, Puck barked when they heard a noise out back. Ginger got up and gazed out the window toward Glory's house to see what had riled up Puck. Glory was out on her back porch using an old broom handle to beat a rug hanging over her clothesline. Ginger laughed about how Glory still used a broomstick over a vacuum. Glory had just cooked, cleaned and entertained, and now she was out on her porch beating a rug. Ginger hoped she had Glory's energy when she reached that age.

Glory was also wearing her favorite old straw hat, and Ginger remembered the first time she saw Glory wearing that hat while standing in her garden. Ginger was just stepping out of the car with the rental agent on a lazy summer day, when she was immediately drawn to the vision of this striking woman standing in the speckled sunlight of a beautiful rose garden that was situated between the two houses. The woman had the beauty and poise of a forties movie actress and emanated the elegance of that era.

Ginger remembered how her thoughts had then shifted to her recently deceased mother and her chest had tightened and her heart ached with fresh rawness. Then the woman turned and looked right at her with the biggest and warmest smile on her face and waved at her like they'd known each other for years. The tightness melted away. The woman's softly wrinkled face made Ginger relax and a peace fell over her as the breeze picked up and sent a cascade of leaves spiraling down around them. Ginger smiled and waved back. She remained captivated by the lovely older woman gently cradling a bright orange rose as the pastel-colored sundress she wore fluttered gently in the breeze and brushed lightly against her delicate skin. Ginger felt a warm sensation wrap around her like a hug and knew at that instant, as the dappled glints of sunlight splashed among the shady tree-lined sidewalk, that this woman was filled with God's grace and would help Ginger mend her aching heart.

Ginger tapped on the window to catch Glory's attention and waved. Glory was at her door with dessert less than ten minutes after that. Ginger savored the last crumbs of blueberry pie before she returned to the couch with Puck and worked on her Bible study lessons until it was time for bed.

~ 4 ~
Little Indian Moccasins

On Sunday morning, the alarm clock rang and Ginger quickly dressed for church. As she was finishing up her breakfast, the melancholy musings were still bumping around in her head. That beautiful Georgia day when she had first seen Glory had been a little over a year ago; and although she was thankful for her blessings, she was troubled that her big, bright, shiny expectations for an exciting new life in the mountains were looking more like an old moth-eaten blanket. She really wasn't *unhappy*—and she was always mindful to be grateful for her growth and wonderful changes in her life—but she wasn't bouncing around with joy tied to a bright red ribbon of hope, either.

She loved Glory. Her heart had mostly mended from her parents' deaths, and she had Puck and her church friends and Bible studies to fill the lonely spaces and keep her busy. So why was she feeling stuck, like she wasn't growing any further? Ginger wondered if this weird thing that was happening to her was a catalyst for something greater. It certainly was getting her attention both emotionally and physically.

She heard Puck barking and then Glory's three quick knocks on the door. She dropped her breakfast dishes in the sink and grabbed her raincoat and purse.

As they settled in the car, Glory asked, "Still feelin' a little blue?"

"Yeah, I just can't shake this feeling like something's a little off," Ginger admitted.

"Maybe you're missin' Florida?" Glory suggested

"No! That's definitely not it." Ginger said with absolute certainty. "I know the Lord led me to Georgia and to you. And I certainly haven't missed Florida for one millisecond. I still ruffle in distaste over the noisy and unpleasant memories of growing up in Daytona and the endless monotony of it all."

"I've heard you say that before, but what in particular was so unpleasant for you?"

"Well, we lived in a small neighborhood that was very close to the Daytona Beach strip. So, every year was the same touristy nightmare. When the snowless winters passed, the beach was a prime spot for the college kids on spring break. We had to endure the drunken non-stop party hooting and hollering all night long for over two weeks. Then summer break would bring the pasty white snow people from the North and their kids that morphed into crimson colored burn patients by the second day, then back to white again after they plastered themselves from head to toe with zinc oxide."

Glory burst out laughing as Ginger continued,

"And then there was the joy of the never-ending, ear-blasting sound of revving motorcycles during Bike Week every year.

So it was constant traffic and pedestrian chaos—kind of like ants on crack that were always in my way and never knew where they were going! I know that's not very nice to say, but add to that the endlessly hot humidity that would settle down on you like a sumo wrestler's chokehold and there in was the perfect cocktail for my daily misery and dreams of escape."

"Well, good thing you didn't grow up somewhere like New York City!" chuckled Glory. "You'd have really gone crazy."

"No doubt about that!" Ginger nodded vehemently. "Being in the crowded city is so different from the politeness and compassion found in small towns that just naturally breathe their welcoming charm all over you. I went to New York a couple of times and was so disillusioned by the animosity and coldness I felt. I remember thinking how odd it was that I was surrounded by all these hundreds of people jammed together, shoulder-to-shoulder, and yet I still felt so isolated. There was no social interaction outside of their assigned cliques or circles and if they didn't think you were of their ilk, they certainly let you know it.

But visiting a small town is like fresh warm laundry just out of the dryer; you want to wrap yourself up and cuddle down into the comfort of it. It's such a relief and unanticipated joy to meet strangers that smile, greet you, and then make you feel at ease, especially when you are traveling in an unknown place."

"I know exactly what you're sayin'," stated Glory as she nodded her head. "I went to New York with Gus for a business trip and enjoyed seein' the sights and museums, but I felt very anxious and hurried everywhere we went. I just couldn't relax with all the noise and the traffic and the horns honkin' and the way they all seemed to be rushin' to get somewhere. Walkin' down the sidewalk was like bein' in an obstacle course. They were bumpin' into me like I wasn't even there and I never once heard a *'sorry, ma'am'*. I was so exhausted when we got home. It took me days to settle down again."

"Yeah, me too," agreed Ginger, "I know some people thrive on that high-energy, big city excitement adrenaline rush thing, but for me it was like having a mosquito stuck in my ear for a week."

Glory laughed. "Well said, honey, well said. Your parents were from the West or Midwest, weren't they?"

"Yes, they moved to Florida from Colorado when I was two. They were opening a new sales market in the southern region and my father's new territory covered Florida, Georgia, and the Carolinas. Being from the frigid cold of Minnesota, my mother adored the beach and the warm weather, so Daytona is where we settled. My father used to say that he thought she might be part reptile since she liked the heat so much."

She and Glory laughed.

"Your daddy was funny," Glory added when she caught her breath.

"Yeah, he was," Ginger agreed, "And he liked the cool weather like I did; so if he was going somewhere for work like in the Carolinas near Cherokee, or Gatlinburg in Tennessee, we would talk my mother into letting me take a couple days off from school and meet up with him for a long weekend."

Glory smiled, "I just adored those little Indian moccasins and long-feathered headdresses they sell in Cherokee."

"Me, too!" exclaimed Ginger, "and I never got tired of the *Ripley's Believe it or Not* attraction in Gatlinburg."

"Oh yes! That's where all those crazy unexplained things were. Kyle and Gus loved that place too."

For a moment, both women were locked in silent memories.

Then Glory continued, "Was your daddy gone a lot? Did that add to why you weren't happy there?"

"Well, he traveled two weeks out of the month, but then he was home for two weeks, so it wasn't too bad. And my mother, as you know, was a very content housewife and raised me with loving devotion. We did have a lot of fun together when my father was on the road—she would call it our *girl time*. I guess the beach was fun when I was young, but even from a very young age I knew I didn't belong there. And then the older I got, the more and more I realized how much I disliked the hot, flat, sandy terrain of Florida. I wanted to be in the peaceful cool quiet of forests, mountains, and snow."

"Did your daddy miss the mountains, too?"

"Yes. But he knew how happy my mom was, so to get our fix, every year my father would take two weeks' vacation and all three of us would load up the car and head to the mountains where we would rent a small cabin in the early summer before it got too hot and crowded. I was so happy being surrounded by the rich green forests, rushing streams, and chilly waterfalls—it was so exciting and mysterious. It was also heaven to have my father's full attention for two whole weeks. We would explore the woods for hours looking for animal tracks, wild blackberries, colored mushrooms, and bird nests. I would collect wildflowers for my mother, and if we were lucky, we would find what my father called a *fairy village* nestled in an old mossy stump."

"You were so blessed to have that enchanted time with your father."

"I was," Ginger nodded. "He always made it into an adventure. We would hike for hours until we would get so sweaty that we would have to jump into the cold rushing streams to cool off while we searched for gold, rubies, and garnets until we were both shivering. We would always laugh at the way our lips turned blue and our fingers morphed into anemic-looking prunes.

Then in the evenings we would watch for fireflies while my father grilled hamburgers and hot dogs. After dinner, we would roast marshmallows over a big fire pit and then play cards or board games. I loved the crisp clear coolness of the evenings when my father and I would take a long walk each night before bed. We would bundle up and head down the small rocky lane in front of the cabin, gazing at all the stars and listening to the mysterious sounds of the night. He would always let me hold the flashlight. When we returned, I would jump into my warm bed in my little footed pajamas all cozy from my bath and my mother and father would smother me in kisses before I drifted off to sleep. I never wanted to go back home."

Glory sighed and put her hand on her heart. "Well, I wouldn't want to go home either. Those are such wonderful memories, Ginger."

"Oh, you've heard my cabin in the woods story plenty of times before, Glory."

"Not with that much detail. No wonder you have such a longin' to recapture those feelin's. And I understand wantin' to recapture our memories. I know you miss your momma and daddy like I miss my Gus."

They were both quiet for a time, lost in their own thoughts of loss, when Glory broke the silence.

"Did you still visit the mountains with your parents when you were older?"

"Yes. I remember taking the trips well into my twenties, but I always reverted back to being my father's little girl the minute he pulled out the marshmallows and sparked up the fire."

"How old was your daddy when he passed? It was heart failure, right?"

"Yes, heart failure. And he was only sixty-eight."

"And now you've lost your momma a little over a year ago, and even though it was from natural causes that doesn't make it any less painful. That could be it, honey."

"What could be it?"

"Why you're feelin' so blue. You may be missin' them more so now that the hubbub of movin' and adjustin' to bein' here and all that distraction has settled down a bit. This is a whole new place and people and culture which are all excitin', but you're still a bit of a fish out of water. It's only been a little over a year now, and you are still lookin' for your little place to call home, right?"

Ginger considered the honest words of her friend. "Hmm, yeah, maybe you're right. I have been reflecting a lot more lately and I just miss my family so much sometimes that I can hardly breathe. I wish I could hear my mother's contagious giggles or feel my father's breath-stealing bear hugs just one more time. He was a really good hugger." Ginger's voice got thick and she felt her eyes well up.

Glory wiped a tear from her own cheek. "I know how you feel, honey. I truly do know how you feel."

Ginger wiped her eyes and nodded, "Yes, you do."

Glory patted Ginger's hand. "I guess we both need the comfort of the Lord today and I praise Him every day that we have each other! You are such a blessing to me, little one."

Ginger's tears welled up again, "And you to me."

Glory smiled at Ginger and squeezed her hand as they turned into the parking lot of the little chapel.

~5~

Family Traditions

After Ginger got home from the chapel, she thought maybe Glory was right. It could be something to do with her life getting a little too routine or stale. Puck yipped at her and trotted toward the back door. She opened the back door to let him out and gazed out over her unattended vegetable garden and sagged against the door frame. Her father would not be very proud of her progress, just a couple of measly tomato seedlings and some wilting lettuce. Without his insight and suggestions, her repeated attempts at growing vegetables every year sadly did not fill the void of his absence. The soil was different here, the temperature was different, but she had no doubt he would know how to whip her garden into shape in no time.

She smiled as she pictured him in his big floppy hat, surrounded by all the varieties of his delicious treasures and the countless times she arrived home from school, pulled on her rubber boots, and raced into the back yard to find him. He would always be standing there with a huge smile on his face, covered in dirt, one garden glove on and one in his pocket, with soil smeared haphazardly on his cheeks, and holding a bucket for each of them to load up whatever fruit, vegetables, or berries were in season. When they were finished filling the buckets, they would trudge over to the back porch to meet her mother and share a pitcher of ice cold lemon tea. She and her mother would comb through recipe books and decide what heavenly creations they would concoct with their harvest, while her father scrubbed their pickings and praised the Lord for His bounty. Fried green tomatoes, cabbage-carrot bunny slaw, strawberry cream cake, and sweet potato pie were some of her father's favorites.

Puck trotted back inside, snorting and rolling on the carpet. The rain had stopped, but some of the bushes were still damp, and he apparently rubbed up against every single one. The phone rang and she hurried to answer it.

"Hi, Heather," Ginger greeted when she recognized the voice on the other line. "Yes, I'm feeling much better today. I'll get Puck harnessed up and meet you down at the farmers' market if you still want to go. Okay, I'll meet you in twenty minutes by the entrance gate."

She gathered her cloth shopping bags and treats and water for Puck and headed to the market. After a couple of hours, she and Heather were getting hungry, so they grabbed some chicken wraps and sat down at a small café table under the shade of some lovely maple trees. She filled a bowl with some water and another with some chicken for Puck which he gobbled down in two seconds flat before he collapsed under her chair for a nap.

Heather began the conversation, "So, I just realized yesterday that you've been here about a year now and I have never asked you how you came to live in our lovely little town. And you know I work in the insurance business because of my daddy, but why did you get into insurance?"

"That's a long story, Heather," answered Ginger.

"Well, Puck and I aren't goin' anywhere right now. Are you?"

Ginger laughed. "It's not really that exciting."

"Honey, everyone is always asking me about you, and I have no information to share with them. So, could you just be a good girl and cooperate? I need some gossip—now spill it."

Ginger laughed again and shook her head. "You are relentless, you know that?"

Heather nodded emphatically. "Yep, so come on now, girl, start talking."

"Okay, but I warned you, it's not very juicy."

"You let me be the judge of that," Heather said with an excited twinkle in her eye.

"Well, okay, then," Ginger relented as she began her story. "I started out working part-time at an insurance agency in Florida for two summers while I was attending the local community college. Eventually they offered me a full time position with a pretty good salary and benefits, so I thought I would put school on hold for a while. But the years passed quickly and college just became an unnecessary drain on my time and finances. Home insurance wasn't very exciting or challenging, no offense…" Ginger looked at her friend.

"Trust me honey, none taken," Heather quipped.

Ginger continued, "But, I made a decent salary and was able to put away a pretty good amount of savings with the goal of purchasing a cabin in the mountains one day. Over the years, I occasionally searched for other job opportunities, but insurance was my area of expertise and Florida was where my mother lived, so that is where I stayed for many more years than I had actually planned."

"So how did you get here?" Heather interjected.

"Well, when both my parents had passed and it was just me, I thought it was finally time to begin a new adventure. So, a month after my mother's funeral, I sent résumés out to several jobs in northeastern states. The mountains had been calling me since I was a kid, and I couldn't wait to answer. Both my parents' deaths had been hard on me, so the adventure of moving to the mountains took some of the pain away and gave me something else to look forward to."

Heather looked sympathetically at Ginger. "It breaks my heart that you went through that all by yourself."

"Well, my church friends down there took good care of me and they were a real blessing when I lost my mother. I do really miss them, and, of course, they didn't want me to move, but the memories of my happiest times were with my parents in the mountains, and there was no talking me out of that. My friends understood that I needed to fulfill my longing for a change of scenery and a cooler climate."

"Amen to that!" Heather agreed, "I took my kids to Disney World in Florida a couple years back, and I thought I might just pass out from the humidity. It was stifling to say the least! It still gets hot here in Blue Ridge, but nothing like that."

"Trust me, I know!"

"So then you saw our advertisement on the internet?" Heather prompted her to continue.

"Yes, and after careful consideration of the job offers I received back, you had the best offer, so here I am."

"Well, of course. I wrote that ad myself and no person in their right mind could have resisted my charms!"

The two women laughed again.

"So now that you've been here a year, do you think you made the right choice? And be honest."

"Well, it isn't as far north as I'd wanted to go, but it was a good start. The Lord led me to this place and I've been blessed with Glory and you and my friends from church."

"So one day at a time is how you're takin' it. That's good, let the Lord make the plans."

Ginger smiled. "Exactly—like right now, I'm sitting here on this beautiful day with the most enchanting socialite in town and my adorable dog is snoozing in the shade below me, and the view of the beautiful Blue Ridge Mountains is right in front of me, so yeah, I should be counting my blessings."

Heather grinned. "Well yes, I am quite enchantin', aren't I?"

They both giggled.

"So how weird was it to move from being a flatlander to the mountains?" Heather inquired.

"I was so excited and ready to move that I didn't really think too much about it, but it did prove to be a bigger adjustment than I expected. You all do have one pace and it is *slow*. I was not familiar with *Mountain Time* or *When we get 'round to it.*"

Heather laughed. "It's definitely slower than Florida, that's for sure. But we like to get to know everything about folks while we can; the work will eventually get done. And of course if it's huntin' season or if somethin' a little shinier and more excitin' comes up, we're definitely gonna chase that first."

Ginger laughed. "I'm not meaning it in a bad way; it just takes some getting used to."

"I'm not sayin' it in a bad way either," Heather agreed. "It's just the truth!"

They both laughed and Ginger added, "It did take me some time to earn everyone's acceptance and trust, though. This was the first time in my life that I ever worried about that."

Heather nodded, understanding. "We're only wary of newcomers because we're just lookin' out for our own. Making sure you're to be trusted before we let ya become one of us. We don't want no big city hot shots judgin' and tryin' to change our small town ways. We done just fine clingin' to our God, guns, and Bibles. And we'll have that with a side of greasy taters and grits, please! If you don't like it, then watch out for my squeaky screen door and rubber boot hittin' you on the way out!"

Ginger burst out laughing. "Amen to that! I was just telling Glory this morning how much I love the way that everyone looks out for their neighbors and helps out whenever they can. Florida is such a big melting pot of immigrants and transplants from other states, so between the tourists and the hundreds of people moving in and out every day, no deep roots have a chance to form. Neighbors live right next to each other and never even say *hello*. But here, everyone seems to know everyone and their business. That took a little getting used to, but I kind of like that now."

"Well, that's how we take care of each other, by knowin' each other's needs and sorrows and pain, and also sharin' the joys. That's what the good Lord intended—community. And that's not some-thin' you can buy, that's a blessin' that's given."

"That's for sure," Ginger nodded.

Heather smiled, "Didn't mean to start goin' on. Back to you, what's goin' on with your cabin? Are you still lookin'?"

"Yeah, but it's moving just below a snail's pace. There always seems to be something that's not quite right. They are either too big or too small, or the land is too steep, or there's not enough privacy, or enough acreage, or the river is just a small side branch instead of a wide rushing river. A lot are in disrepair, or overpriced, or too remote with no electricity or septic tank, etc. The few that were a consideration just didn't have enough of that feeling like… *this is home*. Do you know what I mean?"

"Yes, I do. But just remember, Ginger, the Lord has his own timetable, so you just keep prayin' and it will all work out. You need to find you a husband—that's what you need! *Lord, help me find this girl a husband!* That's what I'm prayin' for!"

Ginger burst out laughing. "I'll take your prayers, but you can keep your matchmaking to yourself! We'll just leave that to the Lord, too!"

They talked and laughed a little while longer, just enjoying the cool breeze and each other's company until the rain started up again, sending them both scurrying to their cars.

After Ginger returned home, the rain had lightened up to just a small sprinkling. She put Puck out back to do his business while she put her farmers' market purchases away. As she opened the door to let Puck back in, she spotted a rainbow fanning out over the mountains. She smiled to herself and said, *Thank you, God, I really needed that!* Her father used to say that rainbows were a sign from the Lord that everything would be all right.

Puck trotted past her and began rolling on the throw rug to get the rain off his fur again. He lolled on his back, snorting and sneezing until Ginger grabbed a towel and had to go through a short game of tug of war before she could get him to stand patiently for his rub down.

By the time she finished up the housework and laundry, the sun had set and it was nearly dark. She took Puck on their nightly walk down the street and relished the chill in the breeze that the rain had brought in. When she got home, she put some more wood on the crackling fire, wrapped herself up in her comfy old sweater, and closed up all the windows before she and Puck settled down on the couch for the evening.

As she snuggled in with her little furry prince, she thought about her conversation with Heather. She *did* like her little house. It was warm, cozy, and safe, and she knew she was supposed to bloom where she was planted—meaning she should be happy and productive wherever she was, and she thought she was doing pretty well with that. But, it wasn't her cabin, and it wasn't on a river, and it wasn't nestled in the mountains, and it wasn't even her *home*—it was just a rental.

The warm fire reminded her of her first Christmas here, a little over four months ago, when, despite the wonderfully cooler temperatures, it hadn't even snowed once. It was just like another Florida Christmas, bitterly cold with no blanket of white to cheer her up. She wanted to live where white Christmases were a normal occurrence, somewhere that it was rare not to get at least two or three good snowfalls during the winter. Glory had not enjoyed telling her that snow was pretty rare in their little town. Only the higher elevations had chances of getting a decent snowfall.

Glory had been so sweet to invite Ginger to spend her first Christmas in town with her and her family, but Ginger had declined and come up with her own plan instead. The snow didn't come to her, so she went to the snow. Christmas had always been a big deal for her family, and it was her favorite holiday. Ginger was determined to have her white Christmas no matter what, while at the same time, keeping her family traditions alive. Every year her father would round up whatever people had no family and invite them all home. Year after year, the house was packed and she loved helping her father give these people the gift of family, even if it was only for one night. She and her mother continued in her father's tradition after his death and she vowed to keep it going in honor of both of them.

The first part of plan B was to decorate every corner of her little house and invite some of the locals from her church and a couple of coworkers for a small party of her own. She was determined to be cheerful on that first Christmas Eve in her new home since now *she* was the one with no family. She had even sewn a small Santa hat for Puck that lasted just long enough for a quick picture before it became his new chew toy.

She played a CD of Bing Crosby's "White Christmas" as she passed trays of ham and cream cheese rolls, turkey and cranberry finger sandwiches, mashed potato and mushroom pastries, and meatballs with turkey gravy to her guests. For dessert she served peppermint eggnog, frosted sugar cookies, and pecan pie.

She and Puck posed for pictures in front of the live tree that she had decorated with cherished ornaments from her childhood. And even though it didn't snow, it was a really frosty night. Her little fireplace kept the house warm and she knew her guests had really enjoyed themselves. Everyone was gone by nine, and she and Puck collapsed on the couch, sharing the last of the sugar cookies while watching *It's a Wonderful Life* until they fell asleep by the fire.

On Christmas morning, she got up early and gave Puck his doggie stocking filled with treats and toys while she loaded her backpack and supplies into her little SUV. Then she and Puck drove to Gatlinburg, Tennessee, for the weekend, where she knew from the weather forecasts that it was snowing.

She had rented a tiny cabin just outside town and the two of them had spent Christmas day trudging happily through the snow on various mountain trails. Puck was fascinated by the snow, biting it, eating it, and digging his nose into it as he bounded, pounced, and rolled to his heart's content. They only stopped long enough for a picnic lunch, which she spread out on a blanket under a snow-covered evergreen. They ate turkey sandwiches with cranberry sauce and sipped on warm apple cider amidst the slowly falling flakes. The snow made her very happy, and sitting there with Puck in that white-covered wonderland was a pretty good Christmas present, if she did say so herself.

She smiled at the memory and then slowly reeled herself back to the present. The thought of those turkey sandwiches was making her stomach growl, and all this reminiscing was starting to give her a headache. She flipped on the news and gave Puck a squeeze and a kiss still happy from the warm Christmas memories. And then she moved lazily off the couch and headed toward the kitchen to warm up the last of Glory's soup.

~ 6 ~

An Unexpected Visitor Comes Calling

Three weeks had gone by since the mossy daydream with no further incidences, but Ginger was still feeling restless and not sleeping well. She awoke on Saturday morning unsettled and fatigued after another night of exhausting dreams. She squeezed her eyes tightly shut waiting for the haziness to clear. Fleeting and distorted nightmares had occurred sporadically throughout her life, but these realistic dreams, or whatever they were, were not letting up. They were actually getting more frequent and more confusing. At least the mossy daydreams had stopped, but a hazy heaviness and feelings of lethargic hopelessness were starting to wear her out.

She did finally go to the doctor last week, but he'd had no real answers for her symptoms. Thankfully the MRI showed no signs of clotting or unusual growths. He said it could be depression from her loss of family and prescribed some popular cure-all happy pills. But she was very skeptical of prescription drugs; the side effects seemed worse than the ailment, so she threw the script in the drawer and forgot about it.

She pondered psychiatric help, but she didn't exactly trust that whole practice and was afraid to admit that she was having all these weird episodes with no reasoning she could decipher. She knew she was sad about the loss of her parents and missed them very much, but she couldn't figure out why that would be causing her to have such odd dreams.

She wasn't really comfortable about the thought of telling a complete stranger about these feelings either, let alone the vivid reality of her recurring nightmares. How was she supposed to explain burning houses and herds of horses running thunderously at her, their eyes wild with panic and fear? And what would they say about the incident with the moss that had worked its way out of her dreams and into her waking hours, where she physically *smelled* the moss and actually *felt* it on her skin?

There was also the old familiar longing that she had been experiencing for years. As long as she could remember, Ginger had yearned for something inexplicable that she was missing. The sensation of having lost something unbeknownst to her was becoming much stronger. She sympathized with the people that could still feel a phantom arm or leg that had been amputated; something was there and now it was gone. The only difference was Ginger had all her limbs accounted for and she was unaware that she was missing something—but her mind just wouldn't accept the mysterious loss. She had never told anyone about any of this in the past, not even her parents. It was too weird. Maybe it was a slow decent into dementia that came from her biological mother.

Ugh, stop it, stop it, stop it! Just get up and get over yourself! She flipped the sheet off in frustration and rolled over right into Puck's wet nose. He liked to put his head on the pillow next to her in the mornings while he waited patiently for her to wake up. He quickly planted a wet tongue right up her nose and across her eye before she turned his face away.

"Oomph, you little devil, you got me again!"

After breakfast she made a grocery list and added a couple things to pick up for Puck at the pet store. Later that afternoon after she had returned from shopping and walking Puck, she settled down on her couch with a grilled cheese sandwich. She was so exhausted from having such restless sleep, that she was starting to suffer physically and mentally. All she wanted to do right then was take a nap, which she never did unless she was sick.

Her tired mind wandered again to a solution to her problems. She had been considering some form of counseling through one of the other local churches to avoid Glory or her friends finding out. Maybe if she did talk to someone, she could finally get some answers or at least some sleep. After she finished her sandwich, she grabbed her laptop and started sifting through pages of options, which led to more pages, which led to even more pages.

"Eenie, meenie, miney, mo—I'm going loony, don't ya know?"

Ginger slammed her laptop shut and tossed it beside her on the couch. Maybe she should get over her issue of worrying about what people will think and talk to Glory or her pastor about this. It obviously wasn't going away. She looked heavenward and whispered softly, *"I know You have a plan and purpose for whatever this is, but I really need Your loving hand and guidance to understand what to do about it."*

Puck cocked his head at her, yipped and snorted—his *I-need-to-go-outside* warning. He had a piece of crust from her sandwich stuck on the top of his nose.

She laughed at him and said, "Okay, okay let's go out back and get some fresh air, but I still need some divine intervention so you'll have to entertain yourself for a while."

She grabbed her Bible and started to head for her lounge chair in the backyard, hoping to get an answer when she heard the doorbell ring. Puck raced to the door barking and growling like a pit bull. She set her Bible down and followed him, telling him to *hush* and *settle down*. She peeped through the hole and noticed a very attractive, yet unfamiliar, face peering back at her.

"Who is it?" Ginger inquired through the closed door.

The voice said warmly, "Hello, ma'am, you don't know me. My name is Hatch McCullough. I'm a representative for a family estate."

She shouted through the door, "You must have the wrong house, Mr. McCullough, my mother passed a year ago and my father is gone as well. I don't have any other family."

The stranger shouted back, "Well, that's what I'm here about, Ms. Thomas. It's a very long story, ma'am. May I come in, or could you come out, so I can explain?"

Ginger realized that the handsome man at the door had just called her by her name. She turned to Puck who had been barking the whole time. "Hush, Puck, settle down now!" He did so unwillingly and kept it to a sporadic half-bark, half-whimper as he stood steadfast in front of the door.

Ginger moved to the window and peeped through the curtain

to see more of what the stranger looked like. He had sandy blonde hair that spilled out in wavy curls from under a faded cowboy hat. His face looked friendly enough from what she could see of his profile—tanned and wrinkled just a bit. Maybe mid-forties she guessed. He had on a white long sleeve shirt with the cuffs turned up to his elbows and very well-fitting jeans. His thighs were muscular and his backside was very nice, indeed. He was tall and really good looking, but then again some thought Ted Bundy was good looking, too.

He started to turn toward the window and she moved back before he could see her. She closed her eyes and prayed silently, *Dear Lord, I'm trusting You that a man that gorgeous is not a serial killer. Amen.*

He knocked softly on the door again. "Ma'am, are you still there?"

She crossed herself and shouted through the door, "I'll come out there. Just give me a minute."

She put Puck on his leash and stepped out onto the front porch holding him back as he barked and jumped at the man. She saw the man's eyes widen as he looked at her and his face went a little pale. She asked him if he was all right and he assured her that he was. He then bent down on one knee and put his hand out to Puck. After some serious sniffing, Puck jumped up and licked his cheek in excited salutations.

The stranger told Ginger that he had two Collies at home and said what a fine looking puppy Puck was. She explained to him that Puck was a full grown Sheltie, but was often mistaken for a baby Collie. He said he didn't know of such a dog and thought his dogs would just love the little fellow.

After exchanging formalities, Ginger sat on her porch swing

with Puck beside her and motioned for Hatch to sit in one of the adjacent chairs. He had a pouch that looked like a saddlebag that he laid in the chair beside him. He took off his cowboy hat, smoothed his hair back, and placed the faded Stetson beside the pouch. He started to take some papers out and then he paused and shoved them back into the bag.

"Ms. Thomas, I…"

"Please, call me Ginger," she interrupted.

"Yes, ma'am," he agreed before continuing. "This is a little difficult for me. Uh, I'm not a lawyer. I just need to ask you some questions and then relay some information. Could I get somethin' to drink by any chance?" He cleared his throat and pulled on one side of his collar.

Ginger blushed with embarrassment. "Oh, of course! Where are my manners? I'll be back in one second."

Ginger went back into the house, took Puck's leash off, and put a pitcher of lemonade and some cookies on a tray. She watched him from inside the kitchen as he paced back and forth on the porch, pausing at the railing every couple of paces to look out at the fading light in the sky. The sun was just starting to set and it wouldn't be too long before the stars started poking their shiny heads out. It was a clear evening with a cool breeze that gently swept the hair on his collar as he gazed at the sky. He seemed nervous in a boyish way. He had a slight accent, from the Midwest, she guessed. He looked like a taller, bigger version of the actor Matthew McConaughey with the same dimples and devilish smile. He must be about six-three or -four, she guessed and very muscular, not like a body builder, just ruggedly solid. In other words he was entirely movie star handsome with a lot of charm thrown in. Whatever he wanted must be a mix-up, but just to be able to look at him a little while longer would be worth dragging it out as long as she could.

Puck stared up at her in anticipation of a treat; she flipped him a piece of cookie and then hurried to the hallway mirror to check her reflection before she went back out. She fluffed her long wavy red hair. She knew she was fairly attractive with her dark green eyes and full lips, but some guys didn't go for redheads. And even though her hair was not the dark copper she wished she had, it was still obvious with her fair skin, that she was most certainly a natural redhead. She had lost ten pounds since she moved here by walking Puck twice a day on the curving mountain roads. She and Puck also did a lot of hiking on the weekends up and down the many Blue Ridge Mountain trails. The combination had firmed her in all the right places, and she hadn't realized it until this morning that she could once again fit into her favorite old college jeans. She stared at her reflection and was glad to see that her makeup still looked fresh and thanked God she hadn't changed her jeans into the old sweats she usually wore on the weekends. She nodded in satisfaction before picking up the tray and summoning Puck back outside. She placed the lemonade on the table in front of the swing, poured them both a glass and offered him a cookie, which he declined.

This time, it was she who initiated the conversation. "Now that I'm dying of curiosity, could you please tell me why you are here, Mr. McCullough?"

"Yes, I'm sorry. Please call me Hatch." He took a ridiculously long sip before he finally set his glass down and spoke again. "First I must ask you, did your parents ever tell you that you were… uhh…" He bit his lip in an anxious way.

"Adopted?" she offered.

He breathed a sigh of relief and nodded.

"And how would you know that?" she demanded.

Ginger was starting to get suspicious now, and Hatch began to look uncomfortable again. He guzzled another long sip of lemonade, obviously avoiding the question, so she offered a little more.

"They told me when I was about six. They said that my real mother had died and that the father was listed as unknown. So, I'll ask you again, how would you know that?"

Hatch shifted to the back of his chair. He leaned forward and rested his elbows on his knees with his hands crossed loosely in front. It was a normally easy position, but at this moment he looked *very* uneasy. He sighed and then sighed again. Ginger now also shifted uneasily in the swing. Puck was trying to get another cookie from her, and she handed him the rest of hers.

Hatch finally spoke. "I think this would be easier if I start at the beginning, and if you don't mind, I will ask you to just listen until I'm done, if that's okay?"

Ginger realized she had been holding her breath; she released it and nodded. "I'll do my best."

As she said this she noticed Glory come to the edge of her porch railing and wave while shouting in her sweet southern drawl, "Is everythin' all right over there?"

Ginger waved back and assured her that all was fine, and she was okay. Glory nodded her head and went back inside. Hatch waved at her too and said *good evening*, which Ginger thought was a nice gesture. He stood up, leaned on the railing, and looked at his boots. Slowly he began telling her a story.

"Thirty-seven years ago a woman had twins. Unfortunately, she was a delicate woman and not very well at the time. She found it overwhelmin' to handle two babies, so as a result she handled it with a lot of mood enhancin' drugs and alcohol."

He raised his head and looked out at the night sky as he continued. "Her husband was a very well-known rancher in Colorado. He loved his wife very much, but the ranch and horse breedin' kept him very busy. He traveled most of the year that the babies were born and hadn't realized how sick his wife had become. From the start she always favored the twin that looked the most like her. The fairer twin was smaller and sickly most of the time, sufferin' with colic and allergies and would cry for hours at night, keepin' everyone awake and on edge.

One afternoon about eight months after the twins were born, a fire started in the barn, and the fairer twin almost died. The woman said she was out showing the baby the horses and had knocked the lantern over by mistake. The husband had finally become aware of her prescription and alcoholic addictions by this time, and he also noted the harshly apparent favoritism she had between the two babies.

Luckily a ranch hand had come in from the fields to switch out a limping horse and saw the rancher's wife runnin' from the blaze by herself. He then heard a baby cryin' inside and got in there just in time to save it, and almost lost several horses that were furiously circlin' the barn in panic and confusion. After hearin' the full report from the ranch hand, the rancher realized his wife's story just didn't add up, and he now feared for the life of the child. So, he arranged for an adoption and had the files sealed."

Hatch shifted his stance to sit on the railing facing the kitchen and crossed his arms over his chest. Ginger's mouth felt dry despite the lemonade. An uneasy feeling was creeping into her gut, and she instinctively wanted to stand up and change the subject. Before she could speak, Hatch began speaking again, so she remained frozen in her seat as Puck climbed onto her lap and nudged her chin with his wet nose.

"As the other twin grew up, she found the mother weak and detached. And since the Father wasn't home very often, she developed some addictions of her own. She was very wild and out of control and was in some sort of trouble all the time. The mother eventually died of complications with her medications, and the father blamed his daughter's reckless actions as the cause. As I said, he deeply loved that crazy woman. After her death he spent a lot more time away from the ranch, leavin' his daughter to mostly raise herself."

Hatch paused and cleared his throat. He moved back to the chair, sat down heavily and took another sip of lemonade. He still wasn't looking at her. Ginger was too scared to move or say anything. She didn't want to be hearing this tragic tale of strangers she didn't know. It seemed like she was being privileged to someone else's private business, and she felt embarrassed. More so, she was scared of the end of this story. It was all too familiar and personal, and she prayed this was all some mistake.

Hatch stood up and moved to the railing again, but this time he was looking straight at her. She did not look back at him. She wished he would just stay seated or stay standing. She wished he would just spit it out and tell her why he was here. She looked down at her lap; she did not want this stranger to see her discomfort. He must have noticed though, because he quickly continued in a weary tone.

"Years after the woman died, her daughter found some old boxes in the back of the attic that belonged to her mother. That's when she found birth certificates and some adoption papers. She was so furious that she confronted her father and demanded to know where her sister was. He refused to tell her on the grounds that it was too late and to just leave things as they were."

Hatch paused again, put his head down and clenched the railing. "Damn it!" He shouted as he banged the railing with both hands.

Ginger jerked backward at his sudden outburst and her foot knocked the table forward, sending their glasses tumbling to the floor. He quickly came over to her help her pick them up.

"I am so sorry," he sputtered. "I tried to do this professionally, but you look so much like her, and this is all such a mess."

Ginger's tears were flowing quickly now as she tried to mop at the lemonade with some napkins. Eventually she gave up and let Puck lick up the remains. She stayed on her knees, realizing she was too weak to stand and just stared at the floor boards of the porch. She took a deep breath and told herself she had to face what she already knew.

"I'm the second twin," Ginger squeaked out.

The stranger laid his hand on her shoulder. "Yes. There was no easy way to tell you this and I fear that I have done a terrible job of relayin' it to you. I must have rehearsed this a thousand times in my…"

Ginger put her hand up to stop him. He paused and let out a long breath. His nostrils flared in frustration at the way he was muddling this up.

"I'm sorry," he apologized again.

He helped her up and she went back to the swing and sat down hard. He leaned on the railing and waited patiently for her to speak.

She finally responded blankly as she wiped the tears from her face. "Before you finish this story – do you have any proof of anything you are telling me? This is all such a shock. And, well, I really don't know you."

Hatch nodded and apologized as he quickly rifled through the saddlebag on the chair. He handed her the detective's report, her original birth certificate, and a picture of him and Grace. They were much younger in the picture but there was no mistaking the girl definitely could be her twin.

She finally looked at Hatch again and said, "Please finish the story. I have to know what happened and why you're here."

He pushed himself off the railing and slowly sat down beside her on the chair. "Okay, but forgive me if I've faltered somewhat. This whole thing is recent news to me, too, and I guess I'm still in a little bit of shock myself. I don't mean to make you cry."

Ginger noticed his eyes showing genuine pain and concern, and she said softly, "I understand. Please don't worry about my reactions. Just finish what you came to say."

He swept his hand over the top of his hair more in a frustrated gesture than to smooth it and continued, "Yes, ma'am. Grace is her name; your sister's name is Grace. I call her Gracie." He swallowed hard to get the lump out of his throat, so he could continue.

"Gracie went nuts when her father wouldn't tell her about you and got into as much trouble as she could just to punish her father. His name was Jake; your father's name was Jake Masterson."

Ginger noticed he used the word *was*, as in past tense. Her mouth went dry again. So he was obviously dead, too. Now she had two sets of dead parents. *Please, God, don't let this get any worse!* she thought.

Hatch continued his struggle to get the words out. His face showed the heavy concentration of trying to put them as gently as possible and in the right order.

"Jake tried to control Gracie's defiance by sellin' her favorite horse. Then he took her car away and even threatened to kick her off the ranch if she didn't straighten up and let it go. But none of that mattered to her anymore. She was obsessed with finding you, and she just wasn't gettin' through to him no matter what she tried. So one alcohol-induced day she decided the ultimate punishment was to set the barn on fire with her in it. She found out through some farmhands what your mother had done to you and that you almost died in that same barn. So Gracie was convinced that maybe out of fear and guilt that he might possibly lose her too, Jake would finally tell her where you were. She knew he was on his way home, and she was sure he would get to her in time and easily put the fire out.

The barn went up much quicker than she thought, and he didn't get home as soon as she expected. By the time he did get there, the fire was out of control. Gracie in her drunken haze tripped over a bucket and hit her head on one of the stalls. Jake spotted her passed out inside the barn and was racin' in after her when a large beam came down and killed him instantly.

I was about ten steps behind him and managed to get Gracie out. She was overtaken with smoke, had a concussion, and some minor burns. She was in the hospital for about six weeks. She came home lookin' like a zombie, barely spoke, wouldn't eat and all her spitfire was gone. For months, she was like an empty shell. Even I couldn't reach her. About three weeks ago, I came in to check on her and she was missing from the house. I searched the grounds on horseback for hours and finally found her late that evenin' just before sunset. She had taken too much of her medication and was lying in a mossy bog next to some fallen trees. When I finally got her back to the house, she was mutterin' something about getting' to the warm sunshine.

Anyway a couple days ago, I got a call from a private detective I hired months ago to find you. He was pretty sure you were the missin' sister and that's why I'm here. I thought I would come here and meet you and that maybe you would consider comin' to see her. She hasn't spoken since that day, and I'm afraid I may have lost her for good."

His voice broke up on the last part of his sentence, and he cleared his throat to cover it as he turned away.

Ginger was stunned. "So the fire and all this just happened recently, and she still doesn't even know that I'm alive?"

Hatch held up a hand in defense. "I was afraid that the detective may have been wrong, or that you wouldn't want anything to do with this whole thing. I didn't want to get her hopes up before I was sure. I also had to meet you first and see your reactions for myself, do you understand, Ms. Thomas?"

"Yes, yes, of course, I wasn't accusing you; this is just a lot to take in all at once. I'm a little overwhelmed..."

His face fell. "I don't mean to put you on the spot, you have no obligation to us, I just hoped…"

Ginger put her hand up to silence him again. "Let me just say again, please call me Ginger. After everything you just told me, I think we can drop the formalities. And before you make any further assumptions, I'll tell you what my reaction to this incredible news is: I definitely haven't registered all of this yet and it's going to take me some time before it all sinks in. But my first thought is if this is true I am overjoyed that I actually have some family left that hasn't died. If all of what you've told me checks out, then, of course, I will help you and my sister with anything I can."

At Ginger's assuring words, Hatch's shoulders finally relaxed and a huge smile spread across his face. "Oh thank you, ma'am—I mean Ginger! I'm so grateful! I booked flights for both of us tomorrow at one o'clock just in case. Gracie is in really bad shape, and I have already been gone too long so I really have to get back. Do you think you can arrange to accompany me that quickly? I know it's short notice, but the sooner the better."

"Okay, well, that *is* short notice, and I will have to confirm some of this information first. I'll have to check with my boss, too, and get Puck settled. So, I will have to get back to you tomorrow."

Hatch picked up the saddlebag and responded, "Of course. My number is in this bag along with all of the ranch information."

"Where is the ranch, anyway, Mr. McCullough?"

He smiled that bright white smile. "Colorado, ma'am, and by the way, no more formalities, remember? It's Hatch."

"Right, Hatch, got it."

He held out the bag. "In here are your adoption papers and

some more pictures that might help you decide."

She took the bag and nodded.

Hatch sighed and said, "I know this is a lot to take in, and I'm a total stranger, but if there's anything else I can give you to prove or assure you that I am sincere in what I'm telling you, then please don't hesitate to call me. And if you decide you can't make it tomorrow – I will understand and make whatever arrangements you decide according to your schedule."

"Thank you. I appreciate that."

He put his hat back on and tipped the brim with his finger and then toward her. "You're welcome, ma'am, and thank you again." With that he got back into his rental truck and drove away.

Ginger stood there in the yard watching the truck until she could no longer see it and then turned and headed into the house with Puck nipping at her pant legs. "Well, guess what, little man? Your mother may not be a looney tune after all."

She walked into her bedroom with Puck close on her heels and tossed the bag onto the bed. Puck circled it and began sniffing it with enthusiasm. She gazed at it in anticipation. Her heart was racing with panic and excitement as she said to Puck, "I think I have a twin sister which means you have an Aunt Grace. If that's really the case, then the Lord has answered my prayers, and we may have a whole new family!"

She eased on to the bed next to Puck and picked up the phone to call Glory. After she reiterated the whole story and requested help in checking the validity of Hatch's claims, she hung up the phone and pulled the saddlebag toward her. Puck had been gnawing on the strap and it was wet, so she wiped the strap on her jeans and slowly opened the pouch.

As she dumped the contents onto the bed, she wasn't prepared for the face in the pictures staring back at her. Grace's heart lurched. There was no doubt in her mind this was her sister. She could feel her like she was right there in the room. If Glory's sheriff friend confirmed that all of the information Hatch had given her checked out, she was going to Colorado tomorrow. The emotions attached to these pictures were too strong to ignore. It may be crazy and she was scared to death, but she decided to trust that the Lord would guide her way.

She was looking at herself standing in those pictures; the hair was darker and shorter, but it was unreal how much she looked like Grace. No wonder Hatch had been visibly shaken when he first saw her. Twins had always been a fascinating mystery to her, the reports of their sixth sense of one another, the way they could communicate. She knew now, it was all true. She had felt it herself; when Grace was in the bog, she actually smelled and felt the moss, and she could feel Grace's confusion and fear. Thoughts and emotions were flooding over her. Relief and anguish were mixing with curiosity and excitement. Answers were flying forward as they crashed into more and more questions. The nightmares she'd been having most of her life were of her own childhood! She had dreamt of the fire the woman had set and saw the horses running frantically around her. She felt sick to think that Grace had grown up alone with these horrible people. What a tragic life her sister had lived! She now knew why she had been feeling so hopeless and tired; it was Grace trying to reach out to her. She wondered why it started coming in so much stronger lately. The phantom longing she'd always ignored—it all made sense now—it was her *sister* that had been amputated. Tears were filling Ginger's eyes now. They had been cut apart from each other without permission. It pained her to think of all these years of wasted time. What would it have been like to grow up together? Did they just look alike or did they like the same things, too? How could she make up for so many lost memories and secrets they could have shared?

She picked up a picture of a tall man with hair the color of wheat, his bronzed leathery face smiling forcefully. He wore cowboy boots and a red shirt with dark jeans held up by a belt with a very big buckle. He held a Stetson hat in one hand and a huge horse with the other. He was handsome—somewhat scary—but handsome. A slighter version of John Wayne, she thought. The sky behind him was so blue; it looked like a post card. She picked up another picture of him and moved her eyes to the small, pale woman beside him with the flaming red hair. Well, it wasn't really red, more of a deep copper, like the color of a sunset just before the sun slipped out of sight. She was stunning in a delicate sort of way, like Hatch had said. Like a porcelain doll that might break if you handled her with less than fragile care. Her mother, she thought, her real mother, the mother that wanted to kill her.

She studied the picture of the strangers again and then closed her eyes and pictured her adoptive mother and father's faces and said to them, *You will always be my real parents, and I sure could use your help handling this.* She felt anxious and glad that her biological parents were dead now. Was that bad? It seemed as if they were horrible people, and she silently told herself to forgive them and not judge what she didn't yet know about them. She looked at the picture again, and it gave her a knot in her stomach.

She sighed uneasily, and Puck moved closer to her leg, sensing her emotions. She stroked his soft head and down his fuzzy back. She was going to miss him terribly and knew that she would need his comfort while she was gone, but also knew it was impossible to take him on this unpredictable journey. It would be a little easier knowing that he would be safe and happy with Glory and Kyle even though she knew he would miss her just as much. The little dog puffed his chest up and let out a big sigh as if he was hearing her thoughts.

Colorado was on the other side of the country and she had never been that far west. It was where her parents lived before they moved to Florida. Where they must have adopted her and saved her from those people! She turned the picture over and read the faded pen strokes—*Jake and Patrice*. Patrice. So that was her mother's name. She thought about how normal her life had been compared to her sister's. Nothing really terrible had ever happened to her, besides her parents' recent deaths, and luckily her parents were the most loving and kind people she had ever known. Her childhood and life thus far would be a boring autobiography compared to the Mastersons'. There was really no need to think too much about her biological parents growing up. She thought her biological mother was dead, which was true, and supposedly no one knew who the father was. She had been happy most of the time, and that was enough for her. Compared to Grace's life, she thought it was unfair that she had escaped. Things would be different after they were reunited; she would make sure that Grace never felt lonely or cheated again.

Those were the feelings she felt when she looked at the various stages of Grace's life in the pictures with their parents. The faces in those pictures reflected detached sadness beneath the brave smiles. There were also several pictures of Hatch with Grace. They were always laughing and hamming it up, his arms around her shoulders, or her perched on his back, him kissing her cheek. She did look honestly happy in those pictures, though, and he seemed to be around from very early on.

Ginger thought about the way Hatch had stood by the railing, staring out at the mountains. He made the perfect magazine ad for some macho cologne. He was so darn sexy. *What was their relationship?* she wondered. There was no ring on his finger, but that didn't mean they weren't married. She had seen the way he felt about Grace by his actions. Her sister was lucky to have someone like him to care so much about her. The thought of seeing him again was exciting, and then she scolded herself for those emotions in case he and Grace really were involved.

"Off limits!" Ginger said out loud to be sure she heeded her own warning. "You've got enough things to deal with already."

She put all the pictures back into the pouch and closed it up carefully. She stood up from the bed and said, "Come on, Puck. I've got a lot to do if I'm going to fly off to Colorado tomorrow. Let's get over to Glory's house and start making a plan."

~ 7 ~

Miss Kitty & Her Cookies

After the sheriff confirmed that all the ranch and birth certificate information was valid, Ginger had him check out the detective that had located her. The sheriff confirmed that the detective was legitimate as well. After speaking to the detective for some time, she finally called Heather to explain the situation. Both Heather and her father had been very sympathetic to her situation, and Heather let her take the time as her paid vacation.

After Puck was all settled in at Glory's, she hugged him tight, kissed Glory goodbye, and rushed off to the airport. She arrived at the gate just in time to see Hatch strolling across the seating area searching the crowd for her. The flight was in first class and very comfortable. Hatch kept her entertained with stories about Grace and the antics they used to pull together growing up.

"So, you've been at the ranch for many years it seems. How did you come to be there in the first place?" Ginger inquired.

"My dad died of lung cancer just after I turned fifteen. Even though I told my mother I would take care of it, she had no interest in keeping the small farm I grew up on in Virginia. My dad and I worked that farm together every day, planting and harvesting and enjoying every part of it. We loved the dirt and the sweat and the connection we made between human and earth. That probably sounds weird and most people don't get it, but it was an important part of us."

Ginger nodded her head. "No, it's not weird to me at all. I know exactly what you're saying. My father and I had that same experience together. He was a master gardener and we had some of our happiest times digging and sweating and becoming part of the dirt and seeds that produce the miracle of growth."

"Yeah, exactly! I haven't really had the time to do any type of planting on the ranch, but I do miss it and would love to start that up again someday."

He paused and a small smile tugged at the corner of his mouth, perhaps from a fond memory of his father.

"So, your mom didn't want to keep the farm?" Ginger prodded him to continue.

"No. She said it reminded her too much of my father, and we needed to sell it to pay off the debts. I knew that was only part of the case. She never really loved the country like my dad and I did, and she spent most of her time in town anyway, so I knew that's where she wanted to live. She wanted to be close to her church friends. She liked the social stuff so she ended up selling the farm to a condo developer, and we moved back to where my mother had lived before marrying my father. But the town life was really not for me. I was bored to death and I really missed being out on the farm. Wide open land was in my blood, so when I was around seventeen I met a guy that was heading out to work a ranch in Colorado for the summer and was looking for other guys to join him. I jumped at the chance to go. I had never been out west before, and at the end of the very first day, I realized that there was nothing better than sitting on a horse looking out at acre after acre and seeing nothing but prairie and mountains. Everything I learned about ranching was interesting to me, and when it ended, I felt I'd had the best summer of my life since my dad died—like I'd reconnected with him somehow."

The flight attendant appeared and asked if Hatch needed anything else. She smiled and kept eye contact with only him while she chattered away and giggled as she cleared their plates. Then she gave him an extra cookie while expertly avoiding acknowledgment that Ginger even existed.

"So, how do you all know each other?" The flight attendant finally purred to Ginger with obviously sneaky intent.

Caught off-guard, Ginger stumbled for an answer.

"We're new friends," Hatch finally said.

Ginger gave the attendant a look that let her know she knew *exactly* what she was up to, and said very carefully, "We don't need anything else right now, thank you."

Ginger smiled sternly then and the attendant gave her a fake smile back and finally moved on to the next passenger. Ginger let out a disgusted sigh and rolled her eyes. Hatch chuckled.

"You think she was flirting with me a bit?"

"Are you kidding? She was purring so loud, I thought she was gonna climb right up in your lap and start grooming you!"

Hatch threw his head back and burst out laughing. "Well, it's been awhile since I had two felines fighting for my attention."

"Ah, correction, there's only *one* feline fluffing her tail in your face. That's not my style."

Hatch chuckled again. "I stand corrected."

Ginger nodded. "Good, now can we get back to the conversation we were having before we were so rudely interrupted by Miss Kitty and her cookies?"

Hatch laughed again. "You're a funny lady." He paused and then cocked his head. "Um, Miss Kitty made me forget what we were talking about."

"Uh huh, I'm sure she did," Ginger smiled. "You were saying that your first summer on the ranch was ending."

"Oh yeah. Well, my buddy returned to Virginia, but I decided to stay on at the Masterson Ranch. Jake had taken to me and offered to hire me on full-time. He had expected to turn his ranch over to a male heir one day and twin girls were not part of his plan, so I became his unofficially adopted son."

"What about your mom?" Ginger looked concerned.

"She was sad at first, but she knew that I was unhappy in Virginia and wanted me to experience as many new things as I could before I settled down, so she relented."

His voice lowered when he shared that his mother had passed on a little over three years ago, and he regretted that he hadn't visited with her more often. He had no blood relatives or family left besides Grace, either.

Once the plane landed and they began to exit, the flight attendant slipped her business card to Hatch. With a sassy grin on his face, Hatch handed the card to Ginger as they were walking away. Ginger walked back and handed the card back to the attendant.

"No thanks, Miss Kitty," she said politely.

The attendant's mouth dropped open in shock and dismay and then managed to sputter in confusion, "Who's Miss Kitty?"

When Ginger returned to his side, Hatch was shaking his head and chuckling with amusement.

"I know that was mean of me, but she was just too much!" explained Ginger. "And just because you're obviously her catnip and enjoy the attention doesn't mean you should encourage behavior like that!"

Hatch just nodded his head in amused agreement and then smiled that big white grin.

"Meow!" Hatch snarled.

Ginger slapped him on the arm. "You know what I mean!"

"Okay, okay…Point well taken, ma'am."

"Good," finished Ginger. "Now, where's baggage claim?"

After they retrieved Hatch's truck, the mood shifted and the drive was relatively quiet during the journey to the ranch. They were both lost in their own anxiety over Grace's condition and hopeful they would be able to bring her a new life. As they drove onto the grand estate marked with large letters over a massive iron gate that read *Masterson Ranch*, Ginger couldn't believe how much land was surrounding her. She asked Hatch how many acres there were and he said roughly over four thousand. She was dumbfounded. *Good God, these people were rich!* Well, she guessed it was her sister who was the rich one now. As they pulled up to the main house she gasped at the size.

"Whoa, how many people live here?"

"Just Grace and I in the main house. The ranch hands live in the bunkhouse, and the other staff members have a house in the back."

She took in a deep breath and thought, *The other staff members?* She was way out of her element here and felt rather intimidated. Hatch must have noticed her apprehension.

"It's okay. It's big but homey, you'll see."

When they walked inside, only a few lights were lit in the main living room. Ginger noticed that the gargantuan clock on the wall read ten thirty. Hatch showed her around and explained that Grace would be sleeping now and it would be best if they waited until morning for introductions. Ginger agreed since she was very tired herself, anyway. Hatch showed her to her room and said breakfast was at six if she wanted to join him, otherwise just let the cook know what she wanted.

"So, you won't be here tomorrow?" she asked in a flustered tone.

"No, I won't be back until about ten, after I check on things and get everyone going."

"Oh, so what should I do until you come back?" she asked. She felt nerves setting in.

"I'm sure you'll find something," Hatch answered. He flashed his charming smile, and with that he was gone.

Ginger put her suitcase on the bed and took out her nightgown. It had been a long day and she felt like a warm bath. She looked around at the huge bedroom, almost the size of her whole house. The large honey-colored furnishings sported the typical western theme. Her bedspread looked like an Indian blanket, which was similar to the large rugs placed over the shiny wood floors that were lighter than the furniture, like light oak or pine. The paintings on the wall were of various Indian scenes. Her favorite was a handsome brave with a bare chest on a rearing horse. His spear was raised in defiance with his long dark hair flying free in the wind. *Hmm, maybe he lives nearby,* she laughed quietly to herself.

She walked into the attached bathroom, which had a large Jacuzzi tub.

"Ah, heaven!" she said out loud.

By the time she had taken off her makeup and put some of her things away, she felt too tired to bother with a bath and just crawled into the large bed instead. Her mind had been in overdrive all day as she battled with the range of her emotions. She had gone from worried to scared to anxious and then to scorn that she wasn't trusting God to handle it. She would relax for a bit and then it would start all over again.

She pulled the covers to her chest and folded her hands on top and began her prayers: *Hi Father, I'm so glad You are here with me tonight. This is too big a thing for me to handle by myself. Forgive me for being such an idiot today and thinking that I have to handle it alone. I know You will take this where it needs to go and I will do my best not to question Your guidance as I do sometimes. And if I do, just nudge me into a wall or something obvious so I will get out of my way and Yours. Let Your healing hands cover Grace and bring her back to those who love her quickly, so we can shed all Your love and light on her brokenness. And please keep my little Puck and Glory safe and don't let him miss me too much. Oh and please, please, please let me stop thinking about Hatch in* that way. *It's too distracting and uncomfortable to deal with Mr. Charming-and-Gorgeous along with everything else. A rest-*

ful sleep for Grace and myself would be nice for a change, too! I love You so much, and thank You for loving me so well. Amen.

She turned to her side and choked up a little that Puck wasn't there next to her. She pulled another soft pillow to her chest and whispered, "Good night, little one, I miss you," and then drifted slowly to sleep.

~ 8 ~

Tucking Stars under Your Pillow

The next morning Ginger awoke disoriented and searching madly on the bed for Puck. Her surroundings finally came into focus, and she remembered where she was. She glanced at the clock. It was eight thirty in the morning, and she had slept like a rock the whole night through—no dreams, no nightmares. Maybe Grace had felt her presence, and it had calmed them both.

With that thought, she smiled and said to herself: *Thank you, Father, for the restful sleep. Please let Your grace shine on my sister and let today be a good one.*

After a warm shower, she put on some light makeup and dressed quickly. As she crept quietly down the stairs, she ran into a woman who looked Indian. Ginger smiled at her, and the woman looked startled. Ginger's "good morning" was met with a stare. Finally, the woman asked if she was finished in her room. Ginger nodded yes, and the woman quickly moved in that direction. Ginger figured she must be the housekeeper, but her room didn't have much to clean up since Ginger had made the bed and put everything away herself.

When Ginger entered the kitchen, no one was around, so she opened cabinets until she found some cereal. She was eating at the large farmhouse table when another woman, who looked similar to the housekeeper, walked in. When the woman noticed Ginger sitting there, she looked a little spooked, too. More wide-eyed staring ensued.

Ginger smiled at her in return. "Hello, I'm Ginger."

The woman frowned and grunted her response. "I am Cook. You no want some eggs?" she asked when she noticed the bowl. "I cook you eggs and bacon and pancakes and biscuits."

"Oh," exclaimed Ginger. "I'm so sorry—I didn't know. I've already had some cereal, but I will take a biscuit."

The woman eyed her with displeasure as she turned the oven on. "You want orange juice?"

"Okay, that would be nice. Thank you."

The woman took out a pitcher of orange juice and set it on the table with a small glass.

"You want honey or jelly on biscuit?" Cook demanded.

"Just butter will be fine. Thank you."

The woman grunted and retrieved the biscuits from the oven and the butter. "You no want anything else?"

"No, thank you, this is fine," Ginger said politely.

Cook nodded and said, "Leave dishes in sink. I wash later." And with that she left the way she had come.

Wow, that wasn't very pleasant Ginger thought quietly to herself. *Not too friendly around here, it seems.*

She placed the bowl in the sink and decided to take a walk around the house before Hatch arrived. The main living room was decorated much like her bedroom, but the paintings were scenes of mountains and frontier wagons and old western towns. The rugs were of the same Indian patterns, and a number of steer horns were mounted around the room. The vaulted ceiling had large beams running up to the peak at about thirty feet tall. The fireplace was monstrous with a large buffalo skin lying in front. Over the mantle was a huge painting of Jake and Patrice. It must have been shortly after they were married, as both looked very young. Patrice was smiling, but she had that same sad shadow behind her eyes that Grace had. A few photos were scattered around of Grace and Jake with different horses.

Ginger scanned the huge room again and breathed in deep; it smelled like the mountains, earthy and rustic, and she loved it. It was a comforting smell, but it still didn't feel real to be here. It was like she was on the set of the old *Dallas* TV show and any minute J.R. would come around the corner and shout, "Well, howdy, little lady!"

She moved toward a thick-glassed gun case that stood along the north wall. Looking inside, she saw all types of antique rifles and an assortment of pistols and arrow heads. Some were very fancy with inlaid silver handles. Continuing to look around the room, she noticed that all the modern conveniences, flat screen TV, stereo system, etc., were carefully disguised to blend seamlessly into the old west décor. She liked that part. It was honorable to keep the traditional look that was so fitting to this region. Hatch was right, besides being so large, it was very warm and homey.

She poked around a few more bedrooms, a large library, and an office that had probably been Jake's. She didn't go in there—she wasn't ready to see anything personal of her real father just yet.

When she came back around to the living room, she noticed the view just beyond the fireplace. It was spectacular. The position of the house was just right to see the wide expanse of open plains, densely treed forests, and postcard-worthy mountain panoramas. She stepped through the large wood-framed glass doors out on to the massive deck to get a better look. The weather was amazing. The springtime air held an occasional breeze and a crisp cool bite that made everything seem so vivid. The towering trees swaying softly on the mountains seemed happy to finally cover their winter skeletons with a brand new coat of lush green leaves. The sound of the wind in their branches was so hauntingly beautiful, it drew her in like a Siren's song. The various wildflowers dancing in the meadows had colors so vibrant her mouth just dropped open in awe at their beauty.

She imagined how it must look in the fall when all the burning reds, dazzling oranges, luminous yellows, and blazing coppers burst into a brilliant showcase of patchwork color along the mountainsides. She noted the vast variety of trees that would don flaming heads of autumn's brilliance. As those trees shed thousands of colorful leaves, the valley below would transform into a glowing carpet of warmth and beauty. That would be a truly amazing sight. And then there would be snow! How wonderful it must be to see the first snowfall transform these mountains into a winter wonderland. The seasons she coveted would be so detailed here. She was daydreaming of standing next to her newfound sister on Christmas Eve, watching the snowflakes descend like dainty little ballerinas of ice, when Hatch found her.

"Howdy! How's it going?"

She jumped as his voice jolted her out of her reverie, and then realized what he had actually said. "Did you just say 'howdy'?"

"Well, yes, ma'am, I did. Are you making fun of the way I talk?"

She laughed. "Well yeah, I guess I am, *pardner.*"

Hatch laughed at her exaggerated imitation of John Wayne and asked her if she liked the view.

"It's unbelievably beautiful; I was just standing here imagining it in the fall and winter."

He turned to look out toward the mountains. "It's pretty damn hard to beat. At night the stars are so bright and brilliant, you just want to reach out and snatch a couple to tuck under your pillow."

"Tucking stars under your pillow? Now that would be truly magical." She smiled at him.

He blushed. "It's something my Daddy used to say when I was little."

"Well, it's a really lovely thought and I will remember it every time I look at the stars," she reassured him.

Ginger smiled at Hatch again, and they were quiet for a few moments before she broke the awkward silence. "I never got to see the seasons change when I lived in Florida, and I still get excited when I see the leaves turn where I live now. I haven't seen snow there either, but I'm really looking forward to seeing that here someday."

"And so you shall. Are you ready to meet your sister? She's partially awake now. I will warn you that she is on a lot of medication, so she will be very sluggish and slow to respond. She fades in and out, so you have to keep talking."

"Okay. I'm so nervous, though."

"That seems natural under the circumstances. I am, too. Shall we?" Hatch motioned toward the door.

She followed him to another branch of the house that seemed to never end. They walked quietly into a large bedroom that was a little more detailed than the one she was staying in. It had slightly darker furniture and more of it, and the paintings were mostly scenes with horses and of bear, deer, and moose pictured with their young. The fabrics and throw rugs were rich burgundies and greens mixed with gold and sapphire. It was comfortable and warm.

The bed was mussed on both sides, and the sheets were twisted and un-tucked, so Ginger assumed that Hatch had probably slept there. At first she didn't see anyone, and then she noticed the dark tangle of copper-colored hair lying wildly against the stark white contrast of the pillow in the far corner of the bed. The sheets were drawn up to Grace's chin, and she was facing away from them toward a large window with a beautiful view, much like the one in the living room. She didn't move or turn toward them.

Hatch approached the bed slowly and sat down next to her as he smiled and smoothed her hair away from her face. Ginger looked away in discomfort at the intimate gesture and felt the bitter sweetness of envy.

He then spoke softly to Grace, "Hi there, remember when I told you I might have a surprise for you when I got back from my trip? I hired a detective to find your sister. And guess what? He found her! Even better, she's here right now and can't wait to meet you. Do you want to meet her?"

Grace still didn't move or respond.

"She's right here in the room with us; do you want to meet her, honey?"

She still didn't respond. Hatch motioned Ginger toward them as he moved to stand at the end of the bed. Ginger moved slowly around in front of where Grace was staring.

"Grace, I'm Ginger, your sister. I have been waiting to meet you. I came here to see you—can you hear me?"

Grace's eyes were glazed over, and a little drool dripped out of one corner of her mouth. Ginger looked worriedly at Hatch. He nodded for her to keep talking. She lowered herself down on the bed and asked her again, "Grace, can you hear me? I'm your sister My name is Ginger."

Grace's eyes moved slowly toward her, and she cocked her head ever so slowly as she narrowed her eyes. She blinked several times, trying to focus. Finally, Ginger saw some clarity cross Grace's face. Then Grace jerked her head back with a squeal and scooted away to the other side of the bed. She moved so fast, Ginger's heart leapt in her chest, and she reflexively jumped off the bed and backed away.

Grace was looking at her wild-eyed now and screaming. "Hatch, it's happening again—Hatch!"

Hatch was instantly at Grace's side. "It's okay, Gracie—look at me, look at me."

Grace had her hands over her eyes now and had buried her head into her knees that were drawn up against her chest. Hatch had a hold of her chin and was raising it toward his face.

"It's not a hallucination or a ghost this time, Gracie. It really is your sister, I promise. It's okay to look, just look at her one more time. Her hair is longer and lighter than yours. Go ahead, I'm right here." Hatch spoke reassuringly to the frightened woman.

Grace opened her eyes slowly and glanced over at Ginger. Ginger stood as stiff as a poker so as not to scare her again and spoke softly. "Hi, Grace, I'm Ginger, your twin sister. I look like you, don't I?"

Grace narrowed her eyes and looked at Hatch and back at Ginger and then back at Hatch again. He moved slowly off the bed, keeping eye contact with Grace as he walked over and stood next to Ginger.

Then he gave her that knee-buckling smile. "She's beautiful just like you, isn't she?"

Grace smiled back at him and then held out her arms toward Ginger, who raced into them.

"Oh Grace, I can't believe we're finally together—I have missed you all my life."

Ginger began sobbing uncontrollably while Grace stroked her hair and held onto her for dear life.

Grace eventually spoke, much more calmly. "It's okay now. I knew you'd come. I knew you'd come and bring me the sunshine."

Ginger slobbered through her tears, "I dreamed about you all the time. I just didn't know about you. No one ever told me about you."

"You knew in your heart," Grace said, understanding.

"Yes, I did, Grace." Ginger agreed, "I did know in my heart."

They stayed like that for a long, long time. Just holding one another, rocking back and forth, each trying to make up for lost time. Grace finally let loose and looked at Ginger. She smiled again and said, "You have prettier hair than me."

Ginger laughed and said, "I always wished that mine was the color of yours."

"I wish we could talk more, but my medication makes me tired and stupid. I need to rest now. You will come back later, won't you?" Grace looked so small and frail, like a little child asking for her mother.

"Of course I will!" Ginger said happily. "I'll even bring some pictures of me, my adoptive parents, and my dog, Puck."

"I love Puck," Grace said sleepily as she covered herself up.

Ginger wondered about this statement—was it the drugs or did Grace dream of Puck, too? She kissed Grace's forehead and whispered that she would be back soon. Grace was asleep before Ginger backed away.

Only then did she realize that Hatch had disappeared. Ginger went looking for him and found him sitting in the kitchen, staring out the window.

"Hey, why did you leave?" She questioned.

Hatch looked up at her and said, "That was personal between you and your sister, and I didn't want to interrupt."

Ginger nodded. "Thank you so much for everything. I am so happy; I just can't believe that she's real."

"Well, she didn't think you were real for a while there, either," said Hatch as they both remembered the look of panic on Grace's face.

"Yeah, that was scary; I thought I said something wrong."

"No, the drugs they first had her on made her hallucinate

sometimes, and it was pretty frightening trying to talk her down. She was like that once or twice a day."

Ginger felt like she could be honest now. "The drugs have got to stop, Hatch. The mixture of pills on her nightstand is dangerous and addictive."

"I agree, but you saw how wild she got, and when she strayed off into the woods that day, the doctors were afraid she might hurt herself, so they prescribed the mind-numbers. I tried everything, but nothing I said or did seemed to reach her. She would seem okay for an hour here and there, like today when she finally realized you were real, but then she would slip away again, get disoriented, forget things we just talked about. I'm hoping that doesn't happen this time, but you may want to prepare just in case. That detective finally finding you gave me one last chance to bring her back. I know you're the only one that can. I just hope it's not too late. I miss her so much."

Tears formed in his eyes, and he cleared his throat and got up abruptly from the table, snatching his hat in irritation. Ginger's heart ached for him. He was obviously uncomfortable with emotions, and it was apparent that seeing Grace slowly deteriorate had been causing him a great amount of pain for some time now. She knew he felt helpless, which was manifesting itself into frustrated anger.

He muttered gruffly before he started for the door and then turned back. "I have to get back to work; she should be awake by dinner. We can eat with her, if that's all right with you."

She nodded and he turned quickly toward the door again. She grabbed his arm. "Hatch, stop. I just want you to know that I don't doubt for one minute that you have done everything you possibly could for her. And I can't thank you enough for taking care of her and for bringing us back together. It's more than apparent how much you love my sister, and I have no doubt that together we can get her well and happy again. What I'm trying to say is that you aren't alone in this anymore. This has obviously been just as hard on you as it has been on her. So, if you need to talk or unload or yell or whatever, I'll be here to listen. I promise showing your tears and feelings won't make you lose any of your cowboy macho. It just makes you a wonderful man with a heart full of compassion and there is no shame in that, okay? "

He smiled a little and nodded. "I appreciate that." Then he changed the subject. "I told Cook to make some chicken soup. It's hard for Grace to keep anything heavy in her stomach. I hope that's okay."

"I love chicken soup, and God knows I won't try and prepare anymore meals myself. I don't think I met with Cook's approval. Is that really what I should call her?"

He chuckled. "Her name is Marta, but she's done all the cooking around here for as many years as I can remember. All the ranch hands call her Cook, so either name is fine. Mahina is her sister, and she keeps the house clean. They are harmless and very sweet, just a little wary of strangers, especially when you look just like their mistress!"

"Oh right, that explains the wide eyes and blatant staring." She imitated their faces for him.

He finally laughed with genuine appeal, and the pain in his eyes dissipated. His face warmed again to her, and Ginger felt happy to see him smiling. He put his hat on and tipped the brim.

"Okay, then, I'll see you at six."

She nodded back and couldn't help staring at the lovely fit of his jeans as he strode out the door with that irresistible mix of masculinity and gentleness.

~*9*~

Lots of Catching Up to Do

Over the next few days, Grace and Ginger spent a lot of time in Grace's room just catching up on each other's lives. The doctor came out to see Grace, said she was looking much better, and gave permission to wean her off some of her medications—just slowly. The days were emotional and sometimes very painful for both women.

"When I discovered your adoption papers and found out that you existed, all of those weird dreams and feelings I had since I was a little girl finally made sense," commented Grace as she looked through photos Ginger gave her. "I dreamed about Puck. I felt your happiness when you moved to some place cooler with mountains. And I am truly sorry that your adoptive parents died."

"How did you know that they died? Did Hatch tell you?" Ginger felt a bit surprised because she knew she had not told Grace about her parents' deaths.

"No, Hatch never told me. I felt the same pain as you over losing them, but when the doctors put me on the mind eraser drugs, the dreams and feelings stopped happening so much. I couldn't feel you anymore and that's when I stopped caring about anything."

Grace stroked Ginger's hair as a tear rolled down her face. Ginger wiped her cheek and clung to her hand.

"But that's when you came through to me the strongest. I slipped into this graphic daydream that I was actually in that mossy bog that Hatch found you in, even down to smelling the moss and feeling it scratching against my skin. It was so real I actually thought I was starting to lose my mind. The previous times were just dreams, but this was during the daytime. Then when Hatch told me about finding you there, I got goose bumps and the hair on the back of my neck stood up."

"That's how it always is with me. The smells, the tastes, the loneliness, even your happiness from Puck. That's why I liked my drugs or alcohol; it helped blur the sensations that I couldn't understand. I figured I was always losing my mind. Maybe that's why our mother was so screwed up and used the drugs for the same reason—maybe we have some twin aunt she didn't know about, either."

"Oh my gosh, with both of our feelings running around in your head, thank God my life was fairly calm most of the time!"

"Yeah, I think that you mostly came through when your emotions were on overload. I didn't like the way you felt with the guy a couple years back."

"Oh, yeah, Robert. He was the last and final loser. I knew he was cheating and lying to me, but it took a long time to admit that to myself. He was so arrogant and sneaky."

"Good thing we weren't reunited as sisters when you knew him."

"Why's that?" inquired Ginger.

"Well, I would've roped that boy up and drug him behind my horse for a couple of hours until I knocked the cheatin' right outta him!"

Ginger burst out laughing in shock. "Oh, Grace, that's terrible!"

"Oh, I wouldn't have hurt him too bad. I'd have only dragged him through a couple of burr patches, maybe over a couple of logs. You know, just a couple of passes through the river. In fact, he'd still be pickin' burrs out of his sorry lyin' butt right now!"

They both burst out laughing as Hatch came into the room, slid onto the bed beside Grace, and cuddled her close to him. "It is so nice to hear you laughing again."

She snuggled into his neck. "Well, you were getting pretty boring!"

"Oh, is that so?" He tickled her and she erupted in giggling protests.

Ginger looked away in discomfort. She was going home the next day to get Puck and return to the ranch in a couple of days. She had arranged it with work to take a month's leave of absence without pay. She couldn't wait to see Puck; she missed him so terribly it hurt.

Deep down inside, Ginger knew she needed the few days away from Hatch, too, since her feelings for him ramped up her anxiety. She felt ashamed that she couldn't control the frequent dreams about him either. Since Grace fell asleep early almost every night, Ginger spent most of the evenings alone with Hatch. It was almost impossible to stay disinterested when he was constantly flashing her that half-grin while telling her some amazing story in that sexy cowboy accent. And he always smelled so good, too, like a combination of leather and horses and some intoxicating cologne.

It was all too consuming just to be near him; she had to get away to clear her head, so when she returned, she could stay focused on getting Grace fully recovered. She was certain that Hatch was in love with her sister, which was something she had to accept and move on from. He wasn't the one God was sending to her, which made her feelings for him so confusing and heartbreaking. He was everything she wanted in a man, and she hadn't felt so comfortable and safe with anyone since her father died.

"Earth to Ginger! Have you been sneaking some of my drugs? You look like a zombie."

Ginger smiled and returned to the present. "Really? I look like the walking dead? Nice compliment, sister! Thank you very much for that!"

Grace giggled again. "No, that would be Hatch before he has his morning coffee; he's even scarier than a zombie!"

Hatch flung the bed sheet over her head and held her under there while she erupted in giggling protests.

Ginger watched them teasing and laughing and tried her best to be happy for Grace. Hatch's shirt was unbuttoned, and her eyes wandered over his tanned chest filled with a light covering of golden hair. Every time he moved, his cologne wafted toward her, and she breathed his scent into her nostrils like a drug. She had to get out; these were forbidden feelings, and she needed to gain control. She jumped off the bed so quickly that she startled Grace.

"Ginger, what's the matter?"

"Nothing. I just need to get packing for tomorrow. I will see you in the morning, Grace. Good night, Hatch. Will you be driving me to the airport tomorrow?"

"No, Tommy will," Hatch responded, "I have a meeting with the vet."

Thank you, God, Ginger said to herself. It would be impossible to sit next to him that whole way and act casual.

"Okay, then. Good night." Ginger hugged Grace awkwardly, since Hatch was still entangled around her and she didn't want to touch him.

As she walked out the door and down the hallway, she couldn't help but overhear Hatch ask Grace if she wanted to watch some TV.

"No. I just want you to hold me until I fall asleep. I love you so much, Hatch."

"I love you, too, baby."

Ginger's heart felt a stab of pain. They were definitely a couple—not married, but still, it was obvious. She had a lot of serious praying to do.

Going Home to Puck

Ginger could not get home from the airport fast enough. After retrieving her luggage from the taxi, she went directly over to Glory's house. When she opened the screen door, Puck flew around the corner like a bullet and began jumping and yipping frantically. She squatted down to see him, and he leaped on her chest, knocking her to the ground. Ginger dissolved into a fit of giggles when Puck started furiously licking her ticklish neck.

Glory stepped into the living room and put her hands on her hips. "Well, my goodness, that's got to be the happiest dog in the whole world! For heaven's sake, Puck, let your mother get off the floor."

Puck turned his head toward Glory's voice just long enough for Ginger to move to the couch. He continued yipping in excitement and wagging his tail so hard it looked like a windshield wiper.

Glory laughed and turned back toward the kitchen. "Let me know when he calms down so we can talk. I fixed us some chicken and yellow rice for dinner."

They ate in Glory's small kitchen with Puck curled up on Ginger's feet. Ginger relayed the details of the entire trip and then told Glory about her plan to take Puck with her back to Colorado for another month or so. They exchanged regrets on how much they would miss each other and ate two pieces of cherry pie each before Ginger finally crossed the yard to her home.

Her sleep that night was restful and comforting, for she was once again all snuggled up with her furry little boy. She awoke the next morning and breathed in his sweet and buttery doggie scent. She hugged him tight to her chest and said, "I missed you so much. You are going to be so surprised at what Mommy has planned for us. We have to get up and get packing; I have a lot to get together before we leave."

Since the car trip to Colorado was the little dog's first, Puck wasn't too happy about the repeated trappings of the car day after day. Ginger stopped as often as possible to let him stretch his legs and run around.

Happiness and relief swept over her when they finally arrived and saw Hatch's pick-up truck waiting for them in the designated meeting place so she could follow him to the ranch. Much to her dismay, she felt the familiar leap of excitement when her eyes found Hatch. She thought she had quelled her feelings for him, but despite over a week of prayers, her feelings hadn't let up one bit. She prayed all the way to the ranch for forgiveness and that the feelings would finally die a natural death. Where was that darn gorgeous Indian from the painting when she needed him?

A few minutes before 4:00 p.m. they pulled into the circular drive in front of the main house. Puck began barking like crazy to get out. Before Ginger was able to emerge fully from her door, two gorgeous dogs encased her in eager greetings. "Oh, look at you two! Aren't you beautiful?"

Hatch came toward them and rubbed each dog behind the ears. "Ginger, meet Cloud and Apache, the best herding dogs in the West."

"They are just stunning!"

Before Ginger could grab an excited Puck, he leaped out of the truck and stood cautiously still as the two larger dogs sniffed and nuzzled him.

Hatch laughed and said, "Cloud will be mothering him in no time. She's a fierce protector."

All three dogs started yipping and chasing and circling each other in a warm dance of acceptance.

"How long have you had them, Hatch? Their coloring is so unusual."

"They are about four years old. I spotted them hanging around one of the dumpsters behind an equipment supply store when they were just pups and couldn't resist taking them home. I know they are definitely part collie and probably also have some Belgian sheepdog, Siberian husky, or Aussie Shepherd mix. I know Apache has some wolf in him. There are a lot of stray mixed breeds in the higher, poorer parts of the mountains. They often drift down for food, like these two when I found them."

Ginger marveled at the beautiful long hair and colors of each dog. Apache was a mixture of sable and dark brown on his lower body and jet black on his shoulders, head, and chest. He was big, too; his head was above her waist. He was gentle with Puck and

Cloud, but she imagined he would be quite terrifying if you ran into him in the wrong place.

Cloud was smaller, but certainly not dainty. It was obvious she held her own with Apache. She was snow white with streaks of gray and tan on her back and tail and some gray and black markings on her forehead and nose. Her eyes were blue and her ears were large and black. The black continued from each ear down each side of her face and on past her chest, like long braids on an Indian squaw. She was quite remarkably beautiful.

"Well, I'm glad they like Puck," Ginger finally said in relief.

"They just think he's a pup," Hatch informed. "They will watch over him like a hawk—Cloud senses danger before danger even threatens and obviously nothing messes with Apache if they want to live."

"How come I haven't seen them until today? I guess I did hear them, but it didn't occur to me that it was the dogs you told me about."

"They are working dogs during the day, and you were also busy with Gracie."

"That's true. Well, we better get in the house so Puck can meet Grace, too."

They entered the big house with all three dogs jumping and chasing each other.

Hatch moved toward the mass of fur and wagging tails. "I better put Cloud and Apache back outside."

"Why? Doesn't Grace like them?"

"Oh, she loves them, but it might be too much confusion."

"I don't think so," Ginger disagreed. "Let's just all go in and give her a big surprise."

"Okay, if you think so."

They moved down the hallway and entered Grace's room. Both Cloud and Apache jumped up on the bed and bathed Grace with lapping kisses. Puck was standing behind them, trying to see what all the fuss was about. When they finally moved away from her, he stopped short. He looked at Grace and then back at Ginger and then he started barking at Grace.

She laughed out loud. "There you are, little Puck! I'm so glad to finally meet you!" She held out her arms, and he leaped into them, smothering her with messy kisses. Then he raced back to Ginger and jumped up on her legs and yipped in confusion.

"It's okay, little one, I know you're not cheating on me!"

They all laughed, and Ginger and Hatch jumped on the bed, too. Just then Cook walked into the room. She flinched at the sight of all of them on the bed and muttered something under her breath. Grace and Hatch laughed at her dismay.

"Oh, come on, Marta, wanna join our party?" Grace teased.

"You all must be smoking some of that *loco* weed. Get off that bed and get washed up for supper. And put those dogs outside!"

Grace and Hatch laughed again, and Hatch jumped off the bed and moved toward Marta. "Are you sure you don't want some big sloppy kisses from Apache? You know he has a crush on you!"

Marta gave him a scowl and then scurried toward the door, laughing when Apache jumped off the bed toward her. "Don't you get sassy with me, you heathen, or you only get one biscuit tonight! And that goes for you too, Apache!"

Grace was hooting in amusement, telling Apache to go get her, and Ginger giggled in relief that apparently Marta wasn't really angry with them. Hatch and the dogs continued to chase Marta down the hallway toward the kitchen with Marta giggling and squealing the whole way.

After she left, Grace told Ginger that her father forbid animals in the house and Cook pretended to share his opinion, but secretly she spoiled the dogs whenever she had the chance. Ginger laughed. She was tickled to know that the intimidating Marta was all bark and no bite. She was just a big softy at heart and would hopefully spoil Puck, too.

Before they began dinner, Hatch put the two larger dogs outside, but Puck whined at the door and barked at Ginger. Since Marta had retired for the evening, Ginger asked if it was okay to keep the dogs in the house for just a little while so Puck would feel safe on his first night in a strange house. Hatch and Grace laughed and said that the dogs had slept in the house every night since Jake's death.

The next morning Ginger awoke to a soft knock at the door. She turned over to find Puck's head on her pillow, Cloud at her feet, and Apache taking up the rest of the bed. She giggled and heard the knock again. She noticed the door was slightly ajar. It was Hatch asking if it was okay to come in.

"Yes, come in," Grace responded, pulling the covers up over her.

When he entered the room, he laughed in a warm tone. "Well, I guess I've lost my sleeping partners. I thought they might be in here."

"They must have come in after Puck and I were asleep."

"Yes, Apache has a talent for opening doors. He just leans that big ole' chin on the handle and walks right in."

Hatch sat on her side of the bed. She felt the warmth of his leg against hers. He reached out to pet Cloud. His cologne drifted over her, and she felt light-headed.

Her discomfort was stifling and she blurted out something to divert his attention. "Well, I'll have to remember that when I'm naked in the room—I mean, when I'm naked taking a bath."

She blushed wildly. *Shut up, Ginger! Stop talking about being naked!* Hatch got up quickly, and she noticed his face was a little flushed, too.

She fumbled for something else to say. "Um, have you seen Grace this morning?"

"Oh, uh, yes," Hatch said, clearly relieved to change the subject. "She told me that she wanted to get outside today. That's really good news—it means she's feeling better. So, if she's still okay by lunchtime, you two can meet me at the waterfall at one. I'll tell Cook to pack a picnic lunch, and don't forget your swimsuits. Gracie loves it there, and it will be good for you both to get out of this house and get some sunshine."

"Are you trying to say that I look sickly, too?"

"No, no, that's not what I meant…"

She laughed then as she realized she had embarrassed him. She threw him a teasing look to stress the point.

"Ah, you are just teasing me."

"Yes, I'm just teasing you. A picnic sounds wonderful. We will see you at one. And I will bring Puck. He loves the water."

"Okay then, see you there. Come on, dogs, time to go to work." Apache and Cloud bounded off the bed with Puck close behind.

"No, Puck, you can't go just yet." Ginger called to her little dog. "Come to Momma. We will see Hatch and the dogs later."

Puck hesitated and whined a little, and then he jumped back on the bed and curled up next to her.

Hatch tipped his hat toward her and said, "Ma'am."

She smiled and nodded back, "Pardner."

He closed the door, and she listened to the sound of his boots descend the stairs. She thought about him sitting so close on the bed, smelling his freshly showered scent…

She slapped her face and shouted, "Good Lord, Ginger, just stop it. You have got to stop it!"

Puck barked at her sudden outburst.

"Your mother's going to hell, Puck, and that's all there is to it!"

~ 11 ~

Food Fight

Ginger loved seeing how Grace's faced beamed as they rode toward the falls. Ginger hadn't ridden a horse in a long time and realized how much she had missed the thrill of it. Her horse was amazing. He was jet black with a splash of white splotches on his hindquarters and hind legs. She was worried about Puck around the horses, but he was staying a safe distance from them and following along just like he'd been doing it forever. He was a herding dog by nature, and she knew he was in heaven with all this outdoor room to run. He'd been chasing and running from the chickens and goats all morning, much to Grace and Ginger's entertainment.

"You and Puck are going to love the falls. It's magical. I used to go there all the time to escape things. It was the only peaceful place I knew."

"It sounds wonderful and it must be nice to have your own waterfall. I can't believe how much land you own!" Ginger exclaimed.

"Oh, I don't own it—Hatch does."

Ginger's mouth dropped open. "*What?*"

"My Dad, I mean, our Dad willed it to Hatch. He knew I didn't care and Hatch was the son he always wanted. He was afraid I would sell it the second he hit the grave. And he was also trying to punish me, or whatever. But all that doesn't matter anyway; it will always be my home. Hatch tried to deed it back to me, but I told him not to. It was more rightfully his anyway. He's always been there to handle everything, including me, and he deserves this ranch. And it was always his dream to run a ranch, certainly not mine—so now he can. I'm just glad to see him so happy these days. You make him laugh."

Ginger's face reddened and she was suddenly terrified that Grace suspected something. Then she began to panic, *oh no, the sixth sense thing, she probably knows*! Ginger stumbled for something to say. "No, it's you who makes him laugh. He's happy because you are feeling better. If you had seen him when he first came to see me, he was so scared he had lost you. He loves you so much, Grace. You are very lucky to have him."

Grace had stopped listening and was looking ahead. "There it is. Isn't it beautiful?"

Ginger breathed a sigh of relief when she realized that Grace wasn't even paying attention to her babbling attempt at a cover-up. As she rounded the corner to see what Grace was pointing at, she gasped. Well, beautiful was not an accurate description of the view—it was awe-inspiring! Ginger had thought maybe the falls were twenty feet high with a little swimming hole at the bottom. Ha! She was staring at a forty-foot-wide rushing white water river that cascaded down a two-tier, sixty-foot-high waterfall, which splashed into a huge swimming lake that eventually moved on down into a wooded valley below.

"WOW!" was all she could manage to say.

Grace laughed and guided her horse over to a beautifully shaded picnic area on the shore complete with an outdoor grill, a couple of thick wooden picnic tables, and several Adirondack chairs scattered about for basking in the sunshine. They unloaded the picnic items from the horses and set one of the tables for three. Grace looked past Ginger, and a big smile crossed her face. Ginger knew Hatch had arrived. Within seconds the dogs had surrounded them, and she heard him yell a greeting.

Ginger took a deep breath and turned around as casually as possible and smiled and waved. Hatch dismounted his horse and tied him to a tree. He then proceeded to take off his hat, his shirt, his boots, his socks, and then his pants! At this point, Ginger realized her mouth was hanging open, and she sat down hard on the picnic bench while trying to tear her eyes away. She looked with panic toward Grace, but she was stripping, too. Ginger looked back at Hatch in just enough time to see his well-defined body, luckily with briefs still on, jumping into the water. He was under a long time and finally came up just short of the waterfall. Grace was in the shallows by this time, and they were both motioning for her to come in.

Ginger felt like an idiot just staring at them, so she quickly undressed and joined Grace in the shallows. The dogs swam toward Hatch, and Puck splashed around the shoreline barking at them.

"Can you swim?" Grace asked.

"Yes, I love to swim."

"Well, what are you waiting for? Go out there and check out the falls."

"What about you? Aren't you coming?"

"Not yet. I'm still a little weak, but you go ahead. I'm fine."

Ginger looked toward Hatch, who was motioning for her to swim out. She looked back at Grace who was waving her to go on. So out she went. The water was so cold and invigorating that it felt wonderful. As she got closer to the thunderous clouds of white spray, Hatch smiled and said something to her. She couldn't hear anything over the roar of the water, so she swam within five feet of him.

"How do you like it?" shouted Hatch above the roar.

"It's unbelievable!" Ginger yelled back.

Even with the water churning like crazy from the force of the falls, Ginger could still see his bare chest. His hair was slicked back, his green eyes seemed to shine right through her, and his brilliant smile was plastered from ear to ear. It was just too much for her heart to bear. She suddenly felt weak and ashamed and ducked underwater to swim back toward Grace. Hatch dove under, too, and grabbed her hand pulling her behind him. The grip of his hand on hers sent waves of sensuous electricity through her body. As they swam farther from the falls, she stayed mostly underwater and could see his body clearly now: his muscled thighs pumping up and down, his strong arm pulling her toward him, his powerful back that led down to his hard waist. When he turned on his back toward her, she quickly looked away. She wrenched her hand away from his and swam the rest of the way by herself. This just couldn't go on, she was out of control, and this was just flat-out torture. When they reached Grace in the water, Ginger was terrified that Grace had seen or sensed that their actions were totally inappropriate. Ginger was all panicky and shaking, and when she finally looked at Grace, she was moving toward Ginger with her own panicked look.

"Are you all right? I thought you were drowning!"

"Oh, no, it's just colder than I'm used to; I just got a little fatigued there for a minute." Ginger realized Hatch had joined them, so she turned to him. "Thank you, Hatch, I needed that little bit of rest time."

"No problem." He was looking at her oddly with that devilish half-smile across his face. "Are you sure you're okay?"

"I'm fine!" Ginger barked. "Just give me a second."

His closeness and fake concern made her uncomfortable and somewhat angry. Was he flirting with her on purpose? She didn't like that. He belonged to her sister, and he better not pull any flirting nonsense! She could lust, but he couldn't, that would be deceiving Grace! Wait a minute—*no, no, no!* What was she thinking? She couldn't lust, either. She suddenly felt sick and realized she was probably imagining the whole thing, or maybe he was just like every other cheating jerk whose eyes wandered the second they had a chance. She didn't really know him at all. What if he was a cheater and tried something with her? How would she tell Grace? This was getting all twisted up, and her chest tightened in panic. Ginger ran as best as she could out of the water and over toward the table. She wrapped herself in a towel and grabbed a bottle of water out of the cooler.

"What is it with you and Hatch?"

Ginger felt the blood drain out of her face at Grace's question. "What do you mean? Nothing—there's nothing with me and Hatch! He just helped me back to shore. That's all!"

"Okay, don't get so defensive!" Grace put her hands up as if to surrender. "It's just so obvious that something happened out there between you two. Do you have feelings for…"

"No, no, no!" interrupted Ginger. "I don't know what you are talking about. Nothing happened, and I don't have any feelings for him, except friendship."

"Don't lie to me Ginger; I feel your feelings, remember? And right now you are having a massive meltdown, so tell me right now what happened with you and Hatch."

"Oh, Grace, I'm so sorry." Ginger took her sister's hands in hers. "Nothing happened, and nothing will! But I haven't been truthful with you, and I'm so angry with myself because I thought I could control it. I should have told you, but it doesn't matter or mean anything. I would never do anything inappropriate or anything that would hurt you. Please don't be mad at me."

Grace stared at her like she had three heads. "Tell me what? What on earth are you babbling about?"

"Hatch!" Ginger exclaimed, throwing her hands in the air. "I'm talking about you and Hatch."

"What about me and Hatch?"

"Well, he's your man or boyfriend or whatever you two are, and I respect that and would never do anything inappropriate to hurt you."

Grace paused and then her eyes narrowed into a dark stare as she stood up and glared at Ginger. "Oh, now I get it, you come here all nicey, nicey and act like you care about me and want to be in my life, but it's really Hatch you want. What? You think you can act all innocent and then steal him from me? Is that your plan? What have you two been doing behind my back? What kind of a sick person are you?"

Ginger's mouth fell open and she felt her face blanch at Grace's attack. "Oh, my God, no! No, no, no! Grace, you have to believe that I would never do…"

Grace's cheeks suddenly blew up like she was holding her breath. She threw her head back and burst out laughing so loud and hard that she scared the birds away that were nearby.

Thinking Grace was having some kind of fit or a seizure, Ginger quickly stood up and moved toward Grace while waving trying to get Hatch's attention.

"Grace! Grace! Are you all right?"

At this point, Grace was bent over with tears streaming from her eyes. She grabbed Ginger and pulled her back toward the picnic bench.

"I'm fine. Sit down! Stop waving for Hatch." She started laughing again. "You are so gullible and clueless!"

"Stop laughing, Grace! I can't understand what you're saying. You're acting crazy and scaring me!"

Grace did her best to stifle another giggling fit. "Okay, okay. I'm sorry, but you are so far off-base and you should have seen your face. I was expecting a flock of bats to fly right out of your open mouth."

"Stop it, Grace! Tell me what you are talking about—and I mean now!"

"Okay, Miss Touchy-touchy, now who's the one acting crazy?

Granted, Hatch is smoking hot, but being with him would be like being with my brother. We grew up together and are very close, but not like that."

"What?!?!" Ginger was dumbfounded. "Are you kidding me? You aren't a couple? I don't believe it! I heard you telling him how much you love him and he said it back to you!"

"We do love each other, but not romantically, and it's a good thing we don't. I saw the way you were looking at him when he was doing his little striptease! You were lusting after my man and you didn't tell me? Bad girl, Ginger, bad girl!" Grace started laughing her head off again.

"This is not funny, Grace; I have been in torture for weeks now! I didn't tell you because I wanted our time to be about us, and I was doing everything in my power to stop my feelings for Hatch. I was terrified it would drive a wedge between us and you might relapse, or never forgive me! I almost had a heart attack out there in the water, worrying that you would misunderstand and might never want to see me again. Besides, it doesn't matter anyway, he's not attracted to me, or he would have said or done something by now. I can't believe I've just made a complete fool of myself and made myself sick to my stomach for weeks now over nothing. That's what I get for not being truthful with you about everything. I am sorry, Grace. That will never happen again. If we can't be truthful with each other, then we have nothing. Can you forgive me?"

"Jeez, Ginger, take a breath! You're my sister, and I don't think you are capable of doing anything that would make me mad enough not to see you again, so lighten up. And I wouldn't have cared anyway. No normal woman can resist his charm. I'm just immune to it. And as far as Hatch being interested, I told him to stay away from you unless *you* made a move! I made him promise to behave, so he didn't scare you away from me. He can't figure you out at all. I've never seen him so messed up. And, of course, I didn't share with him what was so ridiculously obvious on your part. That wasn't my place. Come on, Ginger, this really is funny! I bet you've been prayin' your little buns off over this—I think even God is having a good chuckle right now."

"Maybe so…" Ginger's face finally cracked a small smile and she began to settle down a little. The she remembered. "I can't believe you pretended that you and Hatch were really together and called me a sick person, Grace! That was so horribly mean!"

Grace laughed again.

"Oh, come on, it was just for a second. And I couldn't help it; you were so serious and so pitiful. I'm sorry. It was mean. But, you really should have seen your face, though. Bats in, bats out, in and out…"

Grace imitated Ginger's face and Ginger laughed.

"You're the sick one! In humor, I mean."

"Oh, you have no idea, sister, no idea. So, now back to you and Hatch. He had quite the smile before you spazzed out on the shore. What happened out there?"

"Oh, for heaven's sake, he caught me checking out his body. I didn't mean to because I thought you…anyway, never mind that now. And he's out there with nothing on but his Fruit of the Looms! This is so beyond embarrassing!"

Grace burst out laughing again.

"Well, he had to do something to get your attention, as ridiculously obvious as it was. And it is a very nice body. Trust me, I should know."

"Wait, what do you mean by that? Oh, please don't tell me... You have slept with him, haven't you?"

"Slept together lots of times—yes. Had sex with him—no. We tried kissing a little when we were younger, but it was too weird. But we have skinny dipped together about a million times, and I'm not blind!"

"You've skinny dipped naked together? Oh, I don't even know how to process that."

"Well, skinny dippin' is done naked, otherwise it would just be swim..."

"Oh, for heaven's sake, Grace, I know what it means! I just have a visual now that I'm not comfortable with, so could you just stop talking for a minute?"

"Stop being such a prude; we were just kids horsing around. The man is obviously crazy about you, so stop being such an idiot and go for it! I can't tell you how overjoyed I am to have the two people I love the most so hot for each other. Hatch is so wonderful, and he deserves someone like you. And did you notice how that the cold water thing doesn't affect him at all down there..."

"Grace! I am not talking about this with you!" Ginger blushed furiously. "This is so awkward, and I am still so embarrassed. How am I supposed to act when he comes over here? You cannot tell him this now!"

"Of course I won't tell him now; this is much too good to spoil. Just act like nothing happened and then you can surprise him tonight. He hasn't shut up about you rebuffing him since you got here! He has been beside himself with wounded ego syndrome. I've never seen him so confused and sullen, and I can't wait for him to find out why you haven't responded. I just wish I could see his face when you start the peep show. You could start with a slow striptea…"

"Grace! Just stop. I don't need you to orchestrate my…my… anything!"

"Well, someone has to! You're such a goody-two-shoes old prude since you got religion!"

"I am not! I just wasn't raised to discuss such personal things. My mother would have a stroke! And I didn't *get religion* as you call it; I just don't take lovemaking casually anymore. Besides, isn't he sleeping in your room?"

"No, his room is just past mine."

"Well, even if I were to do anything, it certainly wouldn't be next to your room!"

"Then I guess you will have to lure him up to your room with your feminine ways and that won't take much because he's about as horny as a…"

"Grace! That's enough! I'm glad this is so entertaining for you, but this is the second time in just a month that I have been shocked out of my skin. First, I find out about you, and then I make myself sick over what I now find out was nothing! I'm a little frazzled and way out of my element right now, so just please give me a chance to process all this!"

"Okay, okay." Grace laughed again. "I don't mean to tease, but it's been so long since I had something this fun and entertaining to witness. And besides, I slept with more men by the time I was seventeen than you have in your whole life! Sex is just sex to me. It doesn't have to involve love or commitment. But since that is how you view it, then you should have a barn burner tonight, my sister! Whew, I don't even know if I'll be able to stand the heat! I might have to call the fire department!"

"Quiet," Ginger hissed. "He's on his way in. Just shush now!"

Grace was still laughing uncontrollably when Hatch walked up.

"What's so funny?" He eyed the girls suspiciously.

"Nothing. It's a sister thing. Want a sandwich?"

Ginger stole a quick glance when she offered him the sandwich. Thankfully, his jeans were back on, but he just happened to accidentally-on-purpose forget his shirt. Now that Ginger knew what she knew, it would be a miracle if she could act natural through the rest of their lunch. She shoved her sandwich in her mouth and kept her eyes on Grace, who was still snickering as Ginger flashed her death looks. Hatch kept looking back and forth for some clue about what was passing between them, but they both stayed silent.

Ginger let out a huge sigh of relief when Hatch rode off to return to work.

"Could you have been any more obvious? He knows something is up."

"I'm sorry," Grace apologized. "It's just been so long since I've laughed that hard, if ever. I was just having a little fun and it just felt good to be…happy. Besides, what is the fun of being sisters, if we don't get to embarrass each other once in a while?"

Grace's face had turned gloomy and she began to pack up their lunches. Ginger suddenly felt terrible and realized Grace was right. Teasing each other was what siblings do. She had been jealous of her friends that had sisters. She had to remind herself that Grace didn't have normal boundaries, and it was really great to see her so happy. And despite all the humiliation, it was pretty funny.

"Okay, okay. You're absolutely right. I'm being a big baby, and I overreacted. But did you have to do a lifetime of teasing and embarrassing in one shot?"

Grace perked up again. "Big whiney prude baby is more like it!"

"Yeah, yeah. I will get you back, though. Believe me, your time will come!"

"Ohhh, I'm scared now!" Grace's smile lit up her face.

"I will," Ginger promised, giving her ornery sister a glare as she grabbed the bottle of mustard and squished it all over Grace's chest.

Grace's eyes went wide in total shock before she quickly retaliated, asking, "Is that all you got, sister?"

Grace proceeded to fling her plate of potato salad and baked beans into Ginger's hair and then went into hysterics when Ginger fell backwards off the bench into the dirt, trying to avoid the attack. Ginger sat up, sputtering and giggling and saw Grace clutching her stomach in racking fits of laughter and totally lost it herself. The food fight continued until neither of them could catch their breath between the repeated bouts of laughter. They finally collapsed in exhaustion. By the time they were done, they had more food on them than in them and Puck was licking up the spoils as fast as they threw them. They jumped into the water to rinse off; taking turns splashing at each other and picking food from their ears and hair.

Ginger thought the drugs may have been what made Grace so giddy, but she was overjoyed seeing her sister laughing and so happy, nonetheless. Come to think of it, it had been a really long time since she had laughed that hard and had that much fun, too. She really did need to lighten up. Just because she was thirty-something didn't mean she couldn't still be a kid again every once in a while. She could learn that from Grace.

Thank you, Lord for this very, very blessed day. Just when I think all is lost, Your love and wisdom never ceases to amaze me.

Ginger watched Grace splashing and running along the shore with Puck. It was unbelievable to think that just a little over three weeks ago, Grace was a small, red-headed ghost confined to a bed, drooling on herself and wanting to die. Now here she was, this copper-haired beauty laughing her head off and bursting with life. The past had just melted away between them and it seemed that they had never been apart. *She really is my sister—Amazing Grace!*

~12~

Revelations

Ginger let Grace think she devised their plan for the evening and waited upstairs while Grace waited in the kitchen for Hatch. When he stepped in from the hallway and saw that Ginger wasn't helping Grace with dinner, he was concerned.

"Where's Ginger?"

"Oh, she got a chill today and said she wasn't feeling too good. Just go take your shower; I'll take something up to her later."

He hesitated and then did as he was told. In thirty minutes he was back in the kitchen smelling wonderful and looking extra sexy. Grace had to laugh. *He just has no clue—how delicious is that?*

Hatch saw her sly smile and had to ask, "What is so funny with you today? You have been so weird since lunch."

Grace immediately tried to look normal again. "Oh, nothing, Ginger just told me a joke that only women would get."

"How do you know? Let's hear it."

She shook her head firmly. "No, it's just for girls. Now shut up.

I'm taking Ginger's dinner up to her." She took her time arranging and rearranging the dishes on the tray thinking, *Come on, Hatch; get the hint.*

As if he could read her thoughts, Hatch said, "I can take it up if you want. It looks a little heavy."

Finally! She hid her smile. "Okay, but she may be sleeping, so be quiet. I'm keeping Puck down here with the other dogs, so they don't disturb her."

Upstairs, Ginger was pacing the floor when she heard him knock. She quickly shifted and fluffed the pillows once more. *Lord, give me the right words to say, please.* She stood on the opposite side of the bed and told him to come in.

He bumped the door open with the tray and moved inside the room. "Hi, I see you're up, are you feeling better?"

"I'm fine, thank you. You can just put the tray on the side table over there."

He slid the tray onto the table, turned back toward her and stood there awkwardly. "Do you still want to eat up here if you're feeling better? I can take the tray back downstairs."

She moved onto the bed and made herself comfortable against the propped-up pillows, facing his direction.

"No, that's fine, Hatch. Could you come over here and sit with me? We need to get some things straightened out."

He looked confused and concerned. "Is everything all right? You're not leaving, are you?"

"No, nothing like that. Just sit here with me so I can talk to you. And I will ask you to do me a favor and let me finish before you say anything. That makes it a little easier when you're sharing something important. Like when you first told me about Grace, I didn't interrupt you like you asked, I let you finish remember?"

He nodded and sat down on the edge of the bed and removed his boots, then scooted up next to her. It took him a minute to adjust himself and when he finally looked at her, his face was a mixture of concern and curiosity and he didn't look very comfortable.

He smelled fresh from the shower and she loved when his hair was wet and slicked back like it was now. He looked so handsome, but totally and completely out of his element. She thought to herself: *This is so stupid—I feel like a spider in a web taunting her prey What was I thinking doing this in my bedroom? I should have done this in the barn or out by the falls.*

"I'm sorry for luring you up here, this was a mistake." She started to get off the bed and he grabbed her arm.

"You didn't lure me anywhere. I came of my own accord, so just sit down and say what you have to say."

She sat back against the pillows. "You just look so uncomfortable and that's the last thing I wanted you to be."

"Ginger, I'm a big boy, in case you haven't noticed. I'm uncomfortable because I don't know what you're gonna say, so can you just get on the horse and get to where your goin' with this?"

She laughed, releasing some of the tension. "Okay, cowboy, here goes. But, this ain't gonna be no normal rodeo, so get ready."

His brows knitted together in amusement and curiosity. "Okay, shoot."

She got serious again and looked down at her lap. After she took a deep breath she blurted out, "I just want to start by saying that I am flat out crazy about you and..."

His eyes widened and he started to speak, but she quickly held her hand up.

"Let me finish remember?"

He smiled that half-grin that made her swoon and settled himself deep down into the pillows and said in his most charming cowboy accent, "I'm all ears darlin'."

She summoned all her strength and began again. "As I was saying, I've developed very strong feelings for you, and Grace said you were interested in me, too. But before this goes any further between us, I need to let you know some things up front. This is really serious to me, so it may take me some time, but I will be as brief as I can, so please pay attention."

She looked over at him as he was trying to squelch another big smile, and he nodded for her to go on. She couldn't concentrate on what she wanted to say with his big green eyes messing up her thoughts, so she looked into her lap again and continued.

"Okay, here goes. A couple of years ago, I made some major changes in my life. After my father died, I kind of lost my way and did some really stupid things that I am not very proud of. Then something amazing happened to me and that's when everything in my life changed, and why I changed everything in my life because of it. I committed myself to God and a God-centered lifestyle. And before you make any judgments, please let me explain what that means to me and why it's so important that you understand. I now try to live my life as a person that does my best to emulate Jesus' grace and forgiveness toward others, in thanks for the sacrifice He and God gave for us. That may sound like a canned, stereotypical statement for some, but for me, it's a way of life. Meaning that I pray about everything, I read the Bible almost every day, and I talk to God all the time just like He's in the room with me, because I actually believe and know that He is. I turn to Him first with all my questions, fears, and needs, and I trust His guidance and His love above all others. In return, He has given me peace in my heart and comforted me after both my parents' deaths. I have seen and experienced countless inexplicable miracles that could only be attributed to His divine hand. He answers my prayers when the timing is right, and in fact, I was praying for a family to love in the weeks before you came to my door. You may think that's a coincidence, but I don't believe in coincidences. I believe they are the Father's way of putting us right where we need to be at just the right time in order to receive our blessings or overcome our challenges. In this way, we become strong and tender-hearted enough to understand and fulfill the destiny and purpose He's designed uniquely for each one of us. He's a part of who I am and I won't deny Him for anyone.

"And let me make it very clear that I am not a Bible thumper or a judgmental church lady or someone who pushes my beliefs on others, and I certainly don't hang out at airports with a tambourine like those Moonie cult people. Real Bible-based Christianity means you have a cherished one-on-one relationship with a loving and forgiving God and you do your best to honor Him by not judging or condescending to others. Human-based religions that carry the stigma of using religious fear to gain power or provoke judgment or the fire and brimstone sermons are all false teachings, used by ego-driven imposters to manipulate people's weaknesses and to incite fear and control. That's legalistic religion and not a part of God's love or purpose.

"I'm just a normal person who wants to share God's love with others and also to help others wherever He leads me. That's what makes my life worthy and fulfilled. It makes God happy and it makes me happy. It's also my thanks to God for sacrificing His Son for me, giving me the Holy Spirit in my heart, and the promise of everlasting life with Him. And that may sound too simple or naïve or silly or complicated to some of the cerebral academic types, but that's what Christianity is really about. Trust me, it's not always easy and I still screw up all the time—I'm certainly no saint that has all the answers, but nonetheless, He continues to reward my efforts in more ways than I deserve. He never gave up on me, and I will never give up on Him. So…that's my first revelation, pardon the pun."

She took a deep breath as she looked over at him to see if he laughed or if he was still listening or if he was looking to make tracks out the door. He seemed to still be intrigued by what she was saying, so she continued.

"The second part of that commitment is a baptism that washes away the old and shameful and allows you to start all over as new person. In doing this, I made a promise to the Lord and myself that I would not make love with any man but my husband, should He lead me to one. Casual sex dishonors God by devaluing His honor for me. He wants me to build a life of love and respect with someone very special that will always be worthy and honorable to me. So, I'm willing to wait for someone that will respect my commitment, even if they don't understand it. I'm sorry if that sounds corny, or old-fashioned, or like entrapment, but it's not. It's a vow that I made to God and I can't break it, no matter how attracted I am to you physically."

She finally looked at him, and now he was the one staring at his lap. She had no idea if he was getting any of this, so she continued to try and explain.

"I know this must be a little overwhelming, and I'm sorry if I caught you off-guard because that was not my intention. I never thought I would have to try and explain years of my spiritual growth to you this quickly, but I didn't have a choice. I may have done a terrible job, but please don't let this change the way you act around me. Don't feel like you can't be yourself. I think you are a wonderful man with a very big heart, and I enjoy your company very much no matter what your beliefs are."

She waited a little while longer, but he still wasn't looking at her and seemed to really be wrestling with his response. Her heart was sinking fast, so she finally broke the silence with one last effort to make him understand.

"Hatch, I didn't want my attraction to you to go any further without telling you the truth of who I am and what kind of commitment I'm looking for. And bearing in mind how strongly I feel about you, I felt I owed you that."

She paused again, and he still didn't respond. Her heart hit rock bottom. She had said what she needed to say, and now the rest was up to God. So she bit her lip, gathered all her strength, and did her best not to make more of a fool of herself as she gracefully let him off the hook.

"Well, based on your silence, I now see that your feelings were probably just casual flirtations and I'm feeling a bit ridiculous right now. Please forgive my assumptions and the fact that I have just bared my soul and totally embarrassed myself. I'll totally understand if I just freaked you out and scared you right out of here—you are free to run. No hard feelings."

She smiled a half smile and cocked her head toward him, trying to get him to look at her. He had been silent for so long that she was sure he wanted to run and was probably just trying to find the right words to do it politely. Her heart pounded in her chest as she felt it beginning to crumble into a thousand pieces. She needed to get him out of here before she totally fell apart.

Clutching her shaking hands together she attempted to give him one more quick and easy escape. "Listen, Hatch, you really are a wonderful person, and you don't have to say anything. I know you were just delivering my dinner, and I just dumped all this in your lap. Don't worry about it; I'm a big girl, too. It's not a big deal. Just know that I still value and enjoy your friendship, and that doesn't have to change. We can just move forward, and there doesn't have to be any weirdness between us now. I promise. So that's all I wanted to say, so you can go now. Please just go."

She chastised herself again for doing this in her room. She felt the tears welling up in her eyes, and now she had nowhere to run. She decided to escape to the bathroom to wash her hands for dinner, and then hopefully he would get the hint and leave. As she started to bolt off the bed, Hatch grabbed her arm and pulled her back.

"Whoa there. Just give me a second."

She stopped but kept her face turned away so he couldn't see the panic building inside her as he continued.

"Now just so I'm clear on this. You said you are crazy about me?

She knew she couldn't respond without losing it, so she simply nodded her head.

"Okay. And you'll only make love to your husband. Meaning not until after you're married?"

She finally looked at him in frustration as the tears poured down her face. There it was—the dam had broken. No more pretending she was fine. She finally answered him in exasperated anger. "Yes, Hatch, that's what I said. So if you could just be kind enough to spare me any more humiliation and just get out…"

Now it was his turn to hold up his hand. "Let me finish, Ginger." His tone was firm, and his face was serious.

She bit her lip, wiped her tears on her sleeve, and continued to stare into her lap. She asked the Lord for strength and mercy, not knowing what to expect from Hatch at this point. She was already so devastated by his confusing reactions that she just didn't know how things could ever be normal between them again. Things would most certainly get more messy and painful. This was the last thing she wanted to happen right in the middle of Grace's recovery and would put Grace in a terrible position between them. *What on earth was I thinking? Please forgive me, Lord!* She silently screamed as more tears slid down her cheek.

Hatch gently put his hand under her chin and turned her toward him. The warmth of his touch made her weak, and she fought to keep her eyes closed, hoping to hold back more tears.

"Open your eyes, Ginger."

She knew she couldn't hide her emotions any longer, so she opened them slowly as several more tears made their way down her cheeks. She took a deep breath and looked bravely at the face she loved so deeply. He smiled that devilish half-smile, and she felt those gorgeous green eyes pierce the deepest pockets of her heart.

Her defenses seeped to the floor and were now hiding under the bed—she had nothing left to fight with. She just gave it to the Lord and braced herself for his rejection. *Please, Lord, give me strength.*

He gently wiped the tears from her cheek and repeated his request. "Ginger, please calm down and look at me."

She couldn't fight him any longer and finally took a deep breath and met his gaze head-on. The warmest smile spread across his face as he softly spoke to her.

"I'd be honored to meet any terms or commitments you ask of me, even if I don't understand them. And if being your future husband is what it takes to show you that, then you'll just have to marry me, beautiful lady, 'cause I can't imagine my life without you."

His words caught her so off-guard. Her mouth dropped open, instantly reminding her of the bats going in and out, and she slammed it shut before she exclaimed, "Are you serious? Just like that—you want to marry me? This isn't a joke, Hatch. Did you hear…"

He raised his hand again to silence her protests. "I would never joke about something so serious, and, yes, I did hear everything you said. I'm not as shallow as you think, Ginger. My proposal is not *just like that*. If you'd just let me finish my thoughts…"

He wiped another tear from her face as she nodded.

"Okay then, from the first day I met you, I felt something I couldn't explain. Kind of like a glow or light inside you that drew me in and made me feel safe and warm inside. Your genuine compassion and concern for others humbles me. You have a calming way that makes me feel peaceful and happy. It's a settling and good feeling, like I've never experienced before. It happens to Grace, too; I watch her when you two are together and see her respond to you in ways I never thought possible. In just the short time you've been here, you've filled this big lonely house with love, laughter, and something Grace and I haven't had for a long time—hope. And if that light inside you is from God, then I am very thankful that He chose to shine a little bit of it on me and Grace. Even though I do believe in God, I don't really understand faith in the way you described it. But, if you'll be patient with me, I'd like you to help me understand more about it. The truth is, I love you, darlin', and I will do anything to make you happy."

Tears of joy streamed down Ginger's face as she folded herself into his arms. His soft, warm lips kissed her long and deep. She drank in his scent while she felt the strength and comfort of his arms around her. She pulled away slowly to wipe the tears from her face and catch her breath.

She looked at him. "I can't even begin to tell you how happy I am at this moment, Hatch. What you just said to me was…" Fresh tears rolled down her face, and she paused to swallow the lump in her throat. "Well, my wildest dreams couldn't have imagined anything more beautiful. And even though you took a coon's age to finally respond to me, thank you. If you haven't guessed by my puffy, bloated, and I'm sure, blotchy face, I love you, too."

Hatch laughed and then said, "You still look beautiful to me, and I meant every word. But, seriously, a coon's age? I see you got some country lingo of your own going on. That's some old school country!"

She swatted at him and smiled. "I don't even know where that came from. That's from hanging around with you too much!"

They both laughed and then she got serious again. "Did you

really mean every word? Even the… marrying me part?"

He smiled back and said, "Well, yes, ma'am, I don't think I stuttered! Unless you got something against marrying a cowboy?"

She laughed and snuggled deeper into his arms. "Oh, I've always loved cowboys, but especially an incredibly compassionate and surprising one in particular!"

He pulled her on top of him, so he could see her face. "So, does that mean you'll marry me, ma'am?"

"Yes. That's what that means, pardner!"

"Well, now that that's settled. Let's get back to the kissing part. I plan to take full advantage of that whenever and wherever possible."

She laughed, and then he kissed her with so much passion, she thought she might faint from happiness. They finally paused for a breath and then broke out in a rash of happy and relieved giggles.

"I've been dreaming about kissing you ever since I first laid eyes on you in those tight little jeans!"

"Right back at ya, cowboy!"

"Then why did you wait so long to tell me?"

She looked embarrassed. "I found out only today that you and Grace were not a couple and that I have been making myself sick with guilt over my attraction to you all for nothing."

"Ahhh, so that explains it." He chuckled at her confusion as he embraced her. "That would be like being with my sister."

"That's what she said when I finally told her. After your little striptease at the falls today, she saw my tongue hanging out and confronted me. I was terror-stricken that she wouldn't forgive me or wouldn't believe me that nothing had happened between us. Of course, she took full and cruel advantage of her new sister over that!"

He chuckled again. "It all makes sense now. I suppose she set this whole thing up tonight. It also explains why she was laughing all day at my expense!"

"Well, that, and she pretended that you really were together and had a fake meltdown on me."

"Oh yeah, I can see her working that one."

"I had a real meltdown on her in return when she told me the truth. After I eventually calmed down, I had to admit it really was pretty funny."

"So you enjoyed my little striptease, huh? I saw you checking me out in the water, too, by the way."

"Well, you're kind of hard to ignore, dressed or not."

"So maybe we should go down to the courthouse tomorrow cuz I know I have the patience, but I don't know how you're going to be able to resist all of this?" He motioned down his body.

She smacked him on the arm. "I think I can manage. But one thing I don't have to resist is another one of your kisses, or two, or three…"

He laughed and pulled her close. "Well, yes, ma'am, big wet one coming right up!"

~13~
Not That Kind of Weird

The following morning, Hatch awoke with a start. He looked at the clock on the nightstand and saw that it was 8:00 a.m. "Whoa! I gotta go!" He muttered as he kissed her quickly and began to untangle himself from her.

She grabbed him back toward her. "Whoa, yourself! Grace already told the guys last night that you wouldn't be out today."

"Is that right? Well, you two just got this all worked out, don't you?"

"Are you complaining?" she asked.

"No, ma'am, not in the least." He wrapped his arms around her waist and buried his lips in her neck.

When they finally showed up downstairs, it was 11:00 a.m. Grace was sitting in the kitchen talking with Cook. When she saw them, Grace smiled from ear to ear. "Well, good morning!"

Both Hatch and Ginger turned red with embarrassment. Grace was now laughing with satisfaction and enjoying their awkwardness. Hatch snapped her with a dish towel, and Ginger start-ed laughing, too.

Marta just shook her head and left through the back door while shouting, "Lunch in basket, leftover biscuits and bacon in oven. I no cook breakfast this late!"

They were all laughing now as Hatch grabbed Grace's shoul-ders from behind and crushed her to him, "Well, now that you have me off work today, what did you plan next?"

"Well, I thought you might be up there a little longer, stud, so I told Ronnie to saddle up the horses at noon so we could show Ginger the ranch."

Hatch tickled her and said, "Well, I would have, but I didn't want you to get too jealous, since I'm *your* man!"

"Ha! In your dreams, buddy, you're way too tame for me!"

Ginger cut in, "Okay, conversation getting weird!"

"Exactly," said Hatch to Grace, "and you have no idea how much weirder it's going to get."

"Whoa—what does that mean? Are we talking kinky?"

Ginger rolled her eyes. "Not that kind of weird, Grace."

Hatch winked at Ginger and said to Grace, "Nope, I mean we're engaged and we *didn't* have sex last night."

Grace swiveled around so fast she slammed into Ginger, who was coming up behind her. "What did you just say?"

Ginger tucked herself under Hatch's arm and with huge grins they both said, "We're engaged!"

Grace squealed with joy and couldn't stop jumping up and down and clapping her hands.

"I guess that means we have your blessing! Now can I finally have some grub, please? I seemed to have forgotten to eat my dinner last night."

Grace continued to hop around as Ginger warmed up the leftovers from breakfast. They proceeded to stuff themselves silly between bouts of laughter over Ginger's many instances of misreading Hatch and Grace's relationship until they could barely breathe.

Hatch finally stood up and stretched. "I'll go grab the horses, Meet me out front in ten minutes."

After he walked out the door, Ginger looked at Grace, who suddenly got a puzzled look on her face.

"What?" Ginger asked.

"Wait a minute. Why did Hatch say that you didn't have sex last night? He was joking, right?"

Ginger cut her off. "Never mind that; we'll talk about that later. I need to get ready to go."

Despite Grace's protest, Ginger ignored her and ran back upstairs.

Just after noon, they all saddled up and headed out with all three dogs in tow. The day was beautiful with just a couple of puffy clouds. Ginger marveled at the rich green rolling pastures that melted into magnificent mountain views. Cloud and Apache randomly took turns moving to the front of the horses, then flanking each side, and then dropping to the back while they kept a watchful eye. She realized they were circling like point guards and was amazed at how swift and strong the dogs moved and circled. When Puck got side-tracked smelling some random scent, Cloud nudged him to keep moving. He took this as playful taunts and would then chase and bark at her. He was overjoyed with his new friends and surroundings as much as she was.

She breathed in the sweetness of the air mixed with the sweaty, grassy smell of her horse. The sound of all the hooves hitting the soft green earth was comforting and exhilarating. She felt like she was drugged with endorphins. She gazed at the majesty of the mountains surrounding them with their unspoiled magnificence and sucked every bit of beauty into her hungry soul like a greedy thief. Her happiness was so intense that she imagined any minute she would sprout wings and fly right out of her saddle.

She took a couple of deep breaths to calm herself. Maybe it was the altitude that was making her so delirious, but she doubted that. After the turn of events her life had taken, how else could she feel? She loved horses, she loved the mountains, Puck was at her side, she suddenly had a twin sister and a sexy cowboy that she was crazy in love with—and, oh yeah, she was engaged! She gazed up into the blue sky and thought silently, *Lord, I fear I don't deserve all this happiness, but thank you, thank you, thank you!* The smile on her face widened when she noticed Grace beaming at her with an equally big grin on her face.

"Will you stop spying on me with that sixth sense of yours?"

"I can't help it; you're contagious!"

Ginger smiled and nodded.

Hatch rode ahead of them but turned to appreciate their infectious cheerfulness. He seemed pretty cheerful himself as he smiled at them and pointed to his left. "We are nearing the North Forest Trail. There's some beautiful scenery and wildlife through here."

The trail narrowed and the horses fell into single file. Apache moved to the lead and Cloud fell to the back, keeping Puck in front of her. As they climbed the gently rising trail, the landscape continued to unfold into scene after scene of fantastic views. As they rounded corners of rocky cliffs, the trees suddenly opened up into various panoramic vistas of dark and snowy mountaintops wrapped in blindingly blue skies. Then the trail suddenly dipped down into a canopy of dense shady forest where the temperature dropped and the echoing sounds of birds danced through the trees above.

A layer of goosebumps crawled across Ginger's skin—she didn't know if it was from the sudden coolness or the excitement and mystique that the forest held. She felt like she was in an enchanted fairytale surrounded by an emerald carpet of lacy ferns and mossy-laden trees which had long ago fallen to their demise from some unknown foe. Her ears were struck with the heightened awareness of crunching leaves and rustling bushes as some wary creature scuttled to safety. The mixture of exhilaration and fear of wild beasts that lurked in the dark shadows was swimming through her head when Hatch pointed to the left of the trail. She followed his finger just in time to see a large buck raise his head, snort loudly through his nostrils, and bolt off through the trees in the blink of an eye. Ginger's heart skipped a beat. That had been the first deer she had ever seen in the wild.

As they moved deeper into the wilderness, the wildlife continued to thrill her. The trail led into various larger clearings. They spotted a red fox, a small black bear, a guarded raccoon with her two young'uns, as Hatch called them, and several more deer.

After about two hours, they stopped to have lunch. Grace pulled peanut butter sandwiches, crackers, and various cheeses and cookies from the pack on her horse. They ate in a shady spot near a ridge with a gorgeous view of the valley.

Puck gobbled up half of Ginger's sandwich and then promptly passed out on the blanket. This was the longest walk he had ever been on without a break. Ginger worried about him being too exhausted for the return trip, so Hatch told her to set him across the saddle in front of her. He helped her up and then put a blanket across the front of her and handed Puck up. Puck wasn't sure about this arrangement at first, but then he relaxed and settled in for the ride. When Hatch went to mount his horse, he paused and looked out over the ridge.

"Yeah," Grace said. "Storm's coming. We may have to bunk out at the north shelter for a spell."

Ginger looked at Grace. "Shelter? What does that mean? We won't be back before it starts raining?"

"It's okay. It won't be for long. The storms move through pretty fast this time of year."

Grace and Hatch mounted up, and they started back down the trail the way they came. It didn't take long for the rain to catch up to them. It was only drizzling, but the wind increased and the temperature really dropped. Ginger started to shake and shoved her hands under Puck for warmth.

Hatch increased their speed and cut up a side trail to the left. After about fifty yards, they came into a clearing with a small cabin and noticed smoke rising from the chimney. Hatch stopped his horse short, causing all of them to rack up like bumper cars.

Grace spun toward Ginger and put her finger to her lips in a gesture to be quiet. She then grabbed the reins of Ginger's horse and moved both horses with their riders back into the trees.

Hatch flew off his horse and grabbed a short shotgun he had

stashed in his pack behind his saddle. The dogs circled to each side of him awaiting his command.

He motioned for the dogs to move behind some trees where he joined them and shouted loudly toward the cabin, "You are trespassing on private land! Come out of the cabin with your hands out and identify yourself."

Ginger watched the unfolding scene with disbelief. Did he really just say that? Was she suddenly in an old western movie? Were there cattle rustlers holed up in there that may try to shoot Hatch? Puck could feel her panic; he whimpered and tried to stand up. She held on tight to him and told him quietly that it was all right.

Then the cabin door opened and a very tall, very handsome Indian walked out with his hands up. His hair was jet black and almost to his waist. He smiled and said, "Don't shoot, white man. Me not armed. Me just smoking peace pipe."

Hatch lowered his gun and broke out into raucous laughter. He sprinted onto the porch and hugged the big Indian, slapping him on the back. The dogs licked and greeted him warmly as well.

"You son of a gun! You scared the heck out of us!"

"Us?" The Indian looked puzzled. "Who's with you?"

Grace and Ginger moved into the clearing just as Hatch said, "Surprise!"

Ginger watched the Indian smile from ear to ear when he saw Grace, and then his mouth dropped open when he looked behind her and saw Ginger.

"Wow, I think I smoked too much peace pipe. I'm seeing double!"

Hatch broke out into more laughter and said, "It's not the pipe, brother. It's twins!"

Ginger noticed that Grace hadn't said a word. She silently tied up the horses and carried Puck to the porch. She brushed past the Indian and into the cabin without even so much as a glance.

Hatch laughed again. "Oh boy, brother, you're still knee-deep in cow patties with that one."

Hatch helped Ginger down from her horse as the rain became heavier. They ducked onto the porch, and Hatch introduced her to Running Bear, known to all as Bear.

"So you are a real Indian? That is so…cool."

Both Hatch and Bear cracked up.

"It's not funny; I've never met a real full-blooded Indian before. Well, beside the grunting sisters at the house. You look like the handsome brave in the painting in my bedroom."

"Well, I'm flattered. I just finished my rain dance. How do you like my work?"

Ginger and Hatch laughed, and Hatch slapped Bear on the back.

"Boy, have I missed your stupid humor. Where in the heck have you been these last fifteen years, man?"

"It's a long story, full of many moons and broken teepees."

"Well, it better be a good one, because Little Flame looks like she'd like to break some more teepees right now."

Ginger looked back and forth between the two men. "Who's Little Flame?"

Hatch wrapped his arm around Ginger and kissed her warmly. "I'll tell you later. Let's get inside and get warm."

As they moved inside, Bear punched Hatch on the shoulder and gave him a wink. "I see you wasted no time moving in on the sister. Is she a fiery one, too?"

Grace slammed a pot down on the kitchen stove so hard that they all jumped, including the dogs. "Anyone interested in fresh coffee?"

Ginger walked into the tiny kitchen to help Grace and find out what was going on with her and Bear. When Grace handed her the can of coffee, Ginger gave her a puzzled look. Grace waved her off in a way that told Ginger she was not going to get the answers to this story any time soon.

While they sipped coffee and warmed up by the fire, Bear relayed stories about the rodeo circuit and how he had recently lost his mother. Grace sat in silence, never making any more than glancing eye contact.

Ginger didn't know what was up, but Grace did not like this guy at all. He must have made her very angry or hurt her very badly. It was killing Ginger not to know. As the girls cleaned up, Bear made fast friends with Puck. He was fascinated with the size of him, just like Hatch had been.

As the rain cleared, they all mounted up and headed toward the ranch. It seemed Bear was headed to the ranch before the rain which apparently did not surprise Hatch or Grace.

The ride back was just as fascinating. The rain changed the scenery into different hues of darkness and light glistening off the heavily drenched canopy. The damp earthy smells drifted into Ginger's nostrils, flaunting their rich fragrance with each new breath. She inhaled deeply and again felt comforted by the memories of her father. She felt a light layer of goosebumps tickle her skin and knew her parents were smiling at her happiness. Right at that moment Hatch turned to her and winked just the way her father used to. She felt a catch in her throat and her eyes welled up.

She knew right then that she may not have found her little cabin in the woods, but she had found her home in the mountains and once again whispered a silent prayer of thanks.

When they finally arrived back at the ranch, Grace headed straight to her room with Ginger hot on her trail. "What is going on?" Ginger asked her pointedly.

"Nothing." Grace answered shortly. "We had a fling a long time ago, and I just didn't expect to see him again, that's all."

"Really? Because it looked like a lot more than a little fling."

"Nope, that's it. I'm going to take a shower."

And with that, Grace started stripping and headed into the bathroom, closing the door.

Ginger was dumbfounded—she and Grace had shared so many details about their past, but she hadn't mentioned one word about Bear. Apparently, she was not going to share anymore now either. Ginger stood speechless over Grace's cold dismissal. They had been having such a great time, and Grace was doing so well. She had weaned off most of her medications, and Ginger almost forgot Grace's tendency toward addictions and fragile emotions. The doctor warned her that Grace was still in recovery, so she didn't want to push too hard and risk Grace withdrawing from her. This was going to be difficult, but she knew she needed to be patient. She had not seen this side of Grace and decided she would wait it out and hope that Grace would eventually trust her enough to tell her the real story.

She went back to the kitchen where the guys were talking to Cook about dinner. Much to Ginger's amazement, she witnessed Marta laughing. Bear was apparently charming the pants off of her, and she was giggling like a school girl. As soon as Marta noticed Ginger, the smile instantly faded, and she barked out that dinner was at seven and promptly left the room.

"Well, besides Grunty Cook and Grace, it was an absolutely beautiful day!"

Hatch and Bear chuckled while Hatch engulfed her in his arms. "Marta will warm up to you as soon as she knows that you are to be trusted. And as far as Gracie, well, that's a very long story."

She started to speak and Hatch put his finger over her mouth and turned to Bear. "Why don't you catch up with the ranch hands? They should be in the bunkhouse by now. I'll be out shortly."

"Will do, boss." He turned to Ginger then, "And nice to meet you, Gentle Wind." And with that he turned and headed out.

Ginger looked at Hatch, "I just don't understand what is going on. Grace pretty much just kicked me out and refused to speak any further. What happened with those two? She's pretty angry about someone she's never even mentioned to me? And why is he so calm and jovial about all this?"

Hatch laughed. "Okay, okay, one question at a time. Let's take a walk, and I will fill you in."

They headed out to the back deck. The sun would be setting soon and the sky was starting to take on a pinkish glow. They walked a little way down the hill behind the house and sat on a bench under an oak tree. The dogs settled in on the ground next to them. Hatch grabbed her hand and held it against his thigh as they gazed out over the pasture toward the mountains. Grace could hear the men in the bunkhouse hooting and hollering over Bear's arrival.

Hatch grinned and squeezed her hand. "Hmmm, I'll give you

a quick rundown of what I know, but Gracie will have to fill in the rest. Bear's father and your dad Jake were very good friends. They grew up together. Jake's father purchased this land from Bear's grandfather. Bear worked this ranch with me for two summers when he was around eighteen or nineteen. He and Grace had a very intense relationship the second summer. They kept it a secret from your parents, of course. Eventually Bear had to return to his tribe, and then he left to work the rodeo circuit. He has a way with horses that is incredible—a horse whisperer is what they called him. I lost track of him though after he went on the circuit.

"I don't really know what happened between them, she would never talk to me about it. When he left, Grace didn't talk to any-one for days, and then she lived with someone in town for several months. When she returned, she was more guarded. I tried to talk to her, but when she shuts down, there is no talking her out of it until she is ready. I guess you caught a bit of that today. It's just how she deals with things she can't control. It's either that or the drug or liquor of her choice, which is how she usually copes. I don't think we need to worry as much about the drugs now that you are here, but I'm still keeping a close eye on her. Bear has obviously upset her, and I think if you are patient enough, maybe she'll tell you."

"Didn't you ever ask Bear what happened?"

"That's not my place and guys like us don't poke around in each other's saddle bags, if you know what I mean. He's like a brother to me and Grace is like a sister. I can't choose sides. They both know that I am here if they need me."

"Well, who is Little Flame and Gentle… whatever he said?"

"Oh, that." He laughed. "Bear nicknames people according to

their personalities. Grace is Little Flame because she is like fire. And he sees you as Gentle Wind. Like I told you, you have that peaceful nature, like a gentle wind. It fits, and it's obvious that he really likes you."

"Well, at least there's one Indian that likes me."

Hatch laughed. "I like you pretty well, too."

She smiled and squeezed his hand. "Well, cowboy, I'm going to take a shower, and it smells like you could use one, too!"

Hatch jumped up and pulled her toward the house. "Last one home is a dirty tick on a sow's butt!"

She pulled him to a stop. "Did you just say a sow's butt? Okay, that's just gross. And a dirty tick—really?"

He laughed so hard at her disgusted expression she started laughing at herself. It was really going to take some time to get used to this crazy cowboy lingo.

~14~

Bear and Grace

Dinner was awkward with Grace's absence. Ginger felt like a traitor eating and laughing with Hatch and Bear, but Grace told her she preferred to be alone for a while and would talk to her later. Bear's humor was truly hysterical. He had the Indian stereotype shtick down pat. She and Hatch had tears rolling down their faces with laughter. And *woo*, was Bear as sexy as all get-out! He had a deep, throaty genuine laugh complimented by a big white smile and navy blue eyes that flashed when he spoke. Ginger was jealous of his freakishly long eyelashes that matched his long silky black hair that flew all around his big shoulders when he spoke. No wonder Grace fell so hard for him. He was so grounded and comfortable with himself.

He and Hatch could have been real brothers, they were so much alike—no bull, no pretense, just good, honest, sincere men—very solid, hardworking and genuine. They were so much like her father which seems so rare in this day and age. She wondered about Jake, her birth father. Was he once like them? Did he change over the years? Despite the horror stories, Hatch and Bear seemed to care about and admire him very much.

So many questions she still had to ask. She wanted to like this Indian and couldn't imagine his hurting Grace on purpose. She really wanted to know the full story so she tried one more time that evening to talk to Grace, but she was already asleep. It was late anyway and maybe after a good night's sleep Grace would open up to her in the morning. She and Hatch left Bear flirting with Marta after she brought him a cherry pie. It was apparently Bear's favorite. They headed up the stairs, chasing and giggling with all the dogs in tow, although only Puck was allowed to sleep on the bed that night.

The next morning, Grace was in the kitchen by herself when Hatch and Ginger came down. She looked ragged like she hadn't slept much. Hatch quickly ate a biscuit, kissed both Grace and Ginger on the cheek, and headed out to the bunkhouse.

Ginger sat down next to Grace and stroked her arm. "Please don't shut me out, Grace. It's obvious you are in a lot of pain, but you aren't alone any longer. You have me to share your pain with and I want to help. I love you so much; I just can't stand seeing you this upset. Please talk to me."

Grace's shoulders started to shake and one by one the tears began to roll down her face until she finally broke down completely. Ginger held her tight until the sobbing started to lighten.

"It's too late. The baby's gone."

Ginger's stomach tightened up. "Baby…what baby, honey?"

"Bear's baby." Grace sniffed. "I didn't tell him. I couldn't—he hurt me."

"Oh my God, Grace, you got pregnant and he doesn't know? What did Bear do to you? He didn't rape you, did he?"

"Of course not! He would never do anything like that. I forced him to leave; I said I hated him."

"Why?" Ginger was trying to go slow so she didn't spook Grace, but she couldn't get *the baby is gone* statement out of her mind. This was scaring her. "Grace, please start from the beginning so I can understand what you are saying."

She sighed and blubbered a bit more as she finally began telling Ginger the story. "Bear and I have loved each other from the first time we met. We just didn't know it at first. I was the boss's daughter, and he was raised to respect and revere women, especially white women. Indian and white relationships were frowned upon back then. The elders didn't want the mixed blood on either side. I didn't know any of that then, and I wouldn't have cared anyway. I wanted that beautiful boy and nothing was going to stop me. I flirted with him in every way I knew how. But he never seemed to notice, so I thought that he was just scared of me or shy. At least that's what I told myself when he ignored me, but the real story was that I did not act like any girl he had ever seen before. I drank, I cussed, I rode with no saddle like an Indian, and I sassed my elders and flirted shamelessly with all the ranch hands to make him jealous. He paid no attention to me and that made me nuts, so after some months of me making a fool of myself, trying to get this crazy Indian to notice me, I finally confronted him one day in the barn. I asked him if he thought I was pretty. He hesitated for a moment then tried to walk past me. I shoved him and asked him again. He finally said yes. So I asked him why he never made a move on me. He said, 'Because you act like a dude.'"

She paused and laughed.

Ginger laughed too. "Really he said that to you?"

She laughed again. "Yeah, he did. I asked him what the hell that meant and spit on his boots."

"Oh, Grace, you did not really spit on him, did you? That's terrible."

"That's apparently what he thought, too. He just shook his head at me and walked out. I was absolutely dumbfounded; I could have any guy I wanted, and this guy just walked out. I was so pissed off that I stormed into the house and started slamming doors and swearing obscenities at him. My mother, I mean, our mother came staggering in. She was drunk or high on pills and asked me why the hell I was making so much noise. I told her that dumbass Indian called me a dude. And she said, 'Well, look in the mirror and listen to the way you talk for heaven's sake. You are about as feminine as a goat in heat!' Then she told me to stop making so much noise and turned around and went back to her room."

Ginger thought about her own mother and couldn't believe that Patrice would call her daughter something so terrible and then just leave like nothing happened. Then she remembered that this was the same woman who tried to kill her as an innocent baby. Ginger was concerned that this particular fact was going to hit her someday like a wrecking ball in the stomach and hoped she wouldn't be haunted by it.

"That must have been very painful to hear." Ginger said finally.

"Oh, no, not at all, that was nothing. Actually it was nicer than *whore* or *slut*. Those were her more common names for me."

Ginger flinched again, knowing her adoptive mother probably

had never even heard of those words, let alone used them.

"So, what did you do then?"

"Well, I actually listened to her for the first time in my life. I walked into my bedroom and looked into the mirror. I walked around in front of it, and I talked to myself in the usual way that I talk. I discovered that I did act like a dude! So, I told Dad I wanted to go away to my Aunt Peggy's for the summer. That's Dad's sister. You have an aunt by the way, too. Sorry I forgot to mention that."

Ginger's eyes snapped open. "What? I have an aunt, too? Why haven't you mentioned her until now? Is she still alive?"

"As far as I know. She used to live in town, but she moved away years ago."

"Okay, it just would have been nice to know that before, but never mind that now. Why did you want to go live with her?"

"Well, I heard she was a very prim and proper lady. Dad called her *the spinster* or *old maid*. She and Jake didn't get along because of Patrice, and he didn't know why I would ever want to stay with her, but he was just glad to have me out from under his feet."

"What about Patrice? Was she okay with you leaving?"

"She probably didn't even notice I was gone. We weren't close, remember?"

Ginger didn't think she would ever understand the callousness of this woman that was her mother.

"So, anyway, I went to stay with Aunt Peg, and after some very long days and some very heated arguments, Aunt Peg taught me how to be a lady—not a very good one, but enough so that Mr. Smart-Alec-Running Bear couldn't call me a dude anymore."

Ginger laughed. "What happened? Did he notice?"

"Oh yeah, he did. When I came home late that summer, he was hitching up a horse near the house. I rolled up and stepped out in my brand new dress and high shoes with my freshly washed curls blowing in the wind and my makeup just perfect. I headed right toward him. And, boy, did he notice, all right!" She laughed at the memory. "His eyes bugged right out of his head and his tongue was hanging so far out of his mouth I almost stepped on it."

Ginger laughed and asked, "Did you say anything to him? Did he say anything to you?"

"I just said, 'Hey Bear, how are you today?' Then I blew right past him. He was so shocked he couldn't even speak. He just mumbled something stupid, and when I turned around to hear what he said, he tripped over the horse's strap. I didn't laugh at him, although I wanted to. All I said was 'Okay then, I'll see you around.' When I got into the house, I laughed so hard I thought I would pee my pants."

They were both laughing now because Grace had stood up and was mimicking Bear's mumbling and tripping. Ginger was so happy Grace was laughing again, but she was still worried about the baby part.

"Okay, so, he noticed you weren't a dude anymore, then what happened?"

"Oh, I just casually happened to be at the same places as him occasionally, but never spoke to him in more than a polite casual manner, like I couldn't care less. But I knew the Harvest Dance was coming up, and as far as I heard, he wasn't taking anyone. So, I went with Hatch and his date and just stayed by the dance floor until Bear finally got up enough nerve to ask me to dance. And that was all it took. One touch, one dance, one night and we couldn't get enough of each other.

"I snuck out most nights, and we lay under the stars and talked for hours and hours. We told each other secrets and made each other laugh. He really was shy and so sweet that he didn't even kiss me for a whole month. I didn't care—I just wanted to be with him. He was so real and smart and funny and brave and tall, and as I'm sure you've already noticed, beyond sexy! Only Hatch knew about us. Bear's mother or my father would not have allowed our union. He was to return to his home after the summer and marry an Indian girl and live and work near the tribe. But we were inseparable and had fallen deeply in love, and I didn't think those customs mattered to him. His last summer was coming soon, and I couldn't bear the thought of losing him. We made love every minute we had left. Even until the last moment, I thought he would never leave me. I assumed he would tell his mother, and we would run away and that would be that. But, apparently, I was wrong. He said he had no choice but to honor his mother and father. It was just something he had to do.

"Well, I was not having any of that. I yelled every hateful thing I could think of at him, that he was abandoning me, that he never loved me, that he used me, and that I would tell his mother. I said terrible, terrible things to him and told him to never come back because I hated him and that I just used him. I was so hurt and so stupid and selfish. I didn't understand honoring your family, because honor was something my family never had. I'll never forget the pain in his face. The last thing he said was that he had to go and promised me that he would never stop loving me and that he would come back to me when it was in the stars."

At this point, Grace broke down again. Ginger held her again, telling her it was understandable how she felt. She wiped the tears from Grace's face.

"Tell me about the baby, Grace."

Grace let out a painful whimper and continued. "I was in so much pain after Bear left. I couldn't talk to anyone about it. I was so tired, my body hurt, and I was throwing up all the time. Our wonderful mother caught me running to the bathroom one morning and said in her usual mothering way, 'You better not be pregnant.' I took a test and sure enough I was. I asked my father again if I could spend some time with Aunt Peg. He made the arrangements, and I fled once more. I wanted an abortion, but Aunt Peg convinced me to give the baby up for adoption. So, for seven more months, I held the only piece of Bear I had left next to my heart. The day the baby came, I thought I would literally die from heartbreak. Peg asked me one more time if I was sure I wanted to give him up, and I said yes. As much as I wanted that baby, I knew I couldn't handle it. They took the baby away swiftly, and I never saw him again. He had a patch of silky black hair right on the top of his sweet little head. That's the last thing I had to remember him by. Every day that goes by I feel the loss in my heart, and I still dream of the little patch being torn away. The drugs made the pain go away most of the time, especially when the thought that I almost killed our baby comes to haunt me. Oh God, Ginger…" Grace wailed in pain. "I miss them both so much."

She and Ginger were both sobbing now. Ginger was racked with the pain she felt for her sister but also filled with joy that the baby was still alive somewhere.

"Have you ever asked Aunt Peg where he is?"

"No. I thought about it a hundred times, but I'm too embarrassed to even talk to Aunt Peg. She probably thinks I'm the most horrible person on the earth. Plus, what would I say if I saw him? Why would he even want to know me? I have nothing to offer him, Ginger; I'm not a good person, let alone anything close to a mother."

"Grace, stop talking like that. You made a mistake because you were young and scared. You are a good person in your heart."

Grace just kept shaking her head no, so Ginger suggested they take a ride to the waterfall and get some fresh air. After they had taken a swim and lay quietly in the cool shade for a couple of hours, Ginger finally told Grace what she thought.

"I don't know if you've considered this or not, but I think this is actually terribly romantic."

Grace lifted up on one elbow and just stared at Ginger. "Are you serious? I just poured my heart out to you, and you think losing the love of my life and my child is romantic? That's really screwed up, Ginger!"

"Hear me out for a second. Think about the last thing he said before he left that summer. He would never stop loving you, and he would come back to you when it was in the stars! Well, he's back, Grace! Did you miss that his mother is gone now and there doesn't seem to be a Mrs. Bear with him? The way that man looks and how funny and wonderful he is, the women must have been clawing each other to death trying to snag him. But he obviously was telling the truth when he said all those years ago that he would never stop loving only you. Call me screwed up, but that is the most romantic thing I've ever heard. Why else would he be here?"

Grace welled up and started sobbing again.

"But you have to tell Bear about the baby, Grace. He has a right to know he has a son somewhere. He's seems to be a very good man, and I really think after some time he will understand."

"I can't do it, Ginger. I'm not strong like you. How am I supposed to tell him I wanted to kill his son? I still love this man more than life itself, and when I saw him at that cabin, I thought my heart would explode right there on the spot. I'm not brave enough to tell him after all these years, and I'm still mad at him for leaving me. What if he doesn't forgive me? I will have to lose him all over again! Besides you don't even know if I'm why he came back anyway. Maybe he just wants to buy a horse."

Ginger laughed. "Grace, I would bet my life that he came back for you. And that's all that should matter! Tell him tonight, Grace. Tell him everything you told me. It's the only way you will finally heal your heart and release the pain. You owe him the truth, regardless of the outcome."

Grace reluctantly shook her head *yes* then *no*. "What if he really has come back to me, and then I tell him, and he doesn't forgive me?"

"Can you honestly keep this lie in your heart and expect to have a chance at an honest relationship? No, it won't work, Grace. The truth always comes out, and if it doesn't come from you first, imagine how much more betrayed Bear will feel then! Your heart is sick, and you need to tell him before you can heal it and move on. Even if he doesn't forgive you, at least you will have released this guilt you have been carrying around for way too long. And I will be here no matter what happens."

Grace hugged Ginger, and after another bout of tears, Grace said she would do it. She would tell Bear that night.

Ginger was so relieved. She also asked Grace if it was okay if she told Hatch because Bear may need him. Grace shook her head *yes*.

~ 15 ~

The Painful Truth

After Marta had served dinner, she pulled out another cherry pie. Grace had been quiet for most of the dinner. When Marta put the pie on the table, Grace stood up and asked Bear to take a walk with her. Bear excused himself, assuring Marta he would be back for some pie and to please save him a big piece.

After Grace and Bear left the room, Hatch looked to Ginger to tell him what was going on. She relayed the story to Hatch from the beginning. She could tell Hatch was shocked that Grace had been keeping this from him all these years. Ginger grabbed his hand, and they moved to the main living room to wait.

Meanwhile, Grace led Bear down the back path toward the waterfall. She was walking swiftly when he grabbed her arm and turned her back toward the bench under the big oak tree. He sat her down, and she looked away toward the mountains. He waited patiently until it seemed she just wasn't going to speak.

"Grace, when are you going to stop being so angry and talk to me? I know how much it hurt you when I left. It was the hardest thing I've ever had to do, but I had to honor the commitments to my family. The tribe was doing poorly, and they needed the money I made in the rodeo to help the elders with expenses. I know you don't understand being poor, but that is something that I know very well. Some of my people were sick and needed medical care, the children needed schooling and supplies, and many people could not afford food for their tables. I tried to tell you all this before I left, but you refused to listen to reason."

Grace still could not look at him. "I would have come to the reservation with you. I didn't care where we lived. I just wanted to be with you. If that was not a possibility, you should not have led me on. I still thought up until the last minute that we would be together. I thought your obligation was to me and to us."

"I know it was not fair of me. I was young and reckless, and I didn't think things would go as far as they did with us. You were the boss's daughter, and your father expected you to marry well. I knew that you loved me in a way, Grace, but I just thought I was a summer fling and that you would find some new boy to play with soon after I was gone."

Grace reeled herself toward him with eyes full of fury. "How could you not know how much I loved you? I told you all my deepest secrets, fears, hopes, dreams—everything! I even became a lady for you! "

Bear dropped his head and replied, "It wasn't until Hatch came to see me at the reservation a couple months later and told me how heartbroken you were that I finally let myself believe you really did love me as much as I loved you. But it didn't change the fact that I had nothing to offer you, Grace. I didn't even have a house for us, I was always traveling to the rodeos, and all my money went to the tribe. I had no way to take care of you or provide for you."

"I didn't need you to take care of me! I had plenty of money for both of us."

"I could never take your father's money, Grace. That would not have been honorable."

"Oh, the hell with your honor! If you really actually loved me, you wouldn't have cared about any of that. You should have found a way for us to be together. Maybe that's it, Bear, maybe you didn't really love me. Maybe it was me that was *your* summer fling. Maybe you just couldn't wait to get back so you could go and find your Indian Squaw!"

Bear pulled her chin toward his face. "Grace, I have never loved any other woman besides you."

"Well, I'm sure your mother had a wife all lined up for you."

"I never married, Grace; it would not have been fair to marry another woman when my heart would forever belong to you."

"Liar! If you really loved me, you would have come back for me before now."

"I could only come back, Grace, when the time was right. I have secured a very good business in horse sales and training. And my mother has passed, so I no longer have to worry about dishonoring her by not marrying someone within the tribe. I want to marry you, Grace. That is why I have come back."

Grace felt a lump form in her throat, and her broken heart swelled. "It's too late, Bear; we've hurt each other too much."

"It's never too late when two people love each other. I won't let you go again, Grace. I know you still love me. If you didn't, you wouldn't still be this mad at me."

Grace broke down and started sobbing uncontrollably. Bear engulfed her in his big warm embrace, and, for a moment, it felt like time had never passed. His arms were strong and safe, but she still couldn't trust him to stay once he knew her secret.

"Little Flame, please stop crying. We can't change the past, but we have the rest of our lives to be together. Please give us a chance."

Grace sobbed out, "Oh, Bear, I do still love you. I've never stopped loving you. But I did something awful, and I don't expect you will forgive me."

Grace moved out of Bear's arms and turned away again.

"Forgive you for what?" confusion crossed Bear's face. "What could be so awful? I know about your dad. I don't blame you for that; it was an accident."

"It's not my dad, Bear. It's something worse. I was so angry and hurt. I just wanted to punish you, and I did something unforgivable."

"Grace, you are scaring me now. Just sit down, and tell me what you are talking about."

Grace kept her face turned away from him, toward the setting sun behind the mountains.

"I found out I was pregnant after you left."

Bear turned her to face him. "What did you just say?"

"I said I got pregnant."

"You got pregnant! By whom?"

"By you, dummy!" Grace stood up and began to pace.

"By me?!" Bear was shocked. "You mean that we have a child

and you didn't tell me? Do we still have a child? Oh God, Grace, please tell me that you didn't have an abortion or a miscarriage!"

Grace sat down again. "No, I wanted to have an abortion, but my aunt convinced me not to. I didn't want anything that reminded me of you, and I was scared and confused, and I wanted to punish you."

His voice was harsh now, and he sat down next to her and pulled her around to face him. "What the heck did you do? Where is our child, Grace?"

"I gave him up for adoption, Bear. I don't know where he is. My Aunt Peg handled everything. I just don't know." Grace broke down again in a fresh fit of racking sobs. "I'm so sorry, Bear; I just didn't know what else to do."

Bear leapt off the bench and paced back and forth, screaming at her. "You didn't know what to do? Are you serious? We had a baby together, and you thought that I shouldn't know?" He paced some more, and his voice became angrier. "I've had a son all these years, and you thought I shouldn't know? And you have no idea where he is? What the heck is wrong with you? Why do you always have to be so selfish?"

Grace's sadness turned to white-hot anger as she screamed back at him, "Would it have changed anything? You didn't want me, you rejected me, you left me all alone, and the thought of raising a child by myself in this house was too much to handle! Telling my parents was too much to handle. I couldn't do it, Bear; it was all just too much. I wasn't strong enough."

Bear lashed back at her. "Of course, it would have changed things! You should have let me handle it. I would have figured it out!"

"Maybe so, but I can't change that now." Grace screamed back. "I made a stupid decision, and I have lived with that guilt for over seventeen years! I have two holes in my heart that will never go away, and both have been made by you! I know you can't forgive me, and I will never forgive myself, so just go ahead and run away again. You should never have come back here!"

With that, Grace turned and ran back toward the house. She ran so quickly past Hatch and Ginger, they never had a chance to say a word. Ginger ran after Grace, and Hatch ran out to find Bear. Ginger hurried to Grace's bedroom and knocked on the door.

"Grace, can I come in?"

There was no answer, so she went into the room. Grace was slumped on the bed, sobbing uncontrollably. Ginger lay over her and tried to comfort her.

"Grace, it will be all right. Just give it some time."

Grace shoved her off and jumped from the bed. "It's too late! This is all such a mess. I shouldn't have told him! This is my punishment because I'm a terrible person, and I don't deserve you or Bear! You should just leave. You're the good, sweet twin, and I'm the rotten and selfish twin just like my mother. I'm a screwed up mess, and I don't know how to fix it. None of this is your problem. I'm sorry that Hatch found you. I'm sorry I killed our father. I'm sorry I wanted to kill my child and then just threw him away like Jake did to you! I should have died in the barn that day so everyone would be better off. I destroy everything I touch and hurt everyone I love. Just leave, Ginger. Just leave before I do the same thing to you!"

Ginger jumped up and grabbed Grace's arm pulling her to a

stop. "Just stop it, Grace! Stop it right now. I am not leaving, and I will never leave you. Everyone you ever loved has hurt you. Our mother was a rotten, horrible person that never gave you the love you needed and, let's not forget, tried to kill me. Our father was a cold-hearted bastard to separate us in the first place. He just threw me away without a single thought and then he refused to tell you where I was or even try to contact me himself. They were both terribly selfish and abusive in their treatment of us both. The barn fire was a terrible act of misguided desperation on your part, but Jake's death was an accident. You were just trying to get the attention of a man that cared more about his stupid ranch than his child. And, regardless of Bear's family honor, the pain he caused you was very real! All the people who were supposed to love you did nothing but let you down!"

Fresh tears poured from Grace's eyes as Ginger continued.

"I feel guilty because I was the sister who escaped to loving, wonderful people who gave me everything. I am who I am becuase of the wonderful people who raised and nurtured me but, most importantly, loved me. It wasn't fair that you were left here with people that were incapable of compassion and morality. How could you possibly fathom loving and taking care of a child when you were never shown any love yourself? Regardless of our separation, we have always been linked and always will be. You are my sister, and we are the only family we have left. I love you, Grace, and we will get through this together because that is what families do—they support and stand by one another no matter what the circumstances are—be it good times or bad. I will not let you continue to torture and blame yourself over the cruelty of our parents.

And I will not abandon you the way they did, and neither will Hatch. I know it seems impossible, but I promise you things will get better, and it will take some time, but you have to trust me, Grace. Please, at least trust me. I am here for you, and if you feel me the way you say you do, you know I am telling you the truth. Tell me, Grace, tell me you believe me!"

Grace nodded her head *yes* and then collapsed to the floor like a broken marionette whose strings, attached to a lifetime of pain, had finally been cut. Ginger helped her to the bed and climbed in behind her. They cried together in each other's arms long into the night.

When they awoke the next morning, Puck was snuggled up behind Ginger, and Cloud and Apache were lying on the floor beside Grace's side of the bed. Ginger left Grace sleeping and went searching for Hatch. He was sitting in the kitchen drinking coffee and looking ragged and tired.

"Where's Bear?" Ginger asked quietly.

"Gone. I've never seen him that angry. I begged him to forgive Grace, but there was no talking to him. I know how he feels; I just don't understand why she didn't at least tell me or ask for my help. This all could have turned out a whole lot better if she wouldn't have been so hardheaded and selfish. How could she have wanted to kill Bear's baby?"

Ginger lowered herself into the long bench seat and slid up next to him. "Hatch, I know that you loved Jake, and he was very good to you as far as I've heard, but you have to admit to yourself who he really was. My mother tried to kill me, and instead of getting her help, Jake just got rid of me without a second thought. I was his child, for heaven's sake, and he just threw me away like an inconvenience. Then he left Grace to Patrice's psychotic care, with no thought for the safety of her life, either. How did he know that she wouldn't try to dispose of Grace, too? Grace was basically abandoned to raise herself. There was no structure, no love, and no boundaries or discipline to teach her how to behave. Who Grace has become is a reflection of them. Jake was incapable of showing her love and that is why she doesn't understand love. Patrice was a bitter, angry alcoholic and a drug addict, and you wonder why Grace became one? She doesn't understand the concept of trust or responsibility and she acts tough to mask the fact that she has probably been scared to death most of her life. Grace is thirty-four years old, and she still acts like she's seventeen. She's never been treated as an adult, and she's never had to grow up and be independent. How could she know how to raise a child? And imagine if that child was raised in this unstable house with those people?"

Hatch shifted in his seat and mumbled, "Bear would have taken him and raised him properly."

"Do you really think Jake would have let Bear take a boy child from him? Apparently, in Jake's world, boys and cattle were the only things worth caring about."

Hatch opened his mouth to speak and then closed it and put his head down.

"We can fix this, Hatch. Grace needs you more than anything now, and with our help maybe we can find a way for Grace and Bear to forgive one another. It's so obvious how much they love each other, but it's still an angry, immature teenage love. I think with our help, some time, and some forgiveness, it could develop into a real true love for both of them. Grace needs to know what real love and real family feels like, and I intend to give that to her no matter how long it takes."

Hatch looked into her eyes, and a crooked smile spread across his face. "You're pretty good at this family stuff."

"It's not hard to understand or share when you've been raised by really wonderful people."

He stroked her cheek. "I'm sorry about Jake and what this family has done to you. I guess I've been selfish just thinking about myself and Grace and not about how what they did must feel to you."

Ginger smiled at him. "Well, I've been a little worried about that myself. But so far, I just can't stop thanking God every minute that I was so lucky. My adoptive parents were kind, respectful, loyal, and caring people. They raised me with such loving devotion and honorable boundaries that I can't even begin to imagine them as anything other than my real birth parents. Jake and Patrice seem like immoral strangers to me, and so far I haven't felt any physical or emotional attachment to them whatsoever. And I actually hope that is how my heart will remain. As much as I hate the fact that Grace and I have lost all this time, I'm so glad I didn't grow up here."

"If you did," Hatch said with a smile, "we'd probably be married and have a bunch of kids of our own by now."

Ginger blushed. "As good as that sounds, I think God had a better plan, and things happen for a reason. If I had grown up here, I probably would have been just as damaged as Grace and been no use to her, you, or myself."

Hatch smoothed a lock of her hair. "I suppose that's true. But I sure am glad you're here now."

Hatch held her hand to his lips. His touch was so warm and strong that waves of sensuous heat flowed through her body. His eyes were misty, and his voice came out low and heavy. "I want us all to be a real family, too. I just want Grace to be happy. I miss the feeling and security of people you can trust to be there no matter what, and I am so crazy about you that I will put both the moon and the stars under your pillow every night."

Ginger felt her heart skip, her face went hot, and her breath flew right out the window. Before she could respond, Grace appeared in the doorway looking small and helpless.

"I'm so sorry, Hatch; please forgive me."

Hatch flew off the bench seat and hugged her tight. "It's okay, little one. We will figure this out. It will all be okay now."

Grace started sobbing uncontrollably again, repeating over and over that she should have told him, that she should have trusted him, that she was just so scared. Hatch kept stroking her hair and telling her it was all right, that it would all be okay. Then Grace asked where Bear was. When Hatch said he was gone, Grace spilled what seemed like ten thousand more tears. After hours of tearful apologies and revealed feelings that had been held in for years, the three of them had exhausted all their emotions and decided that they should go for a ride and get some fresh air.

Pretending to Be Normal

Grace reluctantly turned out of the ranch gate toward town. Four months had passed by since Bear left, and the dull, tender throbbing of his absence still lingered like a low grade ache that burned slowly inside her every single day. Without her chemical enhancers to keep the pain at bay, she had been forced to face all her torments head-on. She was sickened over how unruly, frenzied, chaotic, selfish, confused, angry, and mostly wasteful her life had been. It was frightening to admit all that to herself. Anger and retreat had always been her way of protecting herself, and life was easier to deal with that way, but now she realized, it wasn't really a life. It was a waste of life. She had molded her broken and deformed expectations into a razor sharp blade of defense. It had cut deep wounds into the delicate lining of her heart. Blaming everyone else had been an easy escape to avoid self-loathing and unhappiness. After a lot of grueling drama and tears, Ginger and Hatch's patience had finally led her to take full responsibility for her addictions and her bad behavior. She was proud of that at least.

The support and the ever-hopeful forgiving way Ginger had about her made Grace want to change. Ginger said she was beginning to become the woman she was meant to be. *The woman I was meant to be*, she thought to herself. She really had no idea what that even meant. It seemed like some kind of silly cliché, but if it made Ginger happy, it didn't matter. Her real problem was forgiving herself despite Ginger constantly explaining how important it was to her recovery. Ginger repeated over and over how it would come more easily if she sincerely asked God for help, but the "God forgiving" thing was still very confusing to her. She desperately wanted the peace and gentleness Ginger had, but that seemed impossible at this point. And one thing she knew for sure: God or no God, she would never forgive her parents! They had hurt her so much and did not deserve any kind of forgiveness ever!

She looked out over the wild mountains etched with sharp cliffs and dangerous rocks. She still felt like that sometimes—wild and dangerous, ready to crumble into jagged pieces at the slightest shift in her foundation. The only thing that kept her from relapsing was that she did not want to let Ginger or Hatch down. Ginger kept telling her that she had to do it for herself, because she shouldn't want to let herself down. *But how do you let yourself down when you don't even like yourself? Ugh! Just shut up, Grace.* The constant chatter in her head was so tiring.

And that is exactly why she was in the car today. Ginger suggested that she try one of the church counseling groups called Second Chances. She didn't want to go then, and she didn't want to go now. The last thing she needed was some churchy people judging and preaching at her. She used to love being in the spotlight and being the center of attention. Now the spotlight would reveal things she didn't want to illuminate, and the attention would be on her many faults. Ginger said she had to learn to trust again and needed to get out and meet people that had walked in her shoes.

The idea of meeting new people made her want to turn the car around, and she took her foot off the gas pedal. Then she reminded herself about all the time she now had on her hands, being sober. There was never anything to think about, except all the things she didn't want to think about, and she was getting really bored. It was also hard watching Hatch and Ginger together. And she didn't want to keep interfering in their relationship with all her problems. Despite how happy she was for them, it made her desperate, longing for Bear even worse. All these emotions were suffocating her, and she really had nothing else to do today anyway. She gritted her teeth in exasperation at her indecision and then finally stomped her foot back on the gas and turned the radio up as loud as she could stand it.

As she approached the church and turned into the parking lot, she noticed all the people greeting one another with smiles and happy faces, and she immediately dreaded her decision. *This was such a stupid idea! Look at them all. They're just a bunch of fakes! Religious pod people pretending to be normal and happy. What a joke! Sorry, sis, but I just can't do this!*

~17~

Helicopter & Shiitake

Grace quickly pulled into one of the parking spaces so she could turn around and make a quick getaway back home. She was looking behind her, impatiently waiting to back out.

"Hello! You must be Grace." A cheerful voice chirped loudly, followed by a couple of sharp knocks on Grace's window.

As she whirled back around in surprise, Grace saw a mass of spiky gray hair topping a pudgy round face with great big dimples smiling in at her. *No. No. No. This is not really happening. How does Santa Claus know who I am?*

Grace smiled slightly and shook her head *no.*

"Well, sure you are!" exclaimed the stranger. "You look just like your pretty sister! She said to expect you. This parking place is just fine."

Grace kept the fake tight smile on her face as Santa kept talking.

Damn it, Ginger, now how am I going to escape?

"I'm Pastor Fred," she heard the man say. "I'll walk you in and introduce you."

There was no escape. Santa Fred was already opening her door and not taking *no* for an answer. Grace let out a deep breath and told herself she could manage one session, but if they started that judgy preaching at her, she was done!

Inside, the others all sat around in a casual grouping of couches and chairs that felt like a big living room. Someone brought cookies and drinks for the group. The people smiled and greeted her with enthusiasm.

All fakes, she thought to herself.

Pastor Fred opened with a prayer of thanks and blessings for all.

Typical, she mused.

Then he asked if anyone had any testimony or good news to share. A woman named Sue spoke up about her son being sick and asked for prayers. Another man named Bob said his wife was doing really well after her surgery and thanked the group for all the prayers and asked if they could continue to pray for her. They all nodded and seemed happy to hear about his wife. He then thanked several of the people for bringing casseroles and visiting her.

Well, that was nice of them, I guess. Grace was very skeptical of these people that were sharing so much of their personal business. There was no way she would *ever* do that. She was enjoying the observance of them, though.

Another younger man named Jason told how he slipped into temptation and started to drink too much at his family reunion last weekend. "The pressure of family, you know? It's so hard to live up to their expectations."

She watched him shift in his seat and thought, *Here come the excuses and then comes the judgment! Santa Fred won't be so jolly now!*

Santa Fred put his forearms on his thighs and leaned in toward Jason. His voice was soft and understanding. "We all slip up, Jason. The point is that you ask for forgiveness and then remember to go to the strength of the Lord next time you're scared, instead of the false strength of the liquor. God gave you the most incredible talent for singing and that's a gift that doesn't need to meet anyone's expectations but the Lord's. Look to this gift and use the music for strength. I know when He hears you singing in the church band every week that the Lord is smiling and clapping and so proud of you, just like we are. If you want to live up to your family's expectations, then don't give them what they've come to expect."

He smiled at Jason and Jason smiled and nodded back in understanding. "I think I'm finally getting that, Pastor Fred. I could kind of see myself from the outside that day, like I was actually watching myself getting louder and angrier. And when I realized that I was falling into temptation again, I stopped myself and politely told my parents that I was sorry and that I needed to go home and talk to the Lord."

Pastor Fred smiled. "And what did your parents say to that?"

Jason laughed. "Well, it sure wasn't what they were expectin'!" The group laughed, and he continued. "Funny thing was, they didn't really know what to say and that's the first time that has ever happened!"

The group laughed again, and even Grace found herself laughing as Jason continued.

"They don't exactly agree with me talking about God, but I think He was leading me that day to see the truth about my drinkin' and how ugly it was. And at the same time, He was giving my parents a message about how faith really does change a person. I can feel His strength growing stronger in me every day. And I did go home and pray that day and I started writin' a new song. I think I'm starting to get what you all been telling me and I am feelin' His strength. It sure does feel good. Thank you all for helpin' me understand."

The group broke out in to all manner of praises, tears, and prayers of thanks, and even a wink from Pastor Fred to Jason. Grace found herself smiling and nodding before she caught herself. *Stop it, Grace. You're just getting high on the Christian kool-aid. This kid's probably just telling stories for attention.* She crossed her arms tightly to her chest and studied Jason's face and mannerisms. *He does seem really sincere, though.* She could usually tell pretty quickly when addictive people were lying. Her sixth sense thing worked on more people than just Ginger. She was also really starting to like Santa Fred. His little jolly act also seemed to be sincere and he was growing on her—until he turned to her, along with the rest of them.

"Ginger, I wanted to tell you how nice it was to have you here. We want to offer our ears and support if you wanted to share anything with us today."

They all smiled expectantly in her direction.

She blurted out, "Oh, hell no, that's never gonna happen!" Her hand flew up to cover her mouth. He had caught her off-guard and now they were all just staring at her, smiles gone.

"I mean, no thank you. Sorry for the profanity. My sister is always getting on me about that. I'm working on it." She put her head down and hoped they would move on, but instead she heard them all chuckling. When she lifted her head in surprise, a man named Buck who had been silent until now, spoke up.

"That's okay, Grace. It's one of my battles, too. I worked out a plan, though. For instance, when them swear words slip out every once in a while, I stop and make myself repeat a similar word that starts with the same letter. For instance, I'll say: 'Oh Lord, what the helicopter did I just say? Or, oh shiitake, the devil done crawled in my mouth! Please forgive me, Lord!'"

The whole group was beginning to giggle at this point, but Grace wasn't sure what to think about such silliness.

Buck chuckled and finished his comment. "You all may laugh, but it works pretty good fer me. I figure if I can ask for forgiveness while me and the Lord get a good chuckle together, it will all work out. Sometimes the Lord gives me a word so silly that it makes me laugh myself right off my tractor. And that makes my son laugh! If I've learned anything, it's that the Lord does have a wicked good sense of humor and He appreciates a good belly laugh as much as we do!"

"Amen to that, Buck!" Santa Fred had his hands on his round little belly as it shook with laughter at this silly man.

Buck was a big man with gentle eyes that danced with mischief when he spoke. She wasn't sure if he was teasing her or not. He nodded at Santa Fred and then trained his gaze back on Grace once more.

"Sorry I took the floor from ya, Grace. I just wanted you to know that we all have many battles and faults in our pasts. The good news is that when we finally let it go and lay it down at the foot of the cross, it all just becomes part of our testimony. Testimonies we can use when the Lord needs us to help others in their battles. And most important, it teaches us to forgive and not judge others. None of us is free of faults."

18

Airing Your Dirty Laundry

Grace had no idea what Buck was really saying. All she was concerned about was that the attention was back on her again and she didn't want it.

"Well, I'm sure you have a lot less faults to forgive than I do, Buck."

"You think so?"

"Yes. You seem to be a very nice man."

"Well then, let me share my testimony, and then we'll see what you think. Would that be fair?"

Grace heard Ginger talk about the testimony thing several times, but to her it just sounded like airing your dirty laundry to strangers, and she was having no part of that. Her issues were no one's business, and she would do anything at this moment to avoid any further attention, so she quickly agreed.

Buck nodded and began his testimony. "Okay then. You may see a nice man now, Grace, but I wasn't always this way. I was one of the most miserable and mean drunks you ever seen. I was a violent man that used my fists more often than not to solve my problems. I couldn't hold a job, and I spent any money I had on liquor. I had sexual relations with lots of women while I was married. And not only did I cheat on my wife, but I roughed her and my son up pretty good on more than one occasion. I finally wrapped myself around a tree one night and ended up in the hospital. That's where I met Fred." He patted Fred on the shoulder, and Santa Fred nodded.

Grace's mouth had dropped open at "mean drunk" and she felt her chest get heavier and heavier with every word.

Buck chuckled at her response. "You weren't expecting that, were ya?"

Ginger snapped her mouth closed and shook her head *no* as he continued.

"Luckily after a lot of dark days spent on my knees praying for mercy and sittin' in groups just like this, I learned about the Lord Jesus. Only after I accepted His forgiveness could I finally forgive myself. I have devoted my life to service in His name ever since and the Lord has blessed me beyond my expectations. He also helped my wife and son forgive me, and now we have a wonderful life. So with the help of the Lord, my church family, and, of course, Pastor Fred, I got a second chance. And I'm doing my best to grow my boy into an honorable and loving man, so he doesn't end up like how me and my Pa were. That's the power of the Lord, and that's the power of forgiveness, and that's my testimony. I'm not ashamed to share my past anymore 'cause I've been forgiven. And now my past just serves as a reminder of my life without God."

Buck smiled at Grace with those gentle eyes, and she just

couldn't imagine him being violent. He was like Ginger; he had a peace and calm and joy about him. Pastor Fred had it, too.

Then Grace felt confused. "Well, if you are all better, or forgiven, and don't have a problem any longer, why are you still in this recovery group?"

Buck responded warmly, "Because the Lord told me this morning that I needed to come meet someone very gifted and special to Him today, and He was right. It's so nice to meet you, Grace Masterson."

Those words just broke her in two. Tears poured out of her eyes, and she felt some of her hard edges fall to the floor. Her voice finally came out in a small whisper. "I'm not special—I'm a bad person, and I don't have any special gifts to give anyone."

Buck lifted his big frame off his chair and kneeled in front of her as he gently took her hand. "Why don't we let the Lord make that decision? That's what we call faith. Will ya give faith and us a chance, Grace?"

She continued sobbing as Buck handed her his handkerchief. She wiped her eyes, then slowly nodded her head. "I'll try."

Buck smiled and squeezed her hand. "That's all we can ask."

Grace suddenly felt embarrassed that she had lost her self-control in front of everyone, until she noticed that the rest of the group had left the room. She stood and asked where they had all gone.

Pastor Fred put his arm around her shoulder. "They knew you weren't ready to share with them yet and wanted to give you some privacy."

"Oh, that was…nice."

"They were all new to the group at one time, just like you. They didn't want to be here at all, just like you didn't."

Pastor Fred nudged her, and Grace chuckled and shrugged.

He patted his stomach again. "No one wants to share at first either. Jason didn't say a word for over two months. But he kept coming, praise the Lord. All on his own, too. You heard his parents aren't church goin' folk."

Buck interrupted as he nodded to someone behind her in the doorway. "The Lord has something special planned for that young man, too. I heard him in the practice room the other evening. That boy has some serious pipes and writin' talent to boot. The song he was a singin' just 'bout put me on my knees it was so beautiful. My son plays the banjo in the church band, by the way. I hope you will come hear him and Jason someday, Grace. Well, I got to get back to the office. Doris is havin' some problem with the communion biscuit order." He took Grace's hand in his big gentle grip again and gave her a warm wink. "It was a real pleasure meetin' you, Grace Masterson, say a prayer for me will ya?" And with that, Buck was gone.

She looked at Pastor Fred. "He works here?"

"No, he's an Elder in charge of the communion on Sundays, among other things."

"Oh." Grace had no idea what an Elder was. Then she looked at Pastor Fred narrowly. "Does he really do that shiitake thing?"

Pastor Fred laughed and moved her toward the door. "Well, you never know with Buck. He does have a playful sense of humor, and he's pulled my leg more than I care to admit with his practical jokes." He chuckled again. "And that's just part of his charm. Say hello to your wonderful sister and tell her that I'm looking forward to seeing her and Hatch on Sunday. I hope to see you, too. It was so nice to meet you, Grace." He squeezed her arm and flashed his pudgy dimples. "And don't forget that the Lord and I are always available for you; all you have to do is ask."

He waved behind him as he headed down the hall and out of sight. Grace just stood there for a minute blowing her nose and trying to process all that had just happened. Five minutes later she still couldn't come up with a rational explanation, so she finally headed home.

19

The Woman She Was Meant to Be

It had been four months since that first session with the recovery group. Grace was on her way home from a meeting, and it was just starting to mist. The roads were muddy and slick, making the drive home longer than usual. She was okay with that. She always found the ride home a good time to reflect on things as they were. She was still struggling with guilt and anger over Bear and her son, but through her recovery group and time spent with other grace-filled members of the church, she thought she was finally beginning to heal and understand what real faith could bring.

Grace was glad that her new friends and Ginger encouraged her to sign up for some volunteer work. Although reluctant, she decided to help out in a local teen abuse shelter. It had really been good for her. She felt needed for the first time in her life, and that felt amazing. She had finally found her purpose or *her gift*, as Buck called it. With her personal experiences of abuse and addiction, it was easy for her to relate to the kids and helped her sense the ones in real trouble. Her mission was to try and show the kids they had a choice and a chance for something good despite their scorched hearts and disfigured views of life. She felt an urgency and responsibility to stop them before they became as damaged as she was. She had to keep reminding herself that it wasn't her responsibility, that it was the Lord's, and for the most part, she had done pretty well letting Him help her.

The rewards were pretty overwhelming. She still felt like a dimwitted baby in her faith and was still fraught with how to know the Lord on a more personal level. Even though she had been a witness to so many utterly amazing *miracles* right up close, she still found herself questioning God's existence because she didn't always *feel Him inside*. He was still only on the pages of her Bible and in those around her she clung to for understanding. *Be patient,* they all said, *He will come when you are ready.* Patience wasn't one of her virtues. Maybe she just wasn't worthy of His voice.

She turned down the long drive to the big ranch house as the light rain turned to snow. It was the last of November and most of the trees, except the big pines, were just about naked. A few stubborn leaves still hung on for dear life, desiccated and tattered as they twisted in the frigid breeze. She shivered at the thought of how they reminded her of herself—how her life had been, hanging on so hard in the fight to stay attached to her ragged misery. She saw it in the eyes of so many others now. Refusing to let go, to trust, to believe that there is something bigger than what we can see, and instead choosing to suffer in futility. Such a senseless and lonely battle!

She looked out at the parched and dry pastures that were turning white with the oncoming snowfall and thought about how different Thanksgiving had been this year. Who knew it was actually about giving thanks, and not about turkey? She laughed at herself. Her heart turned a little squishy when she remembered the hayrides and the children laughing while they roasted marshmallows around the big bonfire. How wonderful it was for Hatch to invite all the ranch hands and their families for the celebration. The smiles and joy on everyone's faces when they all sat down at the long wooden tables Ginger had set with four twenty-pound turkeys and all that other delicious food. She loved how Ginger began the meal by having each one say aloud what they were thankful for, even if it made her still feel a little uncomfortable hearing their private pleas. She was surprised once again at how they were so honest and genuine in sharing personal prayers in front of everyone. It was so heartbreaking to learn what some of them were going through, but at the same time she was humbled to witness them still giving thanks and praise in the face of such loss and tragedy.

When Ginger first came, Grace thought she was such an oddball with her faith and God stuff. Turns out that most of the good people sitting at the table that day, most of whom she had known her whole life, had some very strong faith as well. How had she missed that? She had also learned something else that day—how to give thanks. This was now a practice that had become vital for her—concentrating on all the good things in her life instead of wallowing in the bad made her feel stronger and more hopeful for the future. It still took great effort to keep looking forward with hope instead of back with guilt, and she still couldn't quite let the past go. She knew that Jesus died so she could be forgiven of all her sins, but it just couldn't be so simple. This was still a hard thing to wrap her head around, and she was embarrassed to admit to anyone that she probably would never forgive her parents for their abuse or herself for almost killing her son. They didn't deserve her forgiveness, and her anger still frequently flared into blaming them and feeling that they were at fault. The recovery group really helped her out on the rough times when she was painfully faltering in guilt. The nights were the worst when the agony clawed at her every time she thought about her child. *Was he safe, was he happy, or was he one of the haunted faces she saw at the shelter? Was he even still alive?*

She turned into the big circular driveway just as the sun was fading and the wind and snow were turning bitter cold. As she turned off the key, she smiled at the warmth and safety of the big old house that used to serve as her prison. There were people she loved and trusted that lived in that house now, and she continued to be awed by that blessed miracle. She could hear Hatch and Ginger calling in the dogs and could smell something wonderful cooking. She was finally able to rest in the comfort that she was no longer alone and had finally banished the fear that she would ever be alone again. Turns out, families came in many shapes and arrangements and didn't necessarily have to share DNA. She now saw many of her friends as family, and they considered her part of theirs too. This discovery, although wonderful, rubbed her with bittersweet pain as it forged up the raw reality that she had destroyed her only chance to share with Bear and her son what she now treasured and understood.

She slammed the door shut and chided herself for drudging up the old familiar pain as she trudged toward the house, doing her best to put on her brave face before she went inside. She smiled and recited her daily prayer through shivering teeth: *Forgive me, Lord, the past is the past; there is nothing I can do about that, and with Your help, I want to let that go and forgive. All things happen for a reason, and I trust in Your plan, and I am thankful for my many blessings. Amen.*

She also prayed that someday she could actually live out that prayer. As she hurried up the stairs, she could see Hatch and Ginger laughing and kissing through the kitchen window. Most of the time her prayer was enough to divert her heartache, but witnessing the love blossoming between those two made it almost impossible not to feel the burn of her losses all the way down to her core.

~ 20 ~

The Spirit of Christmas

In December things really started to change. Grace was not feeling anything but excitement. She couldn't wait to get home and get ready for the evening's festivities. Tonight was Christmas Eve, and it had just started to snow. She and Ginger had planned a giant dinner party at the ranch for all the ranch hands and their families and the teens and counselors from the shelter she volunteered at.

It had all started the first weekend of December when Hatch and Ginger orchestrated a tree cutting party with the ranch hands. They all went out to the woods with wagons and pickups to cut down trees for each family and for the families the church listed that couldn't afford one. Afterward, they all celebrated with hot chocolate and chili. Grace thought it was silly that Ginger had insisted on such a large tree for the ranch house, but when it was finally set up with the backdrop of the mountains through the large picture windows, Grace had never seen anything so beautiful.

When Hatch finally finished wrapping what seemed like a hundred strands of lights and plugged it in, something went all warm and runny inside and Grace felt something she'd never experienced. It was like God had cast a guiding light of hope just for her. She then understood what Ginger called *the spirit of Christmas.* She had not understood why Ginger was such a Christmas freak, but as the weeks went on, she was quickly learning why. The goodwill and Christmas cheer that bubbled over everyone like freshly-opened champagne was such a new experience for Grace, and it was all so exciting and wonderful. She thought that Thanksgiving Day had been a big deal with all the pumpkins and harvest decorations and that fabulous feast Ginger put out, but this was something else altogether.

Jake had usually been out of town in December buying more livestock and her mother hated Christmas, so she had never experienced the magnitude of this collective miracle that transforms the whole country with this kind of frenzied good cheer. And speaking of transformations, her house had been magically transformed into a winter wonderland of amazement. There wasn't one spot that Ginger hadn't decorated with red or green or gold or silver. The house, both inside and out, was stunning, and she had never seen so many lights.

Most importantly, it was Christ's birthday and her time at church had taught her why Christmas was such a special time of year for the people who really understood what it was about. For months, she had been prepping food, gifts, toys, and clothing for the local and international charities the church provided for every year on the holidays. There were so many families in need; it was sobering to say the least. With her teen shelter work and the church, she was spending most of her time in town now and realized that her eyes had been blind to the problems of the world while she was knee-deep in her own.

Grace also realized that she was unaware that there was so much tradition linked to the holiday season, starting with the Christmas trees. There were all sizes and shapes and types to choose from—some real, some fake, some silver! Each one was decorated in its own unique way. There were glass ornaments, and special memory ornaments, and homemade ornaments. The trees might be wrapped in tinsel, strung with popcorn or multi-colored garlands, or tied with bows. The lights could be white or colored or even chili peppers. Some were topped with a star and others an angel.

The best part she decided was the brightly wrapped presents tucked under the tree just waiting for that special morning. The fact that people took the time to pick out just the right gift for those they loved was so thoughtful and foreign to her before now. The food and beverages were special, too. The beverages ranged from warm apple cider to eggnog. Besides pumpkin and pecan pies, there were also weird desserts like mincemeat and something called a fruit cake. The most popular main dishes were a Christmas goose or honey glazed hams or turkey and stuffing like at Thanksgiving. Then there was the never-ending variety of Christmas cookies that seemed to show up along with hot chocolate everywhere she went, all month long.

She was enamored at how cities all across the nation adorned their town squares and neighborhoods in lights and displays. The décor not only included vast arrays of lights, but also Santas, reindeer, snowmen, elves, ice skating penguins, manger scenes, and glorious trumpeting angels that lit up the dark December skies like magic. There was Christmas music and Christmas movies and Christ in the manger with the wise men and the little drummer boy. There was Tiny Tim and Scrooge and the stockings hung by the chimney with care and Rudolph and Frosty and wreaths on the doors with bows and cinnamon-scented pinecones!

Grace was fascinated and overwhelmed with the gravity of it all. Then one day she watched one of Ginger's favorite Christmas shows called *The Grinch Who Stole Christmas,* and as silly as the show was, it all became crystal clear. All her life, her heart had been two sizes too small, but since Ginger and the Lord had come into her heart, it had grown ten sizes tall. And all the Whos down in Whoville showed her that the traditions of Christmas were all wonderful, but the real meaning of Christmas was the coming together of family and friends in charity and love. It was about the sharing, caring, and forgiveness of our fellow man in honor and celebration of the birth of our Savior, Jesus. He is the Christ in Christmas, and His birth changed everything. He was the ultimate gift for all men and the reason she could be forgiven and have her chance for a new life. She remembered her and Ginger sobbing like little babies as they experienced that moment of her understanding together. A small tear ran down her cheek every time she tried to grasp the gravity of that sacrifice by both Father and Son.

Grace gazed out at the beautiful pristine perfection of the new fallen snow—how clean and pure it was—brand-new and untarnished. Then she smiled to herself thinking about her new start. She said a prayer for those she would always miss and still think about every single day, but it was time to move forward. *Lord, she silently prayed, please let Bear and my son have a very Merry Christmas, wherever they are. And thank you for replacing that pain with Your love. Merry Christmas to You and Your Son for all you have done for me. I am forever grateful. Amen.*

She wiped another tear from her eye as she drove up to the lovely sight of pine boughs and red bows strewn along fence tops and porch eves dusted with snow. Just as she emerged from her truck the Christmas lights popped on and turned the snow into a field of shimmering diamonds. Her heart jumped into her throat with the beauty of it all. She grabbed her shopping bags full of gifts and bounced up the stairs to the house with renewed hope and spirit.

~ 21 ~

Winter Wonderland

When Grace entered the house, Ginger was in the kitchen with Marta and Mahina. Luckily at Grace and Hatch's urgings, the two grunty sisters finally accepted Ginger and all her holiday craziness. They had never experienced the holidays like this either and couldn't help but catch Ginger's enthusiasm. Marta eventually welcomed the help in the kitchen and was quickly learning all the new traditional recipes. The grunty sisters had also really enjoyed decorating for Christmas, and tonight they were all dressed up with beautiful gold and rhinestone butterflies clipped into their long braided updos. Ginger had given them the barrettes and shimmering gold taffeta dresses for an early Christmas present which added a big helping of Christmas spirit.

Grace flew down the hall to put on her dress so she could help Ginger in the kitchen with the last minute preparations for the party. When she came out of her bedroom and walked into the giant living room, she was aghast at the sight she beheld. The song

"Winter Wonderland" was playing in the background, which gave her a particular thrill when she heard it. *Sleigh bells ring, are you listening? In the lane, snow is glistening...*

The eighteen-foot tree stood glistening and shining framed by the large set of windows next to the fireplace and once again gave her another warm gush. It was now fully decorated with gold, silver, and red ornaments of every size and shape with bronzed ribbons, poinsettias, bird nests, angels, bells, berries, beads, and cinnamon bundles all dancing along every branch like magic. The star at the top stood majestic and guiding like the star of Bethlehem.

Ten stockings were hanging from the massive mantel topped with fresh pine garland draped with red and gold berries and glowing tapered candles clustered at each end. Various elves and Christmas fairies popped their heads out here and there among the pinecones and greenery. Above the fireplace, a massively decorated wreath joyfully replaced the foreboding portrait of Jake and Patrice. The long coffee table in the center of the room was set with a beautiful gold and silver manger scene complete with livestock and the three wise men. A huge variety of Santas, elves, snowmen, angels, greenery, holly, and lighted candles lined every table, nook, and shelf.

The huge sideboard had been covered with a lacy runner and filled with various heights of gold and silver trays that contained treats of every kind imaginable. There were sugar cookies, chocolate truffles, smoked salmon with cream cheese, crostini, five different varieties of puff pastries, cheeses, pecan tarts, petit fours, mini cheesecakes, brownies, brie, fruit, coffee cakes, mincemeat pie, and smoked oysters. And those were just the appetizers!

Beside the food-laden sideboard was a bar offering champagne, hot apple cider, eggnog, and Christmas punch.

The banister on the staircase was wrapped in more fresh garland and berries, and along the edge of every other stair sat a large red poinsettia with a big gold bow. As Grace's eyes were taking one final sweep across the room, she stopped and shivered at the most beautiful sight of all. It was Ginger and Hatch. He was dressed in a black suit with a white shirt and red bowtie. She had never seen him in anything except jeans, and she giggled a bit, but boy did he look handsome. Ginger looked absolutely stunning in her red satin dress with the fur-lined V-neck. Grace had the same one on in green, and they were both absolutely euphoric about being dressed like twins.

Ginger and Hatch were slow dancing and looked like they had forgotten that the rest of the world existed. They were a prince and princess in a romantic Christmas fairytale. Grace felt so happy for them, but at the same time it made her heart almost break for Bear. She heard the guests starting to arrive, and she quickly wiped her eyes and headed toward the ringing doorbell.

After the last of the guests waved merrily out of sight, Grace joined Ginger on the back deck.

Ginger smiled at Grace. "Well, that was incredibly fun. I think everyone had a great time."

"Are you kidding me?" Grace hooted. "No one at that party has ever seen anything like that. I am still amazed that you put all this together!"

"Well, I didn't do it by myself; we had a lot of help. It was so much fun though, wasn't it? I love Christmas, and I just wanted you and everyone to share in the same joy I do this time of year."

"Well, mission accomplished!" Grace gushed. "I have never been so happy. You have been the best present a sister could ever ask for."

Ginger hugged Grace. "I feel the same way, and I've been doubly blessed. I have my sister and I have a man that is just beyond wonderful. I'm just so sorry I can't give you Bear for Christmas. Hatch has been trying so hard to find him."

"You don't need to worry about me and Bear. You just concentrate on your happiness with Hatch. I will be fine because I have learned that any blessings, big or small, are all gifts that you must cherish and be thankful for. And my blessings have been many. I am truly happy now, Ginger. Of course, I will never stop loving Bear and my son, but the Lord has settled my heart on that. Besides I have you and Hatch, and I love the kids I work with, and I love the people at the church, and I love Santa Fred. They are all so kind and genuine and heaped so much love and support on me, and I thank you for that."

Ginger laughed at her sister's nickname for Pastor Fred. "He really does look like Santa, doesn't he?" Then she looked serious. "Why are you thanking me, though? You are the one that has turned your life around, and you have helped so many of those kids. I am so proud of you."

"Well, if you had not pushed me into counseling, I would still be going crazy with the obsession of me, myself, and I. I needed to see that the world doesn't revolve around my problems and that everyone has been through their own kind of pain. It's how we deal with the pain that matters. And I never would have believed that there are so many people like you that are so willing to give their time and hearts and helping hands for other people with no thought of themselves. I have been blessed to meet so many of those people that it still amazes me how God works."

Ginger smiled and nodded. They were silent as they gazed up at the stars and marveled at the big moon reflecting brightly on the snow-filled wonderland. It had stopped snowing and was stunningly silent and peaceful. Ginger put her arm around Grace, and they huddled together against the chill and admired the breathtaking beauty.

"Oh, my gosh, I just remembered something!" Ginger abruptly broke the silence. "On the first day I came here, I was standing on this deck scared out of my wits about meeting you. I was imagining standing right here looking at the snow with you on Christmas Eve! I even told Hatch and he said, 'And so you shall.' God granted me my wish, and here we are!"

They both smiled and fought back tears as they gazed back up at the stars. Ginger uttered, "Merry Christmas, Lord, and thank you."

Grace quietly followed her with, "Amen."

Just then Hatch appeared and Grace pulled away from Ginger and started jumping up and down with a huge grin on her face.

"Where did you disappear to, Hatch? And why is Grace suddenly acting like a kangaroo?" Ginger smiled at both of them.

"Never mind that. Just come out front. Grace and I have a surprise for you."

Grace was giggling like a kid, and Hatch had an enormous smile on his face.

Ginger now became very suspicious. "What is going on? What are you two up to?"

Grace grabbed Ginger by her coat and dragged her into the living room and out onto the front porch, which was now mostly dark. As her eyes adjusted to the darkness she saw Hatch walking toward something.

"What happened to all the lights out here?"

"Just be patient!" Grace chirped happily through a mass of giggles as she moved to the side of the porch and flicked all the Christmas lights back on. When Ginger's eyes finally readjusted to the light, her mouth dropped open in awe. Hatch was standing proudly next to a beautiful Christmas sleigh that had been decked out in red velvet. It was hooked up to two of their draft horses that had also been decked out in red velvet bows and gold sleigh bells.

"Merry Christmas!" Grace yelled in uncontained excitement.

Hatch moved up to the porch, scooped a most overwhelmed Ginger into his arms, put her into the sleigh, and covered her in blankets. Puck was sitting on the bench seat in a little Santa outfit and woofed an excited greeting. Grace handed her sister a bottle of champagne and gave her a devious wink.

A light snow began to drift down onto a still speechless Ginger as they headed off into the winter wonderland. The snowy trail was ground lit with Christmas lights which led them through the woods all the way to the waterfall. When they rounded the last corner, Ginger gasped at the sight. Hatch had strung Christmas lights in all the trees surrounding the waterfall and had multi-colored spotlights reflecting off the falling waters. It was breathtaking, and Ginger was having a hard time believing it was all real.

She immediately started sobbing.

Hatch grabbed her around the shoulders. "Are you okay?"

"I'm fine," Ginger blubbered. "It's just so…beautiful! I just can't believe you did all this. It's just so beautiful."

Hatch breathed a sigh of relief. "Well, it doesn't hold a candle to you."

Ginger blushed and said, "Thank you, Hatch, this is one of the best Christmas presents I have ever received."

"Well, if you want to give me the best Christmas present I have ever received, then you will say yes again. Since I really didn't have a chance that first night to give you the proper proposal that you deserved, I thought I should do it the right way. So, here goes." He pulled a ring box out of his pocket, snapped it open, and pulled out a stunning diamond ring. Hatch dropped to his knees and said in his John Wayne imitation voice, "Will you marry me, Ginger Thomas, and be my pardner for life?"

Ginger almost fainted with joy and flung her arms around him, happily shouting and sobbing, "YES, YES, YES! A thousand times *yes*, no matter how you ask me, I will marry you, Hatch McCullough!"

Puck started howling and just beyond the trees they heard a joyous *whoopee* followed by a ration of loud giggles and then a loud, "CONGRATULATIONS AND MERRY CHRISTMAS TO ALL AND TO ALL A GOOD NIGHT!" Then they heard Grace's horse galloping back to the house and more whooping fading into the distance.

Ginger and Hatch broke into hysterical laughter.

"She's probably still in her dress!" Ginger blurted between giggles.

"She helped me plan all of this, right down to the lights on the falls. I can't believe she actually kept her promise not to tell you. I thought she was gonna pop out of her skin trying to keep it a secret."

Ginger laughed. "She didn't say a word. I had no clue!"

Ginger suddenly flinched. "Oh Hatch! I just want to stay here in your arms and enjoy this, but I promised the ladies at the church that I would help them with the candles and prep for midnight Mass, and I have to be at the church early…"

He pressed a finger to her lips, stopping her train of thought. "The ladies know all about tonight. Your sister has taken care of all that. We still have plenty of time before it's midnight so how about snugglin' back on down here and keep me warm?"

He pulled out some mistletoe from his pocket and raised his eyebrows at her causing Grace to laugh.

"Do you honestly think you need that to get a kiss?"

He flashed her that melt-your-heart grin and pulled her closer to him. "Just in case, ma'am, I always come prepared."

"Well, Santa already told me that you've been a very good cowboy this year."

She snuggled up close as they welcomed the warmth of each other's lips against the chill of the frosty night air.

22

Christmas is the Time for Forgiveness

On Christmas morning Ginger and Hatch snuggled on the couch surrounded by all the dogs, waiting for Grace to wake up. When she finally came out, she went straight over and jumped in the middle of them in an explosion of giggles and Merry Christmas greetings. After all the presents were opened and the wrapping paper had been cleared away, they ate a big breakfast of chocolate chip pancakes and maple bacon.

Ginger, Grace, and the dogs then piled back on the couches to watch Christmas movies all day, but Hatch had other plans. He shooed them up to their rooms to get dressed, as he had one last surprise for them. When they were dressed, Grace and Ginger went excitedly back to the living room to see what Hatch was up to. He finally came into the living room with some trays of cookies and brownies and then set some coffee up on the bar. He put the Christmas music back on and lit the candles again. Grace and Ginger were on the couch carefully watching all this commotion with curiosity.

The doorbell rang. and they both jumped up. Hatch put his hand up and motioned for them to sit back down. They did as they were told and soon heard laughing voices coming toward them. Ginger leapt off the couch when she saw Glory's smiling face enter the room. She ran to her and wrapped her old friend in a warm embrace.

"What are you doing here?" Ginger exclaimed. "I have missed you so much! How are you? How are James and Kim and Kyle?"

"Well, you can ask them yourself." Glory moved to the side and in came Kyle in a cute little cowboy hat followed by Glory's daughter Kim and her husband James.

"Oh my goodness—Merry Christmas!" Ginger hugged them both and then knelt down and hugged Kyle as Puck circled and barked in excitement to see his old friends again. "What a wonderful surprise!"

Glory grabbed Ginger's hand. "Well, your wonderful fiancé told me how much you were missin' us, so he flew us all out here first class for Christmas. I dare say I have never been so spoiled. They even gave Kyle warm milk and cookies, and we got champagne for free!"

Ginger hugged Hatch and wiped the tears from her eyes. "When did you all get here?"

"A few days ago. We've been sight seein'."

"Where were you last night? Why didn't you come to the party?"

"Oh my goodness, honey, you had enough goin' on and we didn't want to distract you from your big surprise proposal!

Congratulations, by the way! We went to the early Christmas Eve candlelight service at your cute little church and met your adorable Pastor Fred. We're stayin' at the Sagebrush Inn, so we spent the rest of the evening there, enjoyin' first a delicious dinner, and then the cozy fireplace, watchin' the falling snow and minglin' with other guests."

"How long are you staying?"

"Until after the New Year, so there's plenty of time to catch up; but…there's also a little more to our visit."

Ginger looked at her in puzzlement.

Glory continued, "Well, you know James is a veterinarian. And Hatch's longtime vet is lookin' to retire. So Hatch called James last month and presented him with an offer to take the vet's place."

Ginger's mouth dropped open, her head snapped toward James and Kim, and they nodded, smiling. Then she asked, "Are you saying that you're moving here to Colorado?"

James clapped Hatch on the back and said, "Well, we're considering it, and that is the other reason we're here. We wanted to check things out and pray on it as we are waiting to see if this is the Lord's will."

Ginger cut in, "But, Glory, you couldn't leave your wonderful little house with all the memories of Mr. Tobias!"

Glory laughed. "Oh, honey, that's just a bunch of bricks and wood. Gus will always be wherever I am, right here in my heart."

Kim spoke up. "I do have to say, though, if it were up to Kyle, we'd move here tomorrow. When mom updates us on all your stories about the ranch, he is just beside himself with excitement. He never stops talking about the cowboys and the hayrides and riding horses.

Hatch gave him that little cowboy hat the day we got here, and he hasn't taken it off since! And it's all been very exciting for us, too. This trip will be such a memorable Christmas for us all—so Hatch, thank you again for all of this."

Hatch nodded as Ginger squeezed Glory's hand. "I will pray on it, too."

Glory squeezed back. "And no matter what the decision is, I've been missin' my old neighbor and friend and her adorable dog, and I will be back here to help you plan the weddin' regardless."

Ginger's eyes swelled with tears as she hugged her cherished friends. After she gathered herself again, she proceeded to introduce everyone to Grace, who was just as surprised as Ginger.

Grace had heard so much about this family that she felt as if she already knew them. She was genuinely excited to finally meet them.

After they caught up on all the happenings of the past year, they feasted on leftover ham, turkey, mashed potatoes, green bean casserole, sweet potatoes, and pumpkin pie with homemade whipped cream. When they finished, Glory and her family headed back to their little mountain inn with plans for another week of adventure and fun before flying home to Georgia.

As they were heading back to the living room, Hatch's phone rang, and he went into the other room to take the call. When he returned, he whispered to Ginger to wait ten minutes and then grab Grace and head out to the oak tree bench because he had one last surprise. Ginger didn't think her heart could take any more surprises, but Hatch looked so excited that she joyfully agreed.

She and Grace bundled up in excited anticipation and ten minutes later, they headed down the path. When they rounded the corner, they both stopped short in their tracks. Standing next to Hatch was Bear, and standing next to Bear was a handsome younger version of Bear with the same long black hair and his mother's beautiful green eyes. Ginger smiled giddily at Bear and the younger man and moved quickly toward Hatch. Bear moved toward Grace, who was frozen in her tracks with her mouth hanging open, and gently grabbed her hand leading her toward the young man.

"Grace, this is William. He is our son."

William extended his hand and said, "Nice to meet you, ma'am."

Grace burst into tears and flung herself around the boy, and then she took his face in both her hands and kissed his cheeks. Her words came quickly and passionately. "I can't believe it's actually you! You look so much like your father. I'm so sorry I gave you up. It was so wrong of me, I'm so sorry." Then she stepped back in embarrassment.

Bear turned Grace to face him and held each of her hands. "It's okay, Grace, William knows the whole story."

Grace looked up at Bear and asked, "How can you ever forgive me?"

He hugged her into his chest and stroked her hair. "Because for some stupid reason I just can't stop loving you, and, like I said before, we can't change the past, but we still have the future—and I can't imagine my future without you. Merry Christmas, Little Flame."

Grace buried herself in Bear's big warm arms as the tears burst forth in big sobbing torrents. Ginger was also blubbering like a fool, and Bear and Hatch laughed in spite of being a little weepy themselves.

Bear finally spoke. "Well, let's go into the house and have some food. William and I both love turkey. I hope there's cherry pie!"

After they all had settled at the big table in the kitchen, Ginger could not stand one more second of not knowing how Bear had found William. She nudged Grace to ask, but Grace couldn't stop staring and smiling at William.

So, Ginger went ahead and asked. "Okay, first of all, Hatch, when did you find out that Bear was back?"

"Well, I've known for about a month. I didn't tell you because I didn't want you to have to keep it from Grace, and Bear asked me not to say anything."

"Okay. So now, Bear, how did you find William?"

"It took me a bit, but it wasn't too hard. You aren't going to believe this, Grace, but your Aunt Peg has been raising William all this time."

Grace choked on her pie. "What?"

"Peg said she knew it would only be a matter of time before one of us came looking for him. She also had the whole story typed up in her will in case something happened to her so William could find us. She never told Jake because she knew that he would 'ruin the boy' is how she put it."

Grace put down her fork. "This is unbelievable."

"Oh, there's more," Bear continued. "Come to find out that Aunt Peg lived here on the ranch in your bedroom, Ginger. That's a picture of my father above your bed, by the way."

"Oh my!" said Ginger. "So that's why you look like the picture, but why would your father's picture be above her bed?"

"Apparently Grace isn't the only one who fell in love with an Indian."

Hatch, Grace, and Ginger all registered major surprise.

"Whoa," said Grace. "So that's why Aunt Peg never married. She wasn't an old maid; she just loved someone she couldn't have."

"That's right," Bear replied. "Same story as ours: the families would not allow it and so my father moved to the reservation and married my mother and Aunt Peg moved to town to live out her life alone. I think my mother knew more than I realized about the men in *my* family and the women in *this* family. It must have been painful for her, too."

Ginger shook her head in disbelief. "Wow, what a saga this has turned out to be! We certainly have a fascinating history of surprises, don't we?"

Grace nodded her head as Bear continued. "Peg said that when Grace showed up pregnant all those years ago and told her the story, she felt that it was her only way of having what little piece she had left of my father. The grandson that could have been hers, if only allowed. So, she made all the legal arrangements and moved to Idaho."

Ginger's eyes welled up. "Oh, that is so incredibly sad and wonderful at the same time."

"I moved them both back here about three months ago to a little house I own in town. We have been catching up. She's over the moon about you, Ginger. Jake lied and told her you died in that fire by accident, so she wouldn't get involved. She can't wait to meet you."

Grace and Ginger just shook their heads in sadness over their father's cruelty. Hatch still didn't know what to think about all of this.

"Well, I can't wait to meet her, too!" Ginger finally blurted out to break the awkwardness. "What an amazing woman Aunt Peg is and such proof of how the sweetest blessings can came from our losses."

William broke in. "She *is* an amazing woman, and she was a good mother to me, too."

Grace looked at William. "Yes, I can see that she was, and you are an amazing young man, too. Please fill us in on the rest of the story, William. Please tell us about your life."

William told them many stories of his time with Aunt Peg while they finished eating. While everyone else was talking and laughing and comparing stories, Grace was focused only on William. She was totally smitten with this magical creature that was actually her son. He was funny and articulate and smart and respectful. Aunt Peg had given him everything she never could have. He was loved by a woman to whom Grace owed a tremendous debt—a debt she could never repay, but she was bound and determined to try. She would arrange to go see Aunt Peg as soon as possible—it was time for them to heal and reunite the whole family. She hoped Aunt Peg could forgive her, but right now, she wanted to spend as much time as possible with William. She needed his forgiveness most of all, even if that was a very remote possibility.

"William, would you mind taking a walk with me?"

"No, ma'am, I wouldn't mind. I guess it would be okay." He looked at Bear and Bear nodded.

They headed out the door toward the waterfall. Bear, Hatch, and Ginger stood in front of the large windows and watched them until they were out of sight.

"Bear, he is so amazing. Thank you so much for giving us this gift, and thank you for forgiving my sister. You are such a good man for finding William and reuniting him with Grace. I can't even begin to explain how heartsick she has been since you left. She's been showing a very brave face despite her pain and has really changed."

"I know. Hatch has been filling me in, and after my anger subsided, I realized that I was just as much at fault for Grace's decision about William. We were young and stupid, and none of that matters any longer."

Hatch spoke up. "William seems to be taking it pretty well. Was he mad at Grace?"

"At first he was. Peg hadn't told him the whole story. I explained it from the beginning and then told him about how sorry Grace was and that she was making up for it by volunteering at the shelter. William visited there after they moved back, and he was happy when some of the kids from the shelter told him about this cool counselor named Grace that was really great and had helped them a lot. He decided that since she was trying to make amends and was helping other people that he should probably give her a chance."

"Oh, thank God for that." Then Ginger added, "That's all Grace would ask for is a chance."

Bear rubbed his stomach and said, "Well, they could be out there for some time, so I think I'll just have to have some more of that delicious cherry pie! Besides I'd like to hear about a certain Christmas Eve proposal."

They all laughed and went back to the kitchen.

23

The Best Gift of All

Grace and William walked slowly toward the waterfall. It was Grace's favorite place, and she wanted to share it with William. She was suddenly very anxious being alone with him as there were no distractions now to fill the silence. He wasn't talking at all, and she knew it was her responsibility to start.

"William, I know if I said I'm sorry a million times it wouldn't be enough. What I did was selfish and foolish and wrong. I was just a year older than you when I got pregnant, and I was really only about thirteen in my maturity. I don't know if Bear told you about my parents, but they weren't very nice people or very good role models. And I'm not using that as an excuse, but I wasn't mature enough to make a rational decision, and I certainly didn't trust them to make any rational decisions concerning me.

"I was alone and hurt and angry and stupid and selfish and lost. It's still hard to admit and recall what kind of person I was, but I have done my best to make amends for the total destruction of our lives and each other. I'm just hoping that in time you can maybe forgive me, but if you can't, that's okay, too. I'm just so thankful that I finally have some peace in my heart and that you are healthy and beautiful and smart and that you are giving me a chance to apologize, and if that's all I get, then I will accept that." She paused for a moment to let her words settle.

William remained silent, staring ahead and walking slowly beside her with his hands clasped loosely behind his back. His beautiful dark hair was blowing softly in the wind, and his stride was confident and regal. He looked so much like his father at that age that it was almost eerie. Grace remembered walking this same path hand-in-hand with Bear all those many years ago. She was so amazed by the fact that William was filled with so much more maturity and bravery and calm at his young age then they had been. He was truly remarkable. *Thank you, Lord, for this gift. I have no words to express my thanks.* Her heart began pounding with so much overwhelming love and emotion and gratitude for this miracle that was *her* son that she had to tell herself to stay calm and breathe. There was so much more she had to say and learn and makeup for, but she wanted to stay lucid and serene so she didn't scare him off.

She breathed the cool mountain air deeply into her lungs, prayed for guidance and wisdom, and began again. "It took a lot of courage for you to come here today, I know. Ginger and the Lord have taught me that He has his own plans, and we have to trust that He knows what is best for us. Even though it may be brutally painful, we have to take responsibility for our actions, learn from our mistakes, and forgive ourselves and others and just go on as best we can. So that is what I am doing, trying to forgive myself for the bad and be thankful for the good. I continue to do that one day at a time. Some days are better than others, and I still have a long way to go. But meeting you today will be the best day I will ever have. That's what I wanted to say, and I thank you for giving me the chance to do that."

William was still quiet for some time. But he continued walking beside her, so she hoped that that was a good sign. Finally he spoke. "Aunt Peggy told me about them, my grandparents, I mean. I'm sorry they were so cruel. That must have been hard."

"It was, but I reacted the wrong way. I should have done everything I could not to be like them, but instead I became just like them. I was weak and afraid, and I didn't know about faith and couldn't see the goodness in people like Aunt Peg. She was there whenever I needed her, and I didn't even thank her or recognize what a wonderful, caring person she was. And for that I'm sorry, and I will make up for it if she will let me."

"Aunt Peggy is a really forgiving person, I'm sure she will."

"You call her Aunt Peggy. Why don't you call her mom?'

"She told me a long time ago that name was already reserved for someone who would eventually come to know what that means."

"Really? So she still had faith in me? That's truly amazing."

"Yep."

"Well, you can just call me Grace. And if you will just give me a little tiny chance, I will do everything in my power to show you how much I love you and how much I missed you every single day of my life."

He was thoughtful for a minute and then responded. "Well,

since you are my mom, I guess I should just call you that. And I don't know exactly how I feel about all this yet, but I know about the Lord's forgiveness. So, I'm thinking about it, forgiving you that is, and we'll just see how it goes."

Grace smiled from ear to ear, and she felt her heart grow another ten sizes tall.

"That's all I can ask, William. That's all I can ask."

They walked in silence the rest of the way, just happy to be in this newfound journey together.

~24~

Can You Hear Wedding Bells?

The ranch house was at the peak of frenzied excitement. It was June 5th, and in two minutes there was going to be a wedding. Ginger heard Marta grunt that it was time, and she heard the wedding march begin. She turned to face Grace and they both burst out crying.

"We have to stop this. It's the fourth time we've had to fix our makeup!"

"I know, I know. We just can't look at each other, okay?"

"Okay, that's a good idea."

They fixed their makeup one more time and awkwardly avoided each other's gaze as they paused at the top of the stairs. Ginger looked down upon the scene below her, and her eyes filled with tears once again. She let out a little sob and felt Grace nudge her. They both turned to look at the other and laughed through their tears.

Grace shrugged, "Let's just get you down that aisle!"

Ginger nodded. "Okay, here we go."

As they descended down the stairs, Ginger couldn't help but admire how beautiful everything turned out. Their little church wasn't big enough for all the guests, so they had it at the ranch instead with Pastor Fred's blessing. The stairs were wrapped in white tulle with greenery and blush-colored roses that matched Ginger's dress. She finally had the true love she prayed for and the blush-colored gown and roses were in honor of Glory and the Lord's answer to her prayers.

They floated down toward the living room which had been transformed into a candle- and flower-filled indoor reception area with a white draped aisle running through the center that led from the stairs out to the back deck. The guests were lining the aisle and would follow them past the deck which was covered in a white framework pergola filled with white lights, tables, greenery, roses and a dance floor for later on. The guests would soon take their seats in the grassy flower-filled lawn area beyond the deck where additional tents were set up with food and beverage areas.

The altar was nestled under a huge archway of branches and also covered in flowers and lights. The meadow out beyond the massive deck was in full bloom with wild flowers of every color. As she and Grace floated down the stairs, she spotted Glory near the bottom. She had tears of pure joy running down her beautifully smiling face, which made Ginger spill even more tears.

As they approached the foot of the stairs Marta and Mahina stepped onto the aisle in front of them dressed in soft pink gowns, their beautiful black manes were twisted into French braids and piled on top of their heads with little pink rose buds tucked here and there. They each held a bunch of wildflowers and walked slowly toward the altar with big smiles.

As they passed through the doors and onto the deck the music got louder. Ginger paused at the door and took a deep breath as Glory and Grace fluffed her dress one last time before they moved on ahead to take their places at the altar. As the wedding march continued to play, she moved out onto the deck and looked toward the altar, and there she saw the loveliest sight. Hatch was standing to one side in his black tuxedo and shiny black boots with the biggest smile she had ever seen. Beside him was Bear, and then Kyle standing up as straight as could be. Kyle was a very handsome little groomsman. Next to him, looking devastatingly handsome was William, the spitting image of his father, and then finally James.

On the other side of the altar was her beautiful long-lost twin sister smiling like a Cheshire cat, looking like she would pop right out of her skin with joy. But then, of course, she was feeling both sets of their emotions. Marta, Mahina, and Glory were equally giggly, excited, and adorable. Pastor Fred stood in the center with his dimpled smile and round pudgy face beaming at her.

Behind them all, the sky was a brilliant blue, and a cool soft breeze flitted through the crowd just like another wedding guest come to join in the celebration. All their friends and loved ones were smiling and sighing. Ginger felt woozy with joy.

Oh, Father, she prayed, *I am so very blessed. I know my parents are here with me; I can feel them. Thank you, Lord, for giving me this new family. I am beyond emotion and thanks.*

As she moved a little closer, she heard a couple of yips and noticed Puck standing in front of Kyle with a tuxedo bandana wrapped around his neck. He flew down the aisle and trotted up happily beside her. She and the crowd laughed heartily as she continued to float all the way to the altar with her blush-colored bridal gown flowing softly behind her and her little Puck walking her down the aisle.

After the lovely ceremony, the guests feasted on prime rib and grilled chicken. The champagne and dancing flowed readily, and the bride and groom were in their own little heaven. Ginger had just sat down to drink some champagne and rest her feet on Grace's lap when Hatch and Bear approached them, looking very sneaky.

"What's going on with you two?" Grace wondered.

"We have somewhere to take you, so right this way, ladies."

A large wagon covered in white fabric with the same two horses decked out in roses and bells pulled up, and the sisters, looking surprised and curious, were hoisted in. Hatch, Bear, William, Kyle, and Puck loaded in after them, and Hatch took the reins. The guests winked and smiled and waved as they departed toward the waterfall trail. Obviously, they knew what was going on. As they approached the waterfall, the girls expected to stop, but the wagon kept rolling beyond the trees and alongside the river.

Ginger, bursting with curiosity, finally spoke. "Where in heaven's name are we going?"

"Patience, my bride, patience." Hatch said as he pulled them on through a well-trodden trail and over a bridge that was hidden behind some large boulders.

"How have I never seen this trail before? And where did that bridge come from?" Grace demanded.

"Well, you're not really that observant, and you haven't been out here very much lately," replied Hatch.

"That's true." Grace giggled.

With all the holiday rush and wedding plans, Ginger or Grace hadn't been to the falls since Christmas.

Just then the trees cleared, and Hatch stopped the horses. Nestled in a small emerald valley above the waterfall was a brand new, double A-frame cabin. Ginger's heart stopped, and she had to stand up to get it moving again. The flagstone drive leading up to the cabin was lined by flowers and boulders. There was a large deck on the front that wrapped around to the side of the cabin where it overlooked the wide rushing river that flowed down into the waterfall. There were rocking chairs everywhere and right above the door hung a beautifully carved wooden sign that read "Ginger's Cabin in the Woods." At the side of the lovely drive was another flagstone walking path that lead to an arched wooden bridge with more flowers at each end that crossed over the river to a flat, graded sunny area with a scarecrow staked in it that held a sign saying "Ginger's Vegetable Garden."

Grace was jumping up and down and squealing with delight. Hatch was grinning ear to ear, Bear was laughing, and Kyle was leaping off the wagon with Puck on his heels barking frantically. They all knew the story of Ginger's dream cabin in the woods. Ginger, of course, was balling her eyes out with joy. She flung her arms around Hatch, kissed his face at least ten times, and then threw off her shoes as she jumped off the wagon into the soft grass and ran toward the steps leading to the front door.

After they completed the grand tour through every room in the house at least five times, they all finally settled into the rockers on the side deck to marvel at the scenery. Ginger turned toward the front of the house which had a view of the upper waterfall; the side overlooked the river that spilled into one of the lower falls. Her beautiful garden would be beyond that and the back kitchen view ascended up into a rich green forest of hiking trails and mystery. The magical sound of the river would be what she and Hatch awoke to every single day.

She closed her eyes and folded her hands. *Lord, You gave me everything I imagined and so much more. Thank You, thank You, thank You—and I am truly humbled by Your grace.* She then had to sit down before she collapsed from happiness. She couldn't wait to start decorating and planting.

As they all laughed and talked and toasted with more champagne, Ginger realized that they had been gone for some time and that they should be getting back to their guests at the ranch. They all loaded back into the wagon, and with much more tears, laughter, hugs, and joy, they made their way back to the party.

About an hour before dark, the last of the guests left, and the girls told the guys to get into the trucks, because it was their turn for a little surprise. They drove the two miles to the entrance of the ranch and out through the gate. Ginger was driving and she did a U-turn and stopped in front of the large stone entrance and turned off the engine. She got out and pulled Hatch out behind her and faced him toward the gate. He stood there for a minute in confusion before he finally looked up—the high arching structure over the gate read, "Welcome to the McCullough Family Ranch."

Hatch read the sign out loud, "McCullough Family Ranch. Family! We are a family now!"

Ginger came up behind him for a hug and then moved around in front of him smiling with unabashed joy. "Yes, we are a family now—thanks to you and a lot of help from above."

~ 25 ~

More Surprises

A couple of months later they were all together again for a late afternoon housewarming party for Hatch and Ginger. Ginger laid out some more trays of snacks, relishing how happy everyone seemed. So many wonderful things had happened since Christmas.

She smiled at Bear's father and Aunt Peg nuzzling in the corner. Grace had managed to reunite them, and they had just returned from their honeymoon at Disney World in Florida last week. They had purchased the little house in town from Bear and were making up for lost time. Bear's father, Big John, was becoming quite famous for his intricately crafted one-of-a-kind bird houses. They were in high demand, along with his prize tomatoes that were the size of grapefruits. Ginger smiled at their joy. Aunt Peg looked so beautiful tonight; she was the epitome of class and elegance in the same way Glory was. Big John was just as handsome in person as his portrait in Peg's old room. The resemblance of father, son and grandson was undeniable.

William had just recently moved to the ranch to be closer to his newfound parents. He began working with Bear training horses, and it was obvious that he had inherited the same horse whispering gift and equine love his father had. Grace and Peg's relationship developed quickly, and Peg became the mother Grace never had. Since Peg had walked in Grace's same shoes years before, they shared a kindred pain they had both overcome through faith, forgiveness, and one another's love.

Ginger walked down the stairs and over the river bridge toward her garden where she noticed Glory and Kyle standing next to the river. She joined them to see what they were looking at. Kyle and Glory had gone to gather vegetables for the salad and had gotten side tracked watching several fish jumping in the river. Ginger and Glory laughed at Kyle's amazed excitement. After their visit at Christmas, Glory, Kim, James, and Kyle had decided to make the big move. They had settled in quickly and were excited about their new adventure. Glory had joined the local Garden Club and was enjoying the cultural history of the old west. She brought several cuttings from her rose garden in Georgia and had replanted them in a sunny clearing just below her small cottage—her "Little Gingerbread House" as she called it—was set up on a wooded knoll just behind a beautiful old farmhouse James and Kim had recently purchased on a five acre property conveniently located between the McCullough Family Ranch and town.

Kyle had waded into the water at this point and was trying his luck at catching the fish with his bare hands. Marta and Mahina came across the bridge with fishing poles and a bucket of worms and were joyfully subjected to Kyle's contagious excitement and laughter. Ginger and Glory watched in amusement for a while and then left them to fish while they finished gathering vegetables.

After returning to the deck with a loaded basket of fresh pickings, Glory went inside to make the salad, and Ginger went to check on Bear and Hatch. They were just loading the large outdoor grill with burgers and chicken. Grace and William were manning the beverage bar and making sure everyone sampled some of Big John's sliced tomatoes and mozzarella cheese appetizers.

Ginger basked in the warmth and brightness of the day. There was not a cloud in the sky and although it was a little warm, there was slight breeze coming off the river and it felt wonderfully refreshing as it skipped along her skin. Hatch joined her at the railing as they watched Kyle chasing Marta and Mahina with the worms while they pretended to be scared. Ginger and Hatch laughed at their ruse. Ginger was still delighted that the grunty sisters were really very funny and warmhearted women that she now adored and treasured.

Hatch squeezed her close. "Fantastic day for a housewarming, wouldn't you say?

"Unbelievable."

"Meat's about finished. Let's get everyone rounded up and get this chow line goin'." He gave her a wink and kissed her head. She laughed and followed his lead.

After they'd finished dinner and were all settling in to the large Adirondack chairs to digest and relax before dessert, Grace stood up and called for everyone's attention. "I want to run an idea by everyone, and it will affect all of us so I want to be sure I have everyone's attention and agreement."

They all exchanged glances and shrugged shoulders and she continued. "As you all know the shelter that I volunteer for is a very important part of our community. There are so many in need, and the shelter is vital for the lives of so many kids and teens who are in trouble."

Everyone nodded in agreement.

"The shelter building is very old, and the heating and air are frequently in need of repair. We are always overcrowded, and the donations we receive are never quite enough to cover the necessities and food. We need a new, modern, updated facility for the kids and the counselors with more room to develop new programs, purchase equipment, and come up with new ideas to expand the cash flow and donations. So, my idea is to move the shelter here to the ranch house."

Everyone shifted and murmured.

"Now before you say anything, hear me out. Ginger and Hatch have moved out, and Bear and I are also moving to our own house soon. So that leaves eight bedrooms, as well as all the common areas of that big old ranch house just going to waste. Some of the sitting rooms could be converted into bedrooms and meeting rooms as needed. I've already spoken to Marta and Mahina, and they said it would be good to have someone in the house to take care of again. I know Kim wants to resume her teaching, so we could take down the wall between Jake's office and the library which would make a good sized classroom for individual tutoring and home schooling."

Grace was pleased to see Kim's face light up with the possibilities of that idea and then she turned to Hatch, Bear, and William.

"The shelter kids could help out on the ranch when they aren't in school which would help them learn responsibility and a useful trade. Free labor would be a great benefit for you guys in addition to the ranch hands. You would also be great role models for these boys, teaching them hard work, morality and strength of character." They smiled and nodded as she turned to Ginger and Glory.

"I'm thinking of a big vegetable plot out behind the bunkhouse so that Ginger can teach organic gardening and cooking classes. This would teach the kids to be more self-reliant by learning to grow and prepare their own healthy food. Most of them think food only comes in plastic wrappers or cardboard containers."

Ginger looked like a smiling bobblehead the way she was nodding and rubbing her hands together with excitement. Grace chuckled at Ginger's giddiness even though she already knew Ginger would love her ideas.

She focused on Glory and continued her plea. "Glory, it would be wonderful if you could have your gardening club ladies get us started on several flower and herb gardens. And I'll tell you why these are a very important ingredient. I've found the flower gardens in particular just seem to make kids feel so much more calm and open or...*safe,* I guess you could say. The arched garden we built in the backyard area at the shelter has done wonders for the souls of these kids. For them to spend time and dwell within the beauty of the garden walls surrounded by such loveliness and safety after living in some of the violence, filth, and despair they've come from gives them a hope they've never known."

Everyone shook their heads in sympathy and tears formed in many eyes.

"And God willing, we could build another big bunkhouse out

back with a kitchen, large deck, or social area for events and even more beds. It would also allow me to spend more time with the kids and less time driving back and forth. So that's what the Lord has put in my head—McCullough Family Shelter on McCullough Family Ranch."

She flashed one last bright pleading smile. "I know this is a lot to ask, and it will be a lot of work, so if I'm totally out of line here, there will be no hard feelings. It's just a proposal, and you don't have to answer now; I know it's a lot to think about."

She sat back down and watched them all look around at each other to get a general consensus of feelings and then Bear finally spoke up.

"Well, it's Hatch's ranch, so it's ultimately his decision, but I think it's a great idea. I know a lot of the kids on the reservation would really benefit from coming to a place like this when times are tough. It would help the elders, too."

William nodded in agreement.

"I agree, too," said Big John. "If it's okay with Hatch, of course."

Glory chimed in, "My ladies would jump at a project like this. I think the Lord gave you a marvelous idea, Grace."

Ginger, barely containing herself, burst out. "This has so many wonderful possibilities I can't even count them! So I'm definitely in if it doesn't interfere with ranch business, of course."

"Me too!" Kim added with excitement.

Ginger smiled at Hatch in eager anticipation. "I guess it's up to you, honey."

They were all staring at Hatch now, and he let them sweat it out a little longer as he sat there, tilting his head from side to side as if in deep thought. He had them all at the edge of their seats as he took a sip of his tea and poked at a couple of crumbs on the table. He noticed Grace shaking her head and giving him the stink eye along with a half grin. She knew what he was up to, and the old Grace would have been spewing profanities at his teasing by now, but she was staying silent and patient.

He laughed and finally spoke up. "Well, in case no one has bothered to read the sign on the gate, it says that this is a *family* ranch. So this is a *family* decision like all of them, and my vote is yes. I think it's a great idea, Grace. Why should that big ole house go to waste when there's so many kids in need?"

The group raised their hands and cheered. Ginger and Grace leaped up and clapped their hands in elation. Then everyone broke out in murmurs of new ideas and possibilities.

Hatch then stood and bowed his head. They all quieted and joined hands as he led them in prayer. "We ask that you bless this new adventure, Lord. Guide us with your wisdom and grace, and grant us the strength to always serve faithfully in your name. In Jesus' name, amen."

They all repeated, "Amen."

Hatch then raised his glass. "Here's to the new McCullough Family Shelter on McCullough Family Ranch!"

They all raised their glasses and toasted with gusto and enthusiasm.

Ginger then stood up and walked over to Hatch, snuggling under his arm before she loudly addressed the group, "Not to be outdone by my sister…" She smiled and looked at Grace who was now all questioning face and ears in her direction, "I just want you all to know that there will be one more very special addition to the McCullough Ranch in about six months!" She turned to Hatch and rubbed her stomach. "Congratulations, Daddy!"

Everyone's mouth dropped open, and Hatch turned and dropped to his knees and put his hands on her stomach. He looked up at her and asked, "I'm gonna be a daddy?"

Ginger nodded. "Yep, a little cowboy or cowgirl is on the way."

He jumped up with tears filling his eyes and shouted to the sky, "I'M GONNA BE A DADDY!"

At that, everyone stood up and cheered and whooped and hollered congratulations as tears of joy flowed freely and hugs were passed all around.

As they were finally settling down, they heard Kim confirming to Kyle why they were all so happy. He stood up on his chair and looked at Ginger and Hatch with slanted eyes and exclaimed. "Make sure it's a boy to play with and not some crummy girl!"

With that they all collapsed in laughter as Hatch answered, "We'll do our best, buddy!"

Laughter, thanks, and celebration lasted long into the night.

All Work and No Play

It was early September the following year and Ginger had just joined Grace out on the ranch house deck. Ginger placed her son in a small wooden swing William had built as she watched the late summer sunset slowly fading behind the mountains. Jesse began cooing away like a little chicken as Grace typed fervently away on her laptop. Ginger watched the dust billow up behind several pickup trucks passing them by on the short drive that led toward the shelter.

"What's going on down there tonight?" Ginger inquired.

"Winter planting session." Grace quipped.

Ginger nodded. She missed spending time with the shelter kids and her classes, but needed to take the time off after Jesse was born. So much had happened in such a short time. She was looking forward to getting up to speed on all the changes.

"I still can't believe what you've accomplished in about a year, Grace."

"What we've *all* accomplished with a lot of help from the good Lord, you mean."

"Well, yes, but this was your entire brainchild, and I'm still awed by the magnitude of…"

Grace interrupted her. "The shelter needed a new home and I filled the need. The rest was the result of a boatload of divine intervention and a lot of very dedicated and compassionate people."

"Okay, okay. I know you won't take credit for anything, but the Lord did some seriously fantastic work through you, and I'm very impressed and proud nonetheless."

Grace ignored her.

"Bear sent me out here to retrieve you. We are supposed to be relaxing and visiting for a change. We never see you anymore."

"I'm almost finished," she said as she winced and wiped her forehead. "It's too hot to relax these days, and I have too much work to do."

"Well, you are a lot older now, maybe it's hot flashes and premature menopause."

Grace flashed her sister a sarcastic smile. "Very funny!"

"What are you working on, anyway?" Ginger inquired.

"I'm working on a proposal to do a summer program for inner city kids nationwide. Some of them don't even know what a cow pasture is—it's crazy!"

Ginger persisted. "Can't this wait until Monday? I thought you were going to slow down a little."

Grace fanned herself with her notes and said to Ginger impatiently, "If you'd stop nagging me and let me finish these last comments, then maybe I can relax. Okay?"

Ginger put her hands up in surrender. "Okay, okay! You know, crabbiness is a sign of menopause too." Ginger giggled.

Grace shot her a non-amused look, and Ginger just shrugged. "Just saying."

Ginger finally stopped talking. When Grace had her wall up, there was no entry. She was worried about her working so many hours and doing so much all by herself. She seemed to have lost that joyous, carefree, childlike quality that Ginger loved so much. They didn't spend much time together these days, and she couldn't remember the last time they giggled and conspired about anything. She knew the responsibility of the shelter was a tremendous undertaking and had grown much larger than any of them had ever imagined. She suspected that Grace was using all this as a penance to make up for some of the guilt she was still holding on to. She was giving so much of herself to everyone else that she wasn't keeping any joy for herself, like she still didn't deserve her happiness.

Ginger was determined to get her off that computer. "Have you set a wedding date to marry Bear yet?"

Grace signed impatiently. "I promised Bear that it will be before Christmas, so we still have three months."

"I hate to keep bringing this up, but you're living in sin, my sister. You know the Lord doesn't approve of that."

"I'm very well aware, so please don't start the guilt trip on me again. We just can't seem to find a date that everyone's available."

"That sounds like another excuse. You need to just pick one and let everyone else figure out how to attend. And it would also be really nice to know the date so I could start planning a bridal shower."

"I don't want a shower; I told you that. I'm too busy, and it just seems silly."

"Well then, what about the wedding? Have you even thought about that?"

"I just want a small gathering on the deck of the shelter with flowers from the garden and some simple food. Pastor Fred said he would come anytime, day or night to perform the ceremony so what's to plan?"

"You are just no fun anymore! What happened to that crazy girl that galloped through the snow yelling 'Merry Christmas'?"

"We all have to grow up sometime; it just took me a little longer."

"You can still be fun and crazy and spontaneous when you are grown up, too! Come on, Grace, loosen up. You are just too serious these days."

"Ginger, please just let me finish this, and then I will do a happy dance on the table for you, okay?"

Ginger sighed. "I'm just worried about you, Grace. It would be nice to see you smile a little more often."

"Well, don't worry, I'm fine."

Grace went back to her typing, and Ginger decided she best not push it any further. It was dark enough now that she could see the warm scene inside the big windows of the ranch house that Grace was missing. Bear and William were huddled together going over some plans for a new barn and indoor corral area. Word had spread about the magic Indian horse whisperers, and business was booming. Hatch and James were sitting on the couch watching Kyle. He was spinning a new lasso Hatch had given him and was growing up so fast. He had taken to riding and roping like a pro and was definitely going be a ranching man. Big John had Glory and Aunt Peg giggling like school girls with the same corny humor as his son. Marta, Mahina and Kim were just bringing out a couple of pies with whipped cream. Bear was right on their heels so one of them was obviously cherry. Puck was lying beside her on the deck dreaming, when he suddenly yipped, causing Jesse to jump and then giggle. She giggled too and then heard some laughter and singing coming from the shelter in the distance.

The housewarming party that started it all seemed like a lifetime ago. The MFR Bunkhouse Shelter ended up being a much larger project than Grace had ever imagined when she first proposed the idea that night. When the word went through the community, the donations started pouring in, and a large amount of volunteers wanted to help wherever they could. Ginger and Grace were euphoric with the outpouring of support they received. The Bunkhouse Shelter went up fast, and with the addition of all the generous donations, they were able to build a two-story schoolhouse lodge that was three times the size of the ranch library, with extra beds upstairs if needed. The schoolhouse was also used for church services on Sunday mornings and afternoon Bible studies.

The main shelter was designed like a barn with two stories. The top story was divided into two giant rooms with twenty-two bunk beds and three bathrooms in each section. Stairs on each side led down to an open floor plan with a large kitchen, three large dining tables, and a central lounging area. The kitchen opened onto a massive covered deck area with more tables, a large stone fireplace, and various types of seating designed for gatherings, leisure activities, and meetings.

The vegetable gardens were thriving, and the kids were learning to harvest and sell the various crops at the farmers' markets held on the weekends. All the manure from the animals was composting gold for the garden. The kids also built a large chicken house and barn and acquired several cows and goats of their own, so they could add milk, eggs, and cheese sales to the market offerings.

The flower and rose gardens that Glory's garden club had started at the ranch were flourishing as well. So much so, that Glory started a small business called "Shelter Garden Flowers." They were taking orders for weddings, funerals and banquets with all the proceeds going back to the shelter.

The ranch's outdoor mountainous environment proved to have a magical healing effect on the teens. The brokenness seemed to melt away much faster when they were riding, planting, harvesting, cooking, attending classes, or caring for the many farm animals or strays that had also ended up at the ranch. Hatch and James also kept them busy with barn building, painting, pasture and fence maintenance, buying and feeding livestock, veterinary care, and herding. They were too busy learning and working to think too much about their problems.

Grace's influence with healing and forgiveness was growing them into responsible, spiritual, and loving adults. It was truly amazing to see the transformation. Ginger was overwhelmed by the gift of watching these kids find their way back from tragedy to hope. Their path of learning to triumph over adversity and abuse was breathtaking to witness. Seeing them thrive and change and be happy was such a miracle. She just didn't see how people could say that God doesn't exist just because you can't see Him. If they would open their eyes and their hearts, they would see He's everywhere. She witnessed His work every single day in each one of these kids, and in the people that flocked around them as support. She watched these broken and lost souls arrive with so much animosity and pain. But slowly over time, the Lord softened their hardened hearts, turned the tough faces into big laughing amiable grins, and grew the shy withdrawn personalities into larger-than-life leaders.

The wide variety of projects that had developed through the collaboration of ideas and talents seemed endless. They were learning to use both their hands and their heads by practicing trades like construction, design, animal husbandry, team and management skills, finance, sales, bartering, permitting and regulations, well construction and water use, cooking, marketing, farming, and working with the local community and government to facilitate their programs and ideas. Grace and the counselors were great at recognizing the strengths in each of the teens to maximize their interest in the various activities. All were expected to participate in all factions of the Bunkhouse Shelter to teach responsibility and self-sustenance. They all worked, earned money, had rotating chores, and were encouraged to participate in and plan the social activities.

They were also excelling in their school curriculums. Kim was a wizard in securing education assistance and scholarships for all kinds of programs and grants and worked with many philanthropic groups to aid the kids with college and apprenticeship programs. And this was all being done as a local community based project with as little government interference as possible. The atmosphere of personal responsibility, group decisions, trusting others, and offering a helping hand was also showing them that there is kindness, support, and miraculous results when people come together in faith for the good of all.

"Plant the seed, nurture it, and watch it thrive"—it works in human nature as well as in the earth. This was the motto of the MFR Bunkhouse Shelter, and Grace was the living testimony to that very message. The Bunkhouse was big enough that the ranch house was not needed, so it was turned into offices and guest accommodations for the various donors and directors nationwide that were interested in emulating the Bunkhouse Shelter in other communities. It was also the main meeting house for the McCullough family decisions.

They were here tonight to visit, catch up, and discuss a Harvest Rodeo and Halloween Hoedown in October. Since she hadn't done too much to contribute since Jesse was born, Ginger was ready to jump in feet first on this event. She could just see the pumpkin carving, hayrides, and apple dunking for the smaller kids and haunted forest trails with goblins and headless horsemen for the older ones. And that was just the start of her master plan. She heard another round of laughter coming from the distance.

"Sounds like the kids are having fun down there."

Grace nodded. "Yeah, but it doesn't sound like they're getting much crop planning done."

"Maybe you should take a hint from them. All work and no play makes Grace a dull girl."

Grace continued to tap away.

Ginger decided to give it one last try. "I know you want to help all the kids that you can, Grace, but you're just one person. The Lord doesn't want you to spread yourself so thin that you don't even have time to enjoy the blessings He's bestowed on you, some of which are right here in front of your face." Ginger waved both hands and motioned to all the laughter and goings on inside the ranch house.

Grace relented. "Okay, okay. I'm done. Let's get inside."

"Finally!" said Ginger. She told Grace to go ahead as she began to unstrap Jesse from the swing. Her head was still whirling with the possibilities for the rodeo and about what she would dress Jesse as for Halloween when she noticed Puck leap up suddenly and sprint toward the house. As she was lifting Jesse from the swing, she heard Puck start to whine and bark like crazy. She turned to see what had gotten into him and screamed. Grace was passed out on the deck with Puck frantically circling her.

~27~

Second Chances

The doctor finally came into the waiting room. It had been three hours of torturous waiting to hear what was wrong with Grace. The news came as a bittersweet shock. Grace was pregnant, but there were some complications. She had been overly stressed, hadn't been eating or sleeping enough, and apparently hadn't even noticed that she had missed several menstrual cycles. She was also underweight and dehydrated when she passed out. Because she was now forty, she should have been taking extra precautions.

The doctor sent everyone home because they had her on fluids and wanted her to sleep through the night. They needed to run more tests in the morning, as well as share the news with a rested Grace. The doctor promised to wait until they were all back before he said anything to her.

Hatch, Bear, William, and Ginger were back by eight the next morning and, after speaking with the doctor, were all happy to see Grace awake and eating breakfast.

"This food is awful! We need to get our eggs distributed to this hospital. I should call Meggie and get her to bring my laptop so I can contact the…"

Bear sat down on the bed and hugged her until she squeaked. "You will do no such thing. I should have put my foot down long before this. You have to stop running like a wild stallion."

"Bear, don't be silly, I just got dehydrated. I'm fine. Everybody can relax. I'm fine now."

Bear squeezed her hand. "There's a little more to it than that, Flame."

"Why are you all looking so weird and anxious? What is it you're not telling me?" Grace demanded.

Bear held her hand to his mouth and kissed it. "You weren't just dehydrated, little one. We're pregnant again! *You're* pregnant again."

Grace's eyes opened so wide that Ginger thought her eyeballs might roll right out of her head and onto the cold hospital floor. Her mouth fell open and a small peep escaped her lips before her head dropped and she started sobbing. Hatch and Ginger moved to the opposite side of the bed and held her other hand. Bear wiped her tears and smoothed her hair. William exited the room to get his mother a glass of cold water from one of the nurses.

"How did this happen? How did I not know?" she peeped again.

Bear answered, "Well, you know how it happened, but didn't you notice that things weren't happening, you know, down…there?"

Hatch cleared his throat and looked at the ceiling. Ginger quickly cut in. "Okay, boys, that's enough. Let me handle this. Give us a couple of minutes for some girl talk, okay?"

They both agreed. Hatch squeezed Grace's hand, and Bear

kissed her head before they made awkward tracks out the door.

Ginger shook her head. "For heaven's sake, you'd think they were ten years old!"

Grace giggled, which Ginger thought was so nice to hear after all this time. The laughter was soon lost in more tears. "I can't believe I'm really pregnant. I always use my diaphragm."

"Well, I guess this is the one percent chance they warn you about. I know you are in shock, but why are you so upset, honey? Don't you think this is wonderful news?"

"I don't know how to feel. I didn't think I would get another chance. I don't think I deserve another chance. Oh, God, is the baby all right? Is that why you all looked so worried and why the guys are acting so uncomfortable?"

"First of all, I don't want you to ever say that you don't deserve another chance. You should know by now that we all get second chances, right?"

Grace nodded. "I suppose."

"So hold on to that as a blessing. God is giving you a second chance to be a mother, but there may be some challenges this time."

"What challenges? Oh, I knew it. There's something wrong, isn't there?" Fresh tears spilled out on her cheeks as she slammed her fists into her thighs. "All those years of drugs and alcohol—I've hurt the baby, haven't I? Oh God, this is my penance, I'm getting my punishment. I knew it was coming..."

Ginger grabbed her hands and held them tight. "Stop it right now, Grace! I will not have you reverting back to your old guilt! We all have challenges in our lives. It's how you react to the crisis that matters. You now have to practice what you preach to those kids. You know Jesus forgave you for your past, and you must accept God's plan, whatever it may be! There will be a blessing in this somewhere, so you need to reaffirm your faith right now and trust Him. You have to go forward no matter how hard it may seem. You know that no matter how painful it will always work out when you put your trust in Him. You should know that by now! Bear came back to you. William forgave you. Look at your shelter kids! You know the power of His blessings, Grace; you have to trust Him and believe in your heart that He will guide and comfort you, and it will all work out."

Grace was nodding her head, but the tears were still falling. "I do believe it in my heart, Ginger, but I still battle with the fact that I don't deserve it. I know He has blessed me with so many miracles that I can't even count them, but I still don't understand why. I wish I could be truly happy and have the faith that you have. I want that so much, but I'm just afraid that it's all too good to be true, that all the people I love will soon be taken away from me. Then the old guilt of the past mixes with the new guilt of my weaknesses, and it all pushes me back into the darkness."

Fresh tears rolled down Ginger's face as she listened to the struggle that she had long suspected Grace was going through.

"What you are going through is normal, Grace. It's called a 'crisis of faith' and it happens in everyone's journey. The enemy doesn't want to lose us, so he really starts hammering and testing us with all our weaknesses and doubts. We get scared and start questioning whether this newfound faith and hope is real, or if we are even strong enough to live up to the fight. We become overwhelmed when we realize we have to start walking the Jesus walk and not just preaching it. That's our human side still thinking we have to do this life all alone. It's hard to keep our trust in something that's unseen and that is exactly what we have to do. He always gives us the free will to choose Him or choose the fear and doubt of the enemy."

Grace interrupted. "But I did choose Him, Ginger, and the same old bad traits of myself just keep grinding and wearing on me. Will that ever stop?"

"The devil will never stop laying the material pleasures or guilt-ridden emotional baggage out in front of us like an all-you-can-eat banquet. He wants to fill the void in our hearts that longs for the Lord with his putrid decaying slop. But the void never gets filled with that kind of poison, instead it just keeps getting bigger and bigger, so we continue to fill and fill until we are so sick and fat with sin and doubt that we can't even recognize ourselves. That's the promise of the enemy—pain, suffering, heartache and eternal death. All his illusions of happiness are temporary.

"But, if we continue to resist the buffet of lies and keep our faith in the Unseen One, we will eventually overcome. And as you have witnessed, once you commit to your faith journey to find Him, He will begin showing you His strength, His glory, His blessings and His continuing forgiveness. If we keep fighting, trusting, and moving toward Him in spite of the manipulative powers of the enemy, the Lord will fill that void with the comfort of His promise. The promise of joy, peace, happiness and eternal life will always shine through—unless there is something that you are holding on to, Grace?"

Grace wiped away a tear. "I'm just so tired of fighting this war within myself, Ginger. I just can't forgive myself for almost murdering my son, and I can't forgive my parents for what they did to us. They just don't deserve it, and neither do I."

Ginger nodded. There it was, the part she wasn't letting go of, the reason she was not growing in her faith, the wall that remained between her and her final redemption.

"Everyone's journey is different, Grace, just like everyone's purpose is different. We never stop fighting, learning, growing, questioning and even doubting our practice of faith. We are in a daily battle against an enemy that exists for the sole purpose of testing that faith by using our doubts, fears, anger and guilt against us. I still have all that stuff pop up from time to time, too, but then I remember that our individual lives are just a tiny part of a much bigger plan. There are so many atrocities happening in this world right now, Grace, and there is always someone worse off than we are, so we not only have to be strong in our faith for ourselves, but more importantly for them. The Lord's power and strength is reflected through us. We are the warriors of example for Him! That's an honor and a gift that He is entrusting to us.

"God gave us His Son as the ultimate example and sacrifice for our sins. He knew exactly what would happen and He had to witness His Son Jesus being brutally beaten, nailed to a cross, and die right before His very eyes, so *you* could be forgiven, Grace. Imagine watching that happen to William! But God allowed it so He could then raise His Son in victory over death to show us that Satan will NOT win in the end. So honor that gift and sacrifice, Grace, by forgiving yourself and your pain the way Jesus forgave you and those who hurt Him. You can honor them both by accepting His forgiveness and reflecting and sharing that incredible gift in return!"

Grace dropped her head as the tears flowed heavily, and she bit her lip in in shame. "So even after all I've learned and witnessed, I'm still making my life all about me. I still didn't even get that until now. He forgave me, but I'm too stubborn and selfish to do the same. My un-forgiveness of myself and my self-pity is just another form of self-absorption. Why do I still think it's all about me?" She spat out that last sentence as if it were poison.

Ginger handed her another tissue. "Unfortunately, Grace, that's just human nature. We were born into a world that sees the enemy's traps and temptations as acceptable and even worshiped. We cannot fight the enemy by ourselves. No matter how bright the Lord's light is, our little pea brains just can't stop being distracted by the shiny lures of the enemy. It's a daily battle. That's why we can never stop praying and seeking His strength and wisdom. If you stay in His presence by leaning on Him and trusting His promises, you will continue to grow in strength against the enemy. That's how you'll learn to identify and avoid the hook of those shiny temptations."

Grace laughed and blew her swollen and drippy nose. "I feel like a big muddy catfish with ungrateful hooks hanging all over me right now!"

Ginger smiled and stroked her arm. "How about you let Jesus carefully and lovingly pull each and every one of those hooks out of you one by one? If you'll only let Him, He'll patch them all with love and soft bandages, so they have plenty of time to heal."

Grace whimpered. "I feel so ashamed, Ginger, like I accepted all the good of the Lord on the surface, but wouldn't release the bad He wanted to take from me in return."

Ginger smiled. "Congratulations, you're human! Admitting

that out loud is another step toward wisdom and clarity for yourself. But best of all, it's music to the Lord's ears! And don't forget, sweetie, you've had quite a lot of pregnancy hormones bouncing around inside your body in addition to all your sixth sense stuff these past few months!"

They laughed together and then Grace nodded and got quiet again. "I'm scared, Ginger. There's a chance that I might lose this child, isn't there?"

Ginger held up her hand. "We don't know anything yet. The doctor is still running tests, and he will be in shortly to let us all know together what we are up against, so…"

Grace interrupted her. "I just don't know if I'm strong enough to handle it. I don't want to fail if this is a test of my faith."

Ginger wiped tears off both their faces. "I'm scared too, Grace, but we have to have faith no matter what. You just remember that you are not alone! You have the strength of the Lord and me and your family and your extended family. We all love you and will support you whenever you need us. That's some mighty strong blessings right from the start, wouldn't you say?"

Grace squeezed Ginger's hand and nodded. "You should have been the one named Grace."

"I think it suits you just fine. I love you, and we'll get through this together, I promise."

"I love you too. Will you say a prayer with me? I need to honestly forgive myself along with Jake and Patrice. I need your help since they were both of our parents."

Ginger beamed at her amazing sister. "Of course, I'd be honored."

Grace laughed. "And then we can call the ten-year-olds back

in. I think I'm ready now for whatever the news may be."

None of them were really ready for the news the doctor deliverd a few hours later. A series of tests revealed that the child would have Down syndrome, if Grace was able to carry to term. When the doctor gave the option of termination, Bear and Grace didn't bat an eye before they said absolutely not. This child was a gift from God, and they would love it no matter what.

Later that evening Grace had finally convinced everyone to go home and get something to eat and rest. They had been there all day and she was tired.

She had just adjusted her pillows when she heard a familiar voice. "Well, hello there, beautiful. How're ya doin'?"

Grace's face lit up. "Buck! It's so nice of you to visit me! I have missed you and the group so much!"

"Well, we have all missed you, too. But we know you been busy with the shelter, so don't be frettin' over us."

"How did you know I was here?"

"Well, the Lord said I needed to come and see ya. I called the ranch and that's when Ginger said you was here, but didn't say why. I was gonna wait 'til tomorrow cause I didn't want to wake you, but He insisted I come tonight. So here I am. We must have somethin' we really need to talk about!"

Grace blushed and welled up with tears. "Oh, Buck, where do I start?"

Buck tilted his head and patted her hand. "How about the beginnin'?"

Grace wiped her eyes and proceeded to tell Buck about her conversation with Ginger and how she had not been honest and was still denying the gifts of the Lord in her heart. When she finished, Buck just chuckled and mumbled under his breath. *The truth will set you free.*

Grace was confused by his statement. "What?"

Buck took her hand. "The Father reveals things to us in His timing, when he thinks we are ready to *hear* and *understand* what He wants us to learn or do."

Grace nodded. "I've heard that God speaks to people, like you for instance. But I don't really understand that whole thing. He doesn't talk to me, Buck. I've been trying. I see His blessings every day, but I don't hear Him."

Buck nodded. "Remember when I first met you that day and told you how gifted and special you were to the Father?"

She nodded.

"He changed your heart that day, didn't he?"

She nodded again.

"Well, all of them things you been doin' at the shelter is the Lord's work through you. That's why you are special to Him, because He can do special things through you that become His special work or messages for other people. But if you just go through the motions of service as a way to make up for your sins or get more brownie points, then you are wastin' your gifts, and you won't get any joy or happiness out of it. The Lord forgave you for your sins already, so serving Him should be done in genuine joy and not just to ease your guilt or shame. Understand?"

Grace thought about that for a minute and then nodded. "Okay, I think I understand. I'm not special or better than anyone else, but I am very special and unique to God in the way He can get His message out to others through me. But..." she paused to let the pieces of wisdom come together in her mind. "Okay, so if I'm not serving Him in an honest way, then I'm getting His message out, but not in an entirely truthful way, which is not really a genuine reflection of Him and His message. Kind of hypocritical just talkin' the talk and not walkin' the walk."

Buck chuckled again. "Now yer gettin' it. But don't go feelin' bad about that. We all gotta learn in our own way and that can take years or even decades for some. Now remember I also said *gifted*. He gives us all special gifts not only in certain talents, but also a gift within. It's called *truth*."

Grace held up her hand to stop him. "Wait, I'm not following, Buck."

He continued. "You've read the verses: 'The Way, the Truth, and the Life' right?"

She nodded.

"Okay, well, you know that Jesus is the only Way to the Father because of His sacrifice for your sins. And that whoever believes in Him will not perish but have everlastin' life in Heaven. John 3:16, right?"

She nodded again.

"And God is the Life—meanin' everlastin' life—in eternity with Him, right?"

Her brow was knitted together trying to figure out where Buck was going with this. "Yes, I fully understand and believe that."

"Good. But what is missin' there in the middle?"

She repeated the verse to herself. *The Way, the...* She shouted excitedly, "The Truth!"

Buck nodded. "Good. So the Holy Trinity is The Father, The Son and the…" He waited for her answer.

She shrugged her shoulder. "The Holy Spirit, of course."

He continued. "So if Jesus is the Way, and God is the Life…?"

She burst out in excitement. "Oh, my gosh! The Holy Spirit is the Truth!"

Buck laughed out loud as she beamed with her revelation. He questioned, "And what does the truth do?"

She burst out, "It sets you free!"

"Did you get you some truth today, little girl?"

She laughed. "I did! So the Holy Spirit in me made me tell the truth today?"

Buck laughed. "You almost got it. The Holy Spirit doesn't make you do anything. The Spirit just helps you when you're ready to hear the truth. It's the Spirit that helps you understand when you're ready to accept more truth and wisdom from Him. And it's the Spirit that helps you have the courage to keep goin' when them walls or secrets or confessions of truth you been hidin' decide to come a tumbling out of your mouth, like today. And most important, the Spirit intercedes for you when you don't yet fully understand the love of the Father and the Son and what that means. The Truth will set you free!"

Grace put her hand on her chest. "Right inside me is the Holy Spirit of God that I cannot hide or deny the truth from, ever!"

Buck nodded. "Without the Truth between you and the Father, you can't grow no closer to Him. I would say the Holy Spirit is givin' you a double dose of the Lord today for a reason! He must be preparin' you for somethin' very important."

With that, Grace grabbed Buck's hand tightly and proceeded to tearfully tell him exactly why she was in the hospital.

28

Open Your Ears, Eyes, and Heart

Grace was put on a strict routine with lots of rest, special vitamins, and nutrition plans. She was warned again that this was still a very high risk pregnancy that may not come to term. When Grace finally came home, she called together a big meeting for all her friends, family, and the kids at the shelter. Much to Bear's protests, Grace had him drive her to the shelter as she had a message to deliver that could not wait one more day. Everyone was on edge as Grace didn't share too much personal information unless it was really important. Bear helped Grace into a chair that had been placed on an elevated stage area of the large outdoor deck.

After everyone had calmed down and got seated on the large deck of the bunkhouse, she opened her heart. "I want to thank everyone for coming. I invited you all tonight because I have something very important to share with you, so I hope you will indulge me and be patient, as you know I'm not too good at this public speaking business."

She smiled as low laughter spread across the deck. Then everything went deadly silent as all eyes settled back on her. She breathed a heavy sigh and prayed to the Spirit for the right words to share the message she came to deliver.

"First, I want to share a confession with you and ask for your forgiveness." She paused and swallowed hard, waiting for the surprised murmurs to cease and her heart to stop beating so quickly. "I have not been totally honest or open with you all, and I have not been practicing what I have been preaching. So I'd like to speak with you about that before I lose my courage."

More murmurs went through the crowd, and she waited for them to dissipate.

"You all know my testimony and the blessings I've received through the Lord's forgiveness. What you don't know is that until very recently I still really didn't understand that gift. I was willing to accept the Lord's forgiveness, but not really forgive myself or my parents for my past sins and circumstances in return. I was still holding darkness in my heart, which was keeping me from growing stronger in my faith and moving closer to our Father in Heaven.

"So the Lord sent me a message through two very special people who I love and trust very much. They reminded me that Jesus died to forgive my sins against His Father, but the fact that I was not forgiving myself or others for their sins against me, meant that I was dishonoring the whole reason for His death. This hit me pretty hard. *I was dishonoring Jesus!* How was I doing this? First, my prideful nature was still thinking that I should be the judge and jury for others. Then my ego jumped in when I knew it wasn't right and I didn't ask for help. And, of course, my self-pity is always the fall back excuse for everything I don't want to take responsibility for.

"So, very much later that evening when I was laying there in the dark, I imagined—what if Jesus was standing right there before me and asked, *'Why do you not forgive my child? I walked on this earth to show you love, compassion and forgiveness toward all others including those that brought me pain. I went willingly through torture, suffering, and death to show you the ultimate sacrifice My Father endured for that forgiveness. I showed you how to pray to our Father for strength when Satan does not want you to forgive. And I rose from the dead to show you that everlasting life is only possible because of the gift of forgiveness. Yet you continue to deny this gift by not doing the same for yourself and others. You continue to choose anger when I offer you peace. You continue to hold on to your pain when I offer you healing. And you will not let Me fully into your heart, when you know I am the only One that can truly take your burdens away. So, why, my child? Why do you not open your heart and forgive?'*"

She paused to regain control of her emotions and let the crowd absorb the gravity of what she was trying to convey before she continued in a humbled voice.

"How could I possibly answer that question? I felt so ashamed. After I finally stopped crying, things suddenly became very clear, and I asked Jesus to forgive me for dishonoring Him. And then I had the most incredible experience! It was a warmness that was so overwhelming, it actually made me tremble. I broke down like a child at that point, and I felt a lifetime of weight lift off my heart and an incredible feeling of peace came over me. That was when I was finally able to forgive my parents for what they had done. I actually cried and felt mercy for them because I realized that they will never feel the love of their daughters or experience the joy of their grandchildren; they will never have the freedom or feeling of peace in their hearts; they will never know how grace, blessings, and forgiveness can change everything; and, most importantly, they will never get the chance to see the Lord's face in eternity. Their loss hit me so hard that my heart broke for them. And that was it—I was not going to feed that pain any longer, and I let it all go—the anger, the ego, the loss, the guilt, and the most debilitating emotion of all…fear. It all came pouring out of me like a river of sewage, and I forgave myself for things I didn't even know I was still harboring. When it was all done, I prayed like a mad woman for the strength to deny all that darkness for good. And that's how I found that you really can't be a true reflection of God's light and message if you continue to hold anger and darkness in your heart."

She paused to wipe more tears that were joyously streaming down her smiling face. Murmurs and quiet sobs were flooding the room, and her skin tingled and shivered in the presence of the Lord. She felt the Spirit's strength urge her to go on. She had one last message to deliver.

"We are very good at deception though, aren't we? We all know that verse about pointing out the speck in someone else's eye when we have a log protruding out of ours. But we continue to elude ourselves and pretend we are the exception to the Bible's teachings and warnings, but mostly to its compassion! I know there are many here tonight struggling with this same truth. I was the biggest offender, but I am sharing this with you tonight because the only ones we are deceiving, punishing, and dishonoring are ourselves and our Lord Jesus. I know a lot of you have been through unspeakable things, and I'm not here to say that those things will ever be forgotten in this life. But, as I've also told many of you, they are in the past, and you have to accept that. You cannot change them, you cannot fix them, you cannot escape them, and you cannot drink or drug them away! They are a part of you until you decide to let them go and reach for the Lord. I was so fixated with *my* issues, *my* self-pity, and *my* ridicule that I was missing the whole point of true faith. How can I hear Him if my ears only hear my own cries and not His comforting words? How can I see where He's leading me if I'm blinded by my anger and shame? How can He change my heart if I keep filling it with past regrets, rather than with Him? How can I ever know the Truth of the Holy Spirit if I keep lying to myself and the Lord?"

She paused to lower her voice in reverence. "And how can I continue to call myself His daughter without honoring the incredible sacrifice of His Son and fully embracing the gift of His Holy Spirit to dwell within me whenever I need His comfort or guidance?"

Grace's tears were flowing freely and she never felt so strong and so free. There wasn't a dry eye in the house at this point, and Grace wiped her tears and laughed.

"I didn't come to preach tonight, but I guess I'm doing that, aren't I?"

Quiet laughter circled the room.

"What it really comes down to is this: I just want to be happy and enjoy my blessings. I want to feel peace in my heart by filling it with the Lord and not all my anxieties. I don't want to worry about controlling everything anymore because I don't really have the power or the strength to control anything. I don't want to judge, for that is not my purpose. I want to serve the Lord because it makes me proud to have that honor. And, frankly, I am so tired of fighting a war that I can't win by myself, and don't even have to! Only God will ever have it all under control. So, I am putting my faith, trust, and future in His hands, no matter how hard that will still be sometimes. And that means the good and the bad. You all have heard that I am in a very high risk pregnancy. And although I'm still scared, I have to trust the Lord's plan for my child as well and know that His decision is always the right one for me, no matter how painful at the time. In the meantime, I'm choosing hope instead of angst and I ask that all of your prayers reflect that as well. So, as far as I know—I've now aired all my dirty laundry. I'm still Grace, just a little more honest and humbled. Thank you for your many prayers and may God bless each and every one of you. I love you all so much."

She smiled out at the many faces and counted her blessings again. She slowly began to rise to her feet as Bear and William quickly moved to her side.

"And just because I'm not here every day doesn't mean my phone isn't on. I'm just up the road if you want to stop in. I'll always be available when any of you need to talk."

She smiled at the crowd, then turned to Bear and William. "Okay, my beautiful men, help me down off my soapbox now. Thank you all for coming, and I'll ask Pastor Fred to close us in prayer. And from now on," Grace chuckled, "I'm gonna leave the preaching to him!"

In the days that followed, everyone could see that Grace's words were not just a lot of talk. A true peace had come over her that radiated into everyone she spoke to. She delegated all her responsibilities to various volunteers without hesitation, which was something she had struggled with in the past. She put her full trust and encouragement in them and within a couple of days was settled in at home, relaxed, happy, and calm. She started really laughing again and finally took real joy in all the blessings of the shelter and her family. People remarked that she was so tranquil and joyous to be around that it was contagious. Her message had a big effect on a lot of souls that night, which started a whole new journey of healing and understanding for many of them.

Ginger was overjoyed that they now had more time to spend together, even if Grace had also reverted back to relentlessly teasing her, which Ginger was not so overjoyed about. Ginger was still in awe that the immature, crass, little wild-haired waif she first found curled up in the sheets was now this glowing beautiful woman that had given a testimony that rocked that room into something that was not of this earth. The stressed-out, guilt-ridden soul still searching for self-forgiveness was finally healed. The Lord's transformation in her was quite something to behold.

Ginger also noticed that Bear could not stop smiling and was possibly the happiest man she had ever seen. Grace had finally given her whole heart to Bear, and they were married within two weeks after she came home. The ceremony was on the beautiful shore of the waterfall. There was no decorations, no pomp, no frills, just two people madly in love surrounded by all the people they loved, and that was more than enough.

29

Time Moves On

Grace was getting increasingly tired as the weeks went by and rested most of the time. Jesse spent most afternoons cuddling with Grace, so Ginger was able to coordinate most of the holiday festivities. When Ginger would go on and on, telling Grace all the news, she would just smile, nod and rub her big fat belly.

Ginger counted the Harvest Rodeo/Halloween Hoedown as an extreme success. All the attendees had so much fun and couldn't stop talking about it. The attendance was almost too much to handle, but they managed to accommodate all. It brought even more attention to the shelter, and they had to hire more staff to handle the influx.

Thanksgiving was just as eventful when Hatch and Bear decided to have a turkey shoot along with prizes added to the usual campfire and hayrides.

Out of sheer exhaustion by all, they decided to scale down Christmas to just the family at Ginger and Hatch's cabin. Kim and Ginger did most of the cooking with a couple of the shelter girls they hired to help out so Marta and Mahina could have the holiday off. They weren't too keen on the idea until they were invited to a Christmas Eve dance by a couple of the guys from the reservation. Glory called and sent her regrets because she had been invited to the dance, too.

Glory never ceased to amaze Ginger. She was thriving in the community, and everyone fell in love with her as easily as Ginger first did. Her southern charm was hard to resist.

On Christmas day, people just dropped in for a spell and then moved on. Leftovers and light appetizers were put out for the guests along with gallons of warm apple cider as each visitor enjoyed the view out the front windows as snow fell lightly all day.

Puck and Jesse passed out early in front of the fireplace, exhausted by playing in the snow all day amid all the excitement. Cloud and Apache ate a little too much turkey and mashed potatoes and were sprawled out on the floor in sweet slumber as well. Bear and Grace decided to stay over at Ginger's house that evening. The snow had finally stopped, so everyone decided to bundle up in blankets and go outside. It was breathtaking to witness the bright winter moon surrounded by the massive beauty of millions of shining stars in the chilly winter sky. As the glow of another Christmas passed, they enjoyed rocking the night away near the warmth of the fire pit, sharing memories and laughing until their stomachs ached.

The next two months went speeding by. Since Grace was on strict bed rest, Ginger spent as much time as she could in the mornings checking on her, then the afternoons entertaining Jesse and Puck. The late afternoons were spent with the directors of the shelter, and then she would rush home to have dinner with Hatch and Jesse.

Just as she was collapsing into bed after another long day, the call came in, and everything came to a screeching halt. Grace went into labor six weeks early. Ginger and Hatch agreed that they had never prayed so hard in their lives. It was a long and anxious night, but seven hours later baby Chance was born prematurely. And, due to the Down Syndrome complications, he only had a fifty-fifty chance to live. Everyone prayed and remained hopeful.

The following weeks went by in a robotic loop for Ginger. Head to the hospital in the morning to check on Grace, make sure Bear eats, make sure William eats, get back home to spend time with Jesse and Puck, then go back to the hospital for the evening visit, then home for dinner and straight to bed, sleep, start all over again the next day. Between the split shifts at the hospital and Hatch trying to run the ranch and support Bear, Ginger and Hatch didn't say more than *hi* and *goodbye* for weeks.

Through it all Grace remained her serene and collected self. Ginger and Hatch were worried that she would regress, but it was all for nothing. Grace spent more time reassuring everyone else that all would be well than they spent consoling her. She and Bear came home two weeks later with little Chance. He was so tiny, but the doctor said he was a strong little guy, and he was making up for his early arrival by eating like a champ. He had a little black patch of hair, and his little eyes were green as clover. Mahina moved in with them to help with the baby, and Aunt Peg visited three afternoons a week to make sure Grace still rested like she was supposed to.

Ginger was hit with the flu in early April from too much running around and had to stay in bed for a week. Hatch slept in Jesse's room, and Puck was in heaven to have her all to himself again. She realized how much she had missed him. His warm back against hers, his sweet scent, his head on her pillow, and his silly antics were all things that they shared just between the two of them once again. Her furry little prince stayed by her side all week and made the flu tolerable. He had been sleeping in Jesse's room since he was born, but after the flu week he was back to sleeping by her bedside, and she was happy about that.

After the hurried frenzy of the holidays followed by Chance's arrival, life had been at full speed for much too long. Ginger was aching for things to slow down for a while so they could all catch their breath. She wanted to spend time with just her family and celebrate the start of spring. They needed a vacation and decided to take one in their favorite place—their home.

For seven glorious days, Hatch and Ginger checked out from everything and everybody. They rode the horses to the North Trail with Jesse and the dogs and had lunch on a bluff before stopping on the way back for a little rest at the shelter while Jesse napped. They relived the memory of Bear's face when he first saw her and Grace walk up the trail and shared a good laugh. Some days they sunned by the waterfall and had picnics in the shade. They planted herbs, vegetables, and flower seeds and built a small playhouse and rope swing for Jesse in the backyard. They explored the woods behind the house and collected mosses, mushrooms, and wildflowers to transplant into the yard. Hatch even took Ginger on their first official date in town and then went dancing afterward. It was heaven being alone and quiet even if it was just a week. It was the first time since they'd met that they didn't have anyone depending on them.

When they finally ventured back into the mix to check on things, they found that Bear, Grace, William, and Chance had grown in to a strong and loving family. It was like they had always been that way—a normal happy family enjoying the everyday routine of life. The pain of the past had finally healed and was long forgotten. Aunt Peg and Bear's father were on a cruise in the Caribbean, Marta and Mahina were busy with the ranch house activities, and the Tobias family was working on their own various proceedings and the flower business. The extra people they had hired were managing the shelter just fine.

In fact, things were running so smoothly that they took another week off. By the end of the second week, they were all ready to reconnect. Vacations and time spent alone were needed, but everyone really missed each other and was excited to reunite and catch up.

30

Blessings Large and Small

Almost two years later, Ginger sat on the deck of her beloved cabin in the woods enjoying the cool fall weather and the sunshine. The changing leaves were in full color and just starting to drop. She tightened the chenille blanket around her shoulders and breathed in the fresh air as she kicked off her soil-covered boots and slipped on her fur-lined moccasins. Puck snuggled against her legs and flopped down with a big exaggerated sigh. He loved the cool weather and was exhausted from helping her in the garden— at least he thought his digging was helping. She laughed at his silliness and finished recording in her garden journal the names of the various flower bulbs and locations where she planted them.

She put the journal aside and grabbed her cookbook. She had finally had time to do some canning at the end of summer and put up quite a bit of vegetables and fruits for the winter. Her garden had overflowed with all kinds of yummy choices this past year, and she knew her father would be proud. Hatch was even learning to cook and was getting really talented at coming up with his own recipes.

As she pulled up a foot stool and sat back in her rocker, she thought about how much life had changed for all of them. The shelter was basically running itself, and she and Grace only spent time teaching Bible study classes and helping with the big events. Hatch was giving more responsibility to William, and he was taking Jesse with him in the mornings, leaving Ginger four quiet hours before lunch to do whatever her heart desired. Most of her time was spent in her gardens, and she was so happy that Jesse loved the dirt as much as she had when she was a little girl. She heard a fussy whine and reached over to push a lovely wooden swing that William built for Chase.

"He still sounds hungry," she called out to Grace who was inside getting them something to drink.

"He's like his father, always hungry," her sister responded as she walked back outside with two mugs of hot tea.

Ginger rocked the swing a little more, and the baby faded off to sleep. She was happy he would have a little nap before everyone arrived.

"So have William and Meggie settled on a date for their wedding yet?" Ginger asked.

"Yes, the first weekend in June! Oh, and they wanted to know if you would make the cake?"

Ginger smiled. "Of course! I love that they want to have it at the waterfall like you and Bear. It could be the start of a new family tradition."

Grace clapped her hands together. "Oh, I love that! Like our

Sunday barbeques after church. You know, if you think about it, the waterfall is where a lot of our history has already taken place."

Grace put another log on the fire pit and Ginger looked at her. "What do you mean?"

"Well, it's where we were the day I told you that Hatch and I weren't a couple, which led to his proposal that night. And that's also where Hatch took you for your official Christmas proposal. It's where we were when you told me to tell Bear the truth about William."

"Right!" Ginger exclaimed. "And it's also where you and William went the day you were reunited."

"And where Hatch built your cabin where we are right now!" Grace giggled.

Ginger laughed with her sister. "Right, *duh*! And, of course, where you and Bear were married!" She paused a moment before continuing, "Gosh, you're right, the waterfall has been the scene of so many fateful moments. It's been like God's church just for us!"

"Exactly! I told you the first time you came here how magical it was—the only place I felt any peace."

They were quiet for a minute, each reflecting on the memories.

Grace sat down next to Ginger and gazed at her son. "He's so...perfect."

Ginger squeezed her hand. "I know."

Chance had blossomed into the most lovable gift any parent could hope for and was the final redemption for Grace. His innocence and fascination with everything brought wonder back to them all. His brilliant smiles never failed to cheer up even the surliest of temperaments. Ginger was so thankful that Jesse and

Chance were growing up together. They had become inseparable and were learning strong values and morals mixed with mountains of love from all the extended family at the ranch that cherished and mentored them both.

Grace stood up and gently scooped Chance out of the swing. "I'm gonna go lay him down inside."

Ginger nodded.

After Grace went inside, Ginger stood up and moved to the edge of the deck. As she looked out over the railing on the deck of her not-so-little cabin in the woods, she couldn't help but smile. The cool breeze caressed her face, and she knew it wouldn't be long before the coming snows started turning her autumn paradise into a beautiful winter wonderland, and her deck time would soon become rare. She tossed another log into the fire pit and watched the glowing embers float up and disappear into the sapphire sky.

Hearing a beautiful birdsong brought her attention back to the railing where she searched out the source of the lovely tune. She spied the small bird balancing on one of her many birdhouses just past the river. She watched as it fluttered down to the shore then flew to another of her many birdhouses tucked throughout the trees.

She leaned over the railing as some colorful leaves floating slowly down the river caught her eye, and her memory took her back to that autumn day when she first saw Glory. It had only been a little over six years now, but seemed like a lifetime ago. She smiled to herself at all the blessings that had transpired since then. *I know this isn't Heaven, Lord, but to me it's pretty darn close. Thank you so much.*

She followed the swirling descent of the leaves moving down

through the rushing river like little miniature life rafts. And like life, they would get caught up in the rapids on their tumultuous journey to some unknown destination. They rushed past the dangerous rocks, ebbing a little here, flowing a little there, and then once again caught up in the current and swept into small whirlpools, spinning wildly in circles before being spit out and pushed on down to the next obstacle in their path. They would continue on, always fighting to stay afloat whenever the whitewater pulled them down under.

Life is like that, she realized—ever moving, ever changing, and we never know what blessings or challenges are around the next bend. She thought back to the lonely evening sitting in her little rental house in northern Georgia thinking she was going cuckoo and wishing for a family to love. She was like the leaves then, ebbing and flowing, and temporarily stuck in a little whirlpool spinning round and round in turmoil before the rush of change flooded her life and pushed her on to face the next obstacle in her path.

She felt a warm flush move over her thinking about the lessons she'd learned, the miracles she'd witnessed, and the love and joy of her new family. It was sometimes overwhelming to believe, but she'd kept God at the center of her life and just concentrated on being grateful while He'd rewarded her far beyond her imagination. She'd learned the gift of living in a selfless way, as Jesus did, by helping others find peace and trust in the Lord. She thought about her wonderful parents and how much she wished she could share this new life with them. It still hurt to think they would never be able to be grandparents and how much they would have treasured Jesse and Hatch. Her comfort was that she knew the pain and sorrows of this world are all part of the journey, and she would see them again someday. In the meantime, being in the love and support of God's grace and all those He sends to comfort us is the only way to overcome and heal the deepest of wounds. She and Grace had lived that out together.

Puck suddenly started barking and made a beeline toward the stairs to the front yard. Ginger jumped at his outburst and then turned to see what squirrel or bird might have caught his attention.

"Hey, wife, whatcha doing up there all by yourself?"

Ginger turned to see the big wagon pulling up the drive. Hatch and Bear were in the front with Jesse between them waving and smiling as the dogs jumped out the back and ran to greet Puck.

"Oh, just thinking how good looking the men in this family are!"

"Some much more so than others!" Bear shouted as he pointed a thumb at himself.

Hatch punched his shoulder and laughed. "Only if you're into long, girly hair and fluttery eyelashes."

They continued to laugh and taunt each other as they unloaded the wagon. Ginger's heart swelled watching the warm camaraderie of her beautiful family as they piled out of the wagon amidst the barking dogs that were administering their greetings of joy along with the rest.

Hatch shouted up to her as he lifted Jesse off the wagon, "Peg dropped us a big batch of marinated barbeque chicken with baked beans and potato salad for dinner. We just need to grill up the chicken."

Grace came out of the house and shouted over the barking and chaos, "How about a game of horseshoes? Guys against the girls, and, of course, losers have to do dishes!"

Bear shook his head. "Again? I'm starting to get dishpan hands!"

Ginger laughed; she knew the guys couldn't resist the challenge even though they hadn't won a match in months.

Hatch snickered. "You're on, sisters! Good thing we have paper plates and plastic forks!" he quipped as he nudged Bear.

They all laughed as the menagerie climbed the stairs. Ginger grinned from ear to ear as Jesse raced into her arms for a quick hug followed by her handsome husband who gave her a big smooch on the cheek. Bear wrapped his arms around Grace and gave her a crushing squeeze while he told her that William and Meggie were on their way with dessert. Cloud and Apache circled and bumped around them all like pinballs with loving advances and sloppy kisses.

"So how about it, sis—you up for whipping the cowboy and the Indian again?"

Ginger looked at Grace, giggling and grinning in her ceaseless enthusiastic anticipation. She was still mystified that she was looking at herself really, a little thinner and with darker hair, of course, but still, almost identical. Grace's happiness bubbled over onto everyone, and she shined from within like the sun itself. Ginger laughed and pulled her blanket tighter around her shoulders as she felt a small tingle run the length of her body. She knew it wasn't from the cold; it was a shiver of pure joy, plain and simple. *Thank you so much, Lord,* she whispered to herself as Grace snapped her fingers in front of Ginger's face.

"Hey, have you been chewin' on some of them funny herbs of yours? You're looking a little googly-eyed."

Ginger chuckled and shook her head as the guys came out and loaded the wood chips into the large grill.

Grace continued loudly enough for the guys to hear. "I've been practicing my tosses all week, and when we're done with them, there'll be nothing left of those boys but rusty spurs and plucked feathers—just the smell of old leather and cheap cologne. Nothin' but a big ol' pile of chicken bones and cherry pie pits!"

Ginger totally lost it at the cherry pie comment. Grace came up with the weirdest things and never ceased to eventually cause Ginger to laugh so hard she would start snorting, which made them all laugh even harder. The guys were doing their best to keep from laughing as they pretended to ignore Grace's taunts.

Just as the smoke was starting to bellow up, Grace lobbed another challenge. "I hope that's a smoke signal of surrender."

Ginger chimed in between laughs. "Make sure you put some weenies on that grill for the big macho men that can't even beat two little girls!"

The girls doubled over again in laughter which turned into shrieks of surprise when Hatch and Bear began running toward them. Hatch scooped up Jesse and followed the girls as they raced down the stairs and onto the grass where the all dogs joined in the chase.

Bear howled behind them, "How about the old Indian surrender tactic for pale-faced smarty pants girls? I think you all call it *tickling*. Let's see who's a weenie then!"

They all raced around and around the leaf-covered lawn laughing and shouting with the dogs circling and barking with delight as the day settled into night. Their happiness and joy continued to drench the cool crisp autumn air with buckets full of excitement and love. As the evening moved on, the heartwarming sounds of this blessed family sharing, caring, laughing, and living in God's grace echoed high above Ginger's beautiful cabin. It sang out over the beautiful Rocky Mountains and resonated much farther beyond. A smile appeared from far, far above the star-filled night as The One watched this family fulfilling a story that had been written in the pages of Heaven just for them, a very, very long time ago.

The End

Coming Soon!

The Flying Divas

I hope you enjoyed my first book and want to read more! If so, my second book *The Flying Divas* gets even deeper into the questions and answers about what changes everything and why it matters.

The Flying Divas is about six women stranded by a plane crash in the mountains. It centers more on the addictions we have of self-obsession and the insatiable appetite to be validated or recognized as worthy in today's society. It also confronts the dark price we are willing to pay to get there. Some of the women are friends, and some are strangers. They come from varying backgrounds and range from one end of the spectrum to the other on the subject of faith. Emotions get very messy, heated, cruel, catty, and even physical, and there's no escape or diversions to stop the fallout. Being unwittingly snatched out of the cesspool of their lives and forced to face the sludge they have become mired in becomes a non-stop flight to all kinds of turmoil and confusion.

There's nothing like a plane crash in the middle of nowhere with a bunch of hysterical, pampered divas to expose some badly needed reality. A lot of grace can happen in the mountains; I can attest to that personally. Join me in my next book to see how.